LOCKJAW

LOCKJAW

Matteo L. Cerilli

tundra

To horrible towns, to our rage, and to the people we find there.

Text copyright © 2024 by Matteo L. Cerilli
Jacket art copyright © 2024 by Corey Brickley

Tundra Books, an imprint of Tundra Book Group,
a division of Penguin Random House of Canada Limited

Publisher's note: This book is a work of fiction. Names, characters, places and incidents either are the product of the author's imagination or are used fictitiously, and any resemblance to actual persons living or dead, events, or locales is entirely coincidental.

Library and Archives Canada Cataloguing in Publication

Title: Lockjaw / Matteo L. Cerilli.
Names: Cerilli, Matteo L., author.
Identifiers: Canadiana (print) 20230441726 | Canadiana (ebook) 20230441734 |
ISBN 9781774882306 (hardcover) | ISBN 9781774882313 (EPUB)
Subjects: LCGFT: Novels.
Classification: LCC PS8605.E75 L63 2024 | DDC jC813/.6—dc23

Published simultaneously in the United States of America by Tundra Books of
Northern New York, an imprint of Tundra Book Group, a division
of Penguin Random House of Canada Limited

Library of Congress Control Number: 2023936635

Edited by Peter Phillips
Jacket designed by Sophie Paas-Lang
The text was set in Adobe Garamond Pro.

Printed in Canada

www.penguinrandomhouse.ca

1 2 3 4 5   28 27 26 25 24

Penguin
Random House
tundra | TUNDRA BOOKS

"The system isn't broken, it was

Built

This

Way."

—A rally chant

BRIDLINGTON

It was the first night of summer according to the school calendar, and while the sun was easing down behind the mountain range of cul-de-sac roofs, Chuck Warren was on his front stoop, swaying and humming to kill some time. A few kids down the way were playing road hockey, filling the street with the echo of scraping sticks and mildly homophobic taunts. When Chuck turned to look at them, one caught his eye. Chuck waved, but the boy turned away like he hadn't seen. There was an exchange of snickering.

Chuck thought it typical, and went back to humming and rocking, watching the sky fade darker. He hadn't thought they'd ask him to play or anything (he'd had eleven years of outcasting), but a returned wave or something would have been nice. If they were just going to mind their business, they could at least be civil about it.

When Chuck's father came home from a last-minute grocery run, he stepped over Chuck's bike lying in the driveway, but he at least had the decency to offer a "Hey, Chuckie."

Chuck waved at him slowly in the dying light. He usually smiled—for as little as Chuck talked, he smiled quite often. His father noticed his grim silence, lips together, skin cool and pale but not quite clammy. Chuck Warren looked a little like a blank-faced mannequin, or a boy in a trance. It perturbed Mr. Warren, just some, as if he felt something wrong about to happen. Had he stopped that night, asked his son to come inside with him for Cheetos and the ball game, asked his son if he drew anything that day, asked his son if school was going well and "Is anyone bothering you, Chuckie?" things would have gone differently.

Instead, he said, "Don't dawdle, Chuckie," and carried on inside.

Chuck rolled his eyes and went back to sitting and humming.

Chuck watched with rapt attention as the street turned from sunset orange to pre-dusk blue to the purple-black of nightfall. He tapped his fingers against the cold stoop, tightened his already broadening shoulders, and stared at the street lamp across from his two-car driveway and the small grassy median. He felt like there was a wire traced from his eyes to that light, like he couldn't look away. The world was that unlit bulb, seemingly louder than the distant scratch and scrape of hockey sticks and the chuffing of sprinklers on every other lawn. The shadows of the hockey-playing boys were stretching longer, leaking down the road like pooling blood, and Chuck's heart beat faster. Not fear, not yet. He was *thrilled*.

At long last, in what felt like a single moment, the sprinklers all turned off, the first cricket started tuning up, and the street was suddenly suspended in black summer darkness. It was the sort of dark that felt crawled-upon and tight, like worming through close branches.

And then the street lamps popped up gold and paged all kids to return home. But Chuck had other plans.

Those boys down the street swiped their net up and raced inside. In all of the neighborhood houses, in the half-hypnotized state of suburban mundanity, people drew their blinds. Even the Warrens joined them; they didn't recall that Chuck was on the stoop and assumed he was already tucked away in his room. Doors closed, windows were covered, and it was as if every house became a solitary fortress.

Chuck Warren was on the outside, where anything might happen to him. He understood that, but he was used to being ignored.

The entire town of Bridlington was minding its own nightly business when Chuck Warren shot to his feet and righted his bike. He pulled his helmet off the driveway and strapped it on, rustled in a small hedge to find the flashlight he'd hidden earlier, and weaseled it between the helmet strap and the side of his face. It was loose—he wished he had duct tape, but asking his dad would have given him up. He was far smarter than that. He swung onto his bike while the summer air hummed and a few small-town stars popped out above him in the impossibly wide sky.

Chuck lifted his light-up shoe onto the pedal, heaved forward, and sped off down the driveway to carve out into the empty road, racing for the center of town. His face was pale like the dead, but that Chuck Warren smile was back, despite a cold, dripping feeling down his spine. Maybe Chuck knew something was off that night. Maybe he felt something keeping pace with him as he rode for the center of town.

He decided to chance it, for one good summer.

Chuck broke out into the gasping expanse of Main Street, every boutique and shop already locked and abandoned to let him ride straight out to his destiny.

He heard a door close, and he slammed his bike to a nearly somersaulting stop on the corner while the singular streetlight in all of town turned red. He turned his head and saw the diner, just four shops away. Ms. Hoang, the owner and his next-door neighbor, was still locking up. Chuck held his breath and watched her balance her flip-phone against her ear while she fumbled to turn the keys.

"I'll be home soon," he heard her say. The key fit, and she started to turn toward Chuck before he could back his bike up or race off. "No, I know. I know."

She turned, and though the gold light and dark shadows made her face eyeless and ghoulish, he knew she'd seen him. Chuck flashed ice-cold, waiting for her to call him over, or walk him home, or do anything else he thought an adult might and probably should.

She raised her hand to him, cordial but without much intention. He didn't return the gesture, but he knew it didn't matter: she'd only done it to be polite, like a reflex that she seemed hardly aware of.

"I'll be home in a bit," she said into her cell, and she bustled off to the parking lot behind the diner. "We can talk about it then."

Then she was gone.

Chuck wheezed out a shaking breath just as the light above him turned to green. He started off again, barreling east. Sometimes, it was helpful that people really believed in the safe haven of a small town.

Chuck zipped past the tiny movie theater, the coffee shop, the Dairy Queen. He passed the last intersection, and Main Street tapered into a lonely, tree-lined highway with scattershot street lamps all flickering and moth-circled. He passed under the blinking yellow light strung overhead, and the motel emerged on his right, glowing under the crooked *VACANCY* sign. Chuck had never seen the *NO* part lit up, and the parking lot was mostly empty. That night, a single car sat forlorn, and he was slightly fixated by the way the trunk didn't quite close properly, like it was waiting to swallow something into it.

He rode faster, like he was being chased.

Chuck went past the motel's huge back lawn, and then past the drowsy Mac's convenience store and gas station. The sound of racing water grew louder and louder as he pedaled toward the shape of the bridge. The rushing was nearly maddening by the time his bike hobbled up onto the wooden beams.

Blue River shot off on either side of him, moonlit and glistening. But as isolating as that was (a boy on a bridge, with tumultuous water seemingly a hundred feet below, a silently sleeping town behind, and only the dark, toothy shape of the forest to welcome him once he crossed), all Chuck could think about was what lay ahead, and how it made white-hot sparks speed through his veins, made him grin against any cold sweat.

He was suddenly enveloped in the forest's cool shadow, where the street lamps were blocked by rustling leaves. Instead of feeling scared, Chuck turned on his flashlight. And instead of carrying on down the winding road that would eventually take him out past the Bridlington sign and the city limits, he carved a hard, off-road left down into the mouth of a hiking trail channeled between a chain-link fence and the dark forest. It was so thin he felt like he was parting waves of ferns and creeping vines. He went tearing forward anyway, pedaling on the decline. He hit the bottom of the trail and dumped his bike into the weeds with the sound of the river rapids rushing in his skull. The crickets screamed.

On the other side of the path, against the high fence, he saw another bike waiting. She was already there. In one shift of the tree branches, the playing card fastened to the back spokes shone bone-white and blood-red. Chuck froze, wide-eyed in the shifting light. He had been promised such a card. *That* was why he was out so late, chancing a grounding or maybe something worse. He could have simply taken that card and the clothespin it was fastened with, popped them on his bike, and gone home to bed. But that wasn't what this was about, right?

Paz Espino, the owner of that bike, had said that if Chuck snuck off when the street lamps came on, if he came out to Blue River where no one would hear him scream, if he carried on to the most terrifying place in all of Bridlington, he'd get a card the proper way. He'd ride in her rattling crew, and she'd be his friend forever.

A bit of wind blew, creaking the branches together and shifting shadows over the bike in a way that made him feel nearly ill with unease. For the first time in the night, Chuck got a vague feeling that something could be wrong. There was a crack from the woods, and he flinched and peered into the trees but could see nothing but green and dark. He swallowed and turned his head to eye the gap in the fence: one clear spot with no chain-link diamonds blurring the gorge beyond. It looked like a magic portal, one that would take him right to the girl who'd promised him a good summer.

Paz Espino, it should be mentioned, had a reputation for being a notorious loudmouth, and a notorious liar.

But he wanted to believe her—no, he *needed* to. She'd walked up to him that day sitting alone at recess (as he usually did), except this time he was crying because eighth-grader Emily Novak had called him a slur of a very French variety, which was part of her grand tour of thrice-daily playground destruction. Emily had then gone on to call Paz a "dirty little lying—" *thing that rhymes with bike*, and Paz had told Emily to kiss her uncle's ass, which Chuck had expected. Paz was one of those "bad eggs" his mother talked about, with the swearing and the ugly clothes and the rotten attitude.

What Chuck didn't expect was Paz stomping over to him then and crouching down with blunt certainty. The other three members of her rattling crew had gone back to tripping on the double Dutch ropes and laughing anyway. Paz looked at Chuck and his tears. Chuck was stunned into silence, waiting for her to bite his head off or eat his heart raw, like a dog.

"You good at double Dutch?" she asked him instead. It wasn't rude, or loudmouthed, or mean—she smiled, keen but kind. She didn't look like any sort of monster: a sun-bleached ball cap backwards over two braids twisted with fading chalk-dye, her skin a warm copper, her eyes clear brown in the light, wearing a Grave Digger T-shirt and cargo shorts.

Chuck stared at her, thinking it was some sort of joke or prank. He kept waiting for the smile to turn mean. Wasn't this Paz Espino, who told lies about lovely Mr. Meyer? Wasn't she caught stealing chips from the Mac's, and suspected of breaking the coffee shop window? And wasn't she the one his mother said to never play with, because *She's a bad egg, Chuckie—she's bad bad news and don't you ever go tangling with her, but mind your manners.*

Chuck knew he was supposed to fear Paz on the inside, but play it off like pity.

He also knew he was supposed to like Emily Novak.

Paz whooped when Chuck pushed himself to his feet and nodded concession. She called for her friend to drop the ropes and let Chuck have a go, and Chuck did, and he decided he would follow Paz anywhere. That was something like a premonition.

When the teachers broke their game up because someone fell and that someone said Paz pushed them, Chuck's eyes were opened.

"I'm not a liar," Paz told him from outside the principal's office, and she laughed. It was a bright yet nearly ugly sound, with the bitter ring of a person who'd said it before and never been believed. "Course, that's what a liar would say."

That night, past when the street lamps came on, ignored by everyone who'd watched him go, Chuck stared through the magic portal in the chain-link and felt something calling him out there. It was just Blue River, a place he'd passed over dozens of times. So why did he feel like something was creeping up his spine, tightening the muscles along it, a primal preparation for trouble? There was no such thing as monsters, Chuck presumed, and any playground myths about things that haunted old mills were for dumb kids on the junior side of the line. Chuck was no dumb kid, and Paz was waiting. And he'd decided he believed her.

He felt like a ninja (of the Teenage Mutant Turtle variety, which was the only kind he knew of) when he ducked through the gap. The fence jangled around him and he went loping down the steep dirt hill. The metal *DANGER: CITY DRAINAGE* sign stared at him as he went.

Below, Blue River was horribly loud and fast, frothy with rapids and studded with rocks, but there was just enough space between the water and the walls of the gorge for Chuck to run without getting too wet. The mouths of the drainage tunnels in the sloping sides gaped at him. The moon shone down so bright that his flashlight seemed redundant. He raced under the bridge over all the tumbling rocks and cigarette butts and someone's broken bong, focused straight ahead on the night's inevitable conclusion. He drew closer and closer, and his run slowed to a nearly reverent walk.

Slowly, with the methodical laying of each foot on each uneven stone, Chuck arrived at Bridlington's scariest meet-up spot: the old paper mill was half-sunk into the river, a collapsed story of crumbling nothing. It looked like there were ghosts in there, or monsters, but Chuck didn't believe in those. A creeping, more grown-up fear wondered about drifters.

He looked up, though he wasn't sure why. It felt like he was in a daze, like something was moving his neck for him.

Up atop the mill, fearlessly high, Paz Espino stood sideways on the roof and stared out over Blue River and her dominion. She had to be the bravest person in the world, Chuck thought. He swore he saw something bone-white and blood-red sticking from Paz's back pocket, and that made his mind up good and plenty.

Go on, the night seemed to say, though it sounded incredibly real to him over the pounding of his heart. *Are you chicken?*

No way.

Chuck approached the mill's window, just a crude square gap in the cement, and clambered through, scattering shards of stone. His feet hit the uneven ground, and the sounds of the river and forest were immediately quieted to a warbling semi-silence, as if someone had hit him hard in the head and made his ears ring. His flashlight was bobbing along to his frantic breathing, like the strobing lights at awful school dances. The darkness of the mill closed in around him. It was nothing like the wide, moonlit gorge. The air smelled like wet stone.

He turned his head to shine his limited light over the wall closest to him, but the visible tunnel from his flashlight showed no stairs up to where Paz was, only twisting spray paint.

Come on, Chuckie.

He tightened his shoulders, took a slow step forward, and

turned the light to the other side of the mill, so far away. He saw the outline of a rickety metal staircase, steep like a ladder, with the banister lying useless on the ground and twisted into a snake-like, wrenched-wrong shape. It was all shifting and unreal, dancing on the edge of his light, which stretched across the flat expanse of the muddy mill floor. He couldn't see the corners. He could have sworn something moved, but when he turned his flashlight on the spot there was nothing but a broken bottle.

And yet, still, he could hear faint whisperings behind his heavy pulse, though searching for them only made his skin creep.

Chuck breathed stiffly, closed his eyes, and knew there was no going back.

He started his ecstatic sprint to the stairs, never minding what danger lurked in the shadows. He was halfway there—halfway to Paz, to a playing card, to a perfect summer after eleven years as an outcast—when his watch chimed his 9:15 bedtime. It rang loud and obvious in the black silence. He stumbled forward, something caught his ankle, and he went crashing down to his bare knees. He barely had time to register what had tripped him before spindly, hard things crept over his ankles. Fingers. *Hands*.

Chuck heard something laughing in the darkness, a bubbly gurgle, followed by a high-pitched squeal ringing out around the room, creaking and echoing. Something dripped cold on the back of his neck. He smelled not just old stone but blood, and rot.

Chuck had one second to know the end was coming, to regret nothing. And then the ground smashed apart from under him, and he was yanked down into the dark to die bloody.

The rest of the town slept. Except for Paz.

FUGITIVE

The Boy came into town on a string of good luck that he was hardly aware of. All he knew was that he'd finally graduated high school, the summer sun was glinting through his windshield, his AC was cranked, the wind was rustling the canopy of branches that soared out over the road, and he was driving like there were sirens in his wake. His copilot (a dog named Bird) was sticking his head out the window, eyes squinted, feathery fur streaming.

Bird sniffed the air, all hot pavement and cold trees, and a bloody sort of scent that the Boy couldn't catch, and probably wouldn't care to either.

He was feeling good, slick, busy reciting monologues. "Is this a dagger which I see before me," he said, reaching one hand out over the wheel. The heat from his windshield warmed his skin. The Boy was an actor; he had dropped his voice low. "The handle toward my hand? Bird, come, let me clutch thee."

Bird slipped back through the half-cracked window to gnaw the Boy's reaching hand. The sun was dappling through the trees, and the Boy's chest felt tight in a way that was quite all right. He rattled his way through Macbeth's dagger soliloquy, and then something from some teenybopper movie he'd watched as a kid.

The Boy tapped his fingers on the steering wheel and whipped down the smooth curves of the road at a decently illegal speed. He caught his reflection in the sun-washed windshield: his hair was uneven but short, and the wavy texture hid the hack-job. He looked cool, he thought: reinvention was going well. His gas light had come on, so he knew he'd be smart to set up in the next place he crawled into. He passed a blue sign wrapped in vines that proudly proclaimed barely nine thousand residents.

"Bridlington," he said, tasting it. "Sound good enough, buddy ol' pal?"

Bird barked, and panted like he was smiling.

Now what the Boy didn't know about Bridlington was that the local police precinct barely scraped ten people, and they'd kept their major crime rate so low it was like the town was blessed by an almighty spirit of good citizenship and do-right attitude. It was the kind of thing that would probably look great on a billboard, and it meant that all six beat cops strained at their leashes and bit down hard on petty things like smoking under the bridge, riding ATVs around private farmland . . . or speeding. Bridlington's very own chief of police particularly enjoyed popping out his tripod chair and some paperwork next to the Blue River bridge, right where the speed limit abruptly sunk to something far more residential. Every local knew this; the good captain was mostly concerned with catching arrogant newcomers.

And so the Boy raced closer and closer to the bridge, the speedometer only going higher. He was ecstatic, electric—nothing would stop him when the forest opened up and released him into searing sunshine that burned his eyes. The car thundered off cracked pavement and onto the strange new rhythm of wooden planks. Blue River tore off in either direction.

It felt like being suspended for a moment, hovering in nothingness.

When the Boy's car hit road again, and kept on rocketing, no one stopped him. Fortunately for the Boy, the other benefit of sitting next to the bridge was that the captain had an eye and an ear on that old abandoned mill, and he had gone sauntering down there after thinking he saw someone. Which meant his tripod chair was empty and tipped over in the Boy's renegade wake.

The Boy had gotten lucky.

Besides the great majesty of Blue River and the less-than-great husk of the mill, the first thing Bridlington offered the Boy was a Mac's convenience store and gas station, which was exactly what he needed. He hauled left into the sparse parking lot and up to the pumps. The first was striped in tape with a sign that probably said something about it being out of order, but the sun was too bright on the stark-white paper.

"Boooo," the Boy said, and drove up to the next. Bird started sniffing fiercely again. With the windows down, the air reeked of chalky, dry cement. The Boy shut the car off, shot two finger-guns at Bird, and let his voice sink as low as it could possibly go without turning to gravel and scrape. "Be right back, copilot."

Bird smile-panted. The Boy kissed his nose very quickly before swinging out of his car and slamming the door behind him.

Thunk!

(*Thunk, thunk, thunk, thunk*)

The sound seemed to float off around the gas station, rattle the chain-link at the edges, and reverberate across the street to where the forest stretched a little past the gorge. Then it was only silence aside from the faint sizzle of the deliriously hot day.

Everything seemed still, a little too far from the town and from the river. The Boy's skin was prickling under his hoodie and jeans—he wanted to believe that was just sweat, but it felt like more than that. The air was hot in a thick way, like the bubble of stale air that rises from something rotting on the side of the road. Deep below the pavement, the soil and stone squirmed with something wrong, a premonition of another unseen catastrophe in the making.

The Boy blew air through his lips. Was he really losing his head so soon? "No way, man," he said to himself. There was nothing in the air but the distant sound of birds across the street and the even more distant rush of Blue River. The Boy turned to the gas pump, picked up the hose (he only had cash, which unfortunately meant having to deal with paying in person), and filled his matchbox-small car while Bird tumbled into the driver's seat.

Bird was a dog in the plainest sense of the word, which was to say he didn't look particularly special: he was a caramel sort of brown with a little white, had floppy ears and eyes like black marbles, and was decidedly medium-ish-large-sized with possible spaniel-shepherd-sheepdog-retriever origins. He wasn't exactly an "asset," couldn't drag Timmy from the well or play basketball or whatever. All Bird knew was "Stay," which the Boy assumed wouldn't be helpful in a crisis. But he was a happy-go-lucky little bastard who was clouding the glass with his usual panting smile, and it made the Boy feel like he was doing all right.

"You and me, dude," he said like he was in some stupid teen drama, meaning for it to come out sarcastic and ironic. But it came out very sincere, and entirely truthful.

Bird panted, licked his own nose, and panted more. The hose hiccuped. The Boy hooked it into the stand and popped the car door open.

Bird came spilling out. He dove and dipped in front of his Boy, claws clicking on the hot pavement that the Boy could feel through the rubber treads of his Converse.

"Don't get all sappy on me," the Boy said, but let Bird gnaw at his fingers.

Even under the overhang of the gas station, creaking and groaning despite the lack of wind, the sun was too bright. It turned everything flat and gray and hot. The Boy shoved his hands deep into the kangaroo pocket of his new hoodie, slouched in on himself so the fabric made a flat plane over his chest, and kicked his way across the empty parking lot. He started whistling, some old theme song to some old show.

Then there was a voice. He couldn't place it at first. It seemed to come from everywhere, or nowhere, or inside his skull:

"Hey, guy."

The Boy swallowed his whistling and half a scream, but

couldn't hide the lurch of his shoulders or stumbling of his feet. He'd thought he was alone. As he squinted through the pavement heat lines and into the shade from the Mac's overhang, he first saw a mess of bikes with cards in the spokes thrown next to the icebox, and then he saw a few shadows lit by the orange-red of the *OPEN* sign. For a moment in the sparse darkness, the figures seemed strange, like they were being pieced together Frankenstein-style as he looked at them. Faces bloomed from the dark, and small hands, and keen eyes, and bloody-red teeth.

His eyes adjusted to the shadows rather than the blinding light. Properly now, he saw four kids sitting on and around the out-of-season saltbox, passing a huge red slushy among them. Cherry: the smell was sickly sweet and strong. The kids were all quite a bit younger than the Boy—probably just getting into their middle-school years. They seemed very "small town": the boy on the saltbox was wearing a camo shirt that could only have come from a Bass Pro Shop, the girl next to him had ugly chunky sandals and one arm in a sling, and the kid with the slushy was missing two teeth in the front. Welcome to Podunk. Feeling entirely unthreatened now, the Boy sauntered into the shadows, approaching the sidewalk lip.

The one who had spoken pushed herself off the box to stand in front of the door. She was streaked with a little mud on her legs and arms, her dark hair was pulled into two thick braids studded with bits of twigs, her knees were bandaged with Spider-Man Band-Aids, and there was another on her cheek that took the Boy a second to recognize: Lightning McQueen from *Cars*. *Ah yes*, thought the Boy, *the classics*.

"I like your dog," the girl said, very simply, without moving.

Bird stopped his prancing and took to staring right at the girl, wiggling his nose with fierce intensity. The other three kids stared back from the box.

"Thanks," the Boy said, amiably enough. There were worse welcoming committees. "His name's Bird."

"Like the animal?" she said. "The animal that isn't a dog?"

"Well, a dog named Dog feels a little too obvious," said the boy called the Boy.

She tilted her head as if considering that, or him.

He'd always been a fast-talker, a little charming or at least disarming, and he tried to rely on it. "He's friendly," he offered. "You can hang with him while I pay."

The girl stared expectantly. She said nothing in response. The neon of the Mac's sign hummed. She sucked at her teeth, and didn't stop blocking the ad-plastered door. "Why are you in Bridlington?" she asked. She gave him a *very* obvious size-up.

"Good a place as any," he said, which was unfortunately true. "I think. Haven't had the chance to look around yet."

"You look like a weirdo."

"Right back at'cha," he dared to say.

It garnered no response, which didn't sit well. The group of them stared harder. One of them shook out his blue-pale hands with a grin, and it made Bird take a step backward. For a second, the Boy remembered that security cameras are a thing that exist, considered to himself that he didn't have proper ID, and wondered if talking to kids was way more trouble than it was worth.

Then one of the kids on the saltbox smiled and stuck out a

hand, and Bird's tail started wagging. He trotted off to them. The hand-shaker (the kid with missing teeth, a weedy-looking boy wearing a cross necklace) gave his slushy to the girl with the sling so he could scratch at Bird's ears.

The Boy could have gone on with his day, but something about those two kids prickled worse than their staring. "What happened there?" he asked, using his elbow to indicate the sling around the girl's cold-brown arm. The other was striped right up to the elbow with colorful elastics and jelly bracelets. "Something cool?"

She tilted her head at him very, *very* slowly. The Boy looked painfully honest in that moment . . . painfully himself.

The girl moved the collar of her pink shirt higher. The Boy caught a flash of a faint plum-red bruise before it was hidden. "Sure," she said carefully. She smiled, sharp, her eyes half covered under straw-dry hair. "Real cool."

The kid with the missing teeth snickered and shook out his hands again. Bird shook himself too and all the kids laughed, tapping at his nose and scratching his ears. The tension had snapped like a wafer, and the Boy's shoulders relaxed. He had, unknowingly, staved off death for a while.

"You usually go around asking questions?" the girl in front of the door asked.

"Looked like it hurt," was all he managed to say. "I broke my arm when I was your guys' age. Weirdo to weirdo, it sucked major ass."

They all nodded, like a small, approving council. Swearing at them seemed to give him favor, and he felt like this was good favor to have. He saw it in the first girl's clear brown eyes: a sliver of something keen, and "too smart for her own good."

"I'm Paz," she said. She straightened up, very businesslike for an eleven-year-old. "I like your dog, and I think you seem like not an asshole."

The Boy laughed. "Glad I'm Not-An-Asshole," he said, clicking his tongue. "You had me on the ropes for a second."

"Good," she said. "What's your name?"

The Boy's brain fumbled. He could have lied, but whatever kinship Paz was seeing in him, he similarly saw in her. A cosmic link, from weirdo to weirdo.

He shrugged. "Don't have one."

None of them gawked.

"Hmm," Paz said, tapping her toes. "You need a name."

"Obviously," he said. It felt like a fun game, and he had always liked kids this age, though he couldn't remember ever being one. "You got any ideas?"

Paz tilted her head and jerked her thumb back to the toothless boy. "Ben reads a lot," she said, "so he knows names. And he can make sure you don't have the same one as anyone else here."

The Boy waved a hand. "Spin the wheel, Benny," he said, to an approving little smirk from Paz. "What'll it be?"

Ben shook his hands harder, which seemed to help him think. He screwed up his face and made a high sound in his throat. "Asher," he finally said, because apparently all the average names were taken. "Or Gordon." *Yup*, the Boy thought. *All the average names are taken.*

"There's definitely no one here named that," said the girl with the sling.

The Boy shrugged. Why not? "Asher Gordon sounds fine to me."

The kids all grinned, even the quiet one still on the saltbox.

"Good," Paz said. She leaned in a little more, conspiratorially. "Weirdo to weirdo, I don't think anyone's going to give you much trouble as long as you keep to yourself."

That crept through him slowly, and now the fine hairs on his arms were itching against his thin hoodie. The gas pump overhang gave a low, slow creak like something tightening its muscles. What sort of trouble was there to get into?

"There's a motel just up the road on the left," she said. "My dad owns it, and it's cheap." She leaned back on one leg and gave him another very obvious scan that seemed to suggest (and rightly so) that she thought he was in need of "cheap."

"Thanks," Asher said, nodding and trying to look sincere. "I'm gonna go pay. Stay, Bird."

Asher stepped for the doors.

"Wait," Paz said.

He turned to look at her, and she was standing rigid, hands balled in fists at her sides. She seemed hesitant to tell him something, looking around like someone might overhear.

"Be careful," she finally said. Her eyes were all keen again, and he thought they looked as unstoppable and deadly as that river he'd passed: too huge, with too much possibility. "People here won't watch your back if something happens. We will, though. We can keep you safe."

He furrowed his brow. Bird barked once, and it shook the chain-link on the edges of the gas station. It startled him.

Oh, he suddenly thought. *It's some sort of game, like some movie or whatever.*

Asher Gordon nodded, made sure to add a polite but still sort of wary "Thanks, dude," and then turned on his slightly gummy heels and walked into the deliciously AC-ed convenience store.

He could still feel Paz staring at him, and the momentum of the metaphorical knife barely missed. But then he heard the jangling of bikes, the rattling of cards in spokes, and Paz's crew was gone.

To him, they were just kids like any others. He didn't know what had already happened, and that was the problem.

BRIDLINGTON

In the moments directly after Chuck Warren's death, Paz had felt the first drop of fear enter her veins. It was like that soft-looking bit of ice that grows from the middle of a freezing water bottle, sending fractals creeping out, touching more and more of the water around it. Water to ice. Liquid to solid.

Paz had stood on the top of the paper mill, hearing Chuck's scream race around in her head. It had been cut off suddenly along with his ringing watch, but it echoed longer and longer, a baseline beneath the tempo of her heartbeat slamming in her chest and in her temples and against her lungs. She couldn't breathe more than shallow mouthfuls. She had frozen solid, staring down at Blue River.

She told herself to move. *Don't just ignore it. Don't just stand there!* She felt like she was curled up in bed after a nightmare, debating if it was better to run to her parents' room and chance the thing that hid under the bed, or stay still and hope it didn't notice she was awake. Her eyes were wide, her skin clammy and cold, but she felt her body like you might feel winter chill radiating from a window: only a vague suggestion of what's beyond. She knew her pulse was hammering and there was sweat in her eyes, but it was all too far away to feel properly.

Come on, scaredy-cat, she thought. *Just* move.

This was supposed to be a good summer—a great one. They were going to steal stickers from her mom so it wouldn't be just Ben who would fill out his summer reading log, and she and Ellie were going to marathon all their favorite shows all night, and they were going to raid the movie theater and the Mac's like a storming cavalry. Finally, they were going to pool Sammy's and Paz's chore money to get *Mario Kart*, because they only needed one cartridge, and the four of them didn't plan on being apart long that summer. No, the five of them. They were supposed to have Chuck. She was the one who had double-dog-quadruple-to-the-googleplex-million *dared* him to come out in the first place. And now she was alone.

Paz Espino stood on that roof, heart pounding so hard she tasted bile, the trees at the top of the gorge whispering and Blue River chuckling. There was no way she could jump from the roof to get away. She'd have to go through the mill, and find out what happened.

Maybe he was still alive, she reasoned. That got a bit more blood into her muscles.

Paz, despite the terror trying to numb her from the stomach out, needed to figure out what happened.

Paz turned on the headlamp stolen from her father and tightened with a pink hair tie. Then, she slipped back across the cement roof to the gap of the access. Her lungs were still competing with her heart, and it felt like she was trying to breathe in snow or river water. The cricket sounds of the forest followed.

Carefully, she eased into the gloom, ready to race back up to the open safety of the roof. She stepped down half the stairs, moved her light around, waiting for something horrific to leap out from the shadows or scuttle from the light. Nothing did. Still, there was no sign of Chuck, only the usual broken bottles and spindly tree branches. Except now, where there had once been nothing but the thick sheet of dirt that covered the floor, there was a perfectly round chasm right in the middle of the room.

Paz gasped. Her next breath caught in her throat and came out as a gurgling moan. Her skin was crackling-cold; moving felt like breaking frost from her joints. She reached the ground and walked carefully forward, stutter-stepping gingerly over the branches. They dragged tentative fingers against her ankles, but they were just branches. Yes. Just branches.

It was a warm night, but she half expected to see her breath. "Chuck?"

No answer. Her light trembled, and she could have sworn she saw movement down in the gap, like something watching from below the surface. There was an uncanniness about the dark in there, like it was just slightly left of what it should be, and she could only tell by the faint reek in the air.

Chuck could still be alive. She kept that in her head.

Paz Espino, eleven and three-quarters, stepped forward and stared down down down into the dark. She hoped she could just laugh at herself for being so stupid and letting fear recreate every monster movie she'd ever seen. She hoped she'd see Chuck

Warren, a little bruised up but fine, and she'd put the playing card from her pocket into Chuck's spokes and he'd be a real member of the crew. And then nothing else would have to matter.

Instead, she smelled rot. She smelled blood. A bubbly, breathing sound echoed up to her ice-cold ears. Down in the dark pit, too far for her flashlight to reach, she saw the glow of a yellow-orange eye.

Her entire body locked. She felt the air pressing hot against her clammy face. The breathing sound grew louder, rushing through her and building pressure. It sprayed the bloody smell upward, so thick she thought she'd reek of it forever. The eye moved closer, glowed brighter. The whole world rumbled—that *thing* was coming for her next.

Paz Espino was no coward, but she knew this needed more than a little girl with a bike and a flashlight. She needed help.

Paz scrambled from the mill window and ran with her arms pumping and her shoes tumbling and her breath coming out in frantic, choked gasps. She practically clawed her way up the gorge wall and biked home as fast as flight. In what seemed like only a single heartbeat, she was slipping back through the high and small window of the motel bathroom in the suite she shared with her sister and racing, muddy and sweat-soaked and frantic, to her parents' door. She'd been tight-lipped for some time, but there was no "tattling" or "making up rumors" now that there was proof someone was really in trouble, and if she could just—

"Paz," she heard, sounding very immediate in the silence. "I've been waiting up for an hour. Where were you?"

She managed to turn. Her sister, Marcela, was sitting up in

bed with her earbuds in and her iPod in her hands. With just a bit of white parking lot light coming in through the curtains, Paz could see only one of Marcela's eyes. She saw it take in all the mud and Paz's twitching terror, and then go wide as a jaw-breaker. "Paz," she said, warningly. "What did you do?"

"Nothing!" Paz shrieked. She wasn't crying then but she was *oh so close* in the way where her lungs felt too big against her ribs and her eyes stung and she couldn't stand still. "Marcela, I didn't do anything—I didn't—we can still save him if we—"

Marcela was already up out of bed and striding for Paz. For a moment, Paz was terrified she was about to be bowled over like a raccoon on the northern train tracks, but Marcela grabbed her in her arms and hugged her fiercely. It felt half like love and half like a restraint to anchor her down.

Her parents' door opened.

Paz, shaking and sweating so profusely that it looked like tears, stared at her dad, and her mom wandering up behind him.

The words tumbled from Paz's lips. "A monster," she said.

A monster, a monster.

All at once both of Paz's parents seemed to notice, under the protective shell of Marcela, the headlamp, and the mud, and the twigs caught in Paz's shoelaces. Something had happened that wasn't just a nightmare. Something had happened, and Paz was in the middle of it, like she always seemed to be.

"We were at the m-mill," Paz choked out, her voice a shiver. Marcela tensed around her, so tight it almost hurt. Her parents seemed blurry and far away. And Chuck. Oh, Chuck. Her mother made a dry, choking sound and her father's eyes dimmed.

She just had to tell them what happened, and then they could get out to the mill and kill the thing. "Chuck Warren came to the m-m-mill and a monster got him—"

It all happened in segments for Paz; her mind was slipping away from her. Every moment was impossible to hold on to and collided with the next. All from within Marcela's arms, Paz Espino wailed to her parents. And then:

"Chuck could still be alive. We have to tell the police," Paz's mother said, framed in the doorway to their room. Paz was shaking and rocking, wished Marcela would relax her hold so she could *move*.

"It wasn't Paz's fault," her father said. But it was more than that. Paz already had a reputation for being a liar. She was surprised Marcela still cared for her.

"It was a monster!" Paz screamed.

"Come on, Paz," Marcela said. Had it sounded cold, Paz might have told her where she could shove it, would have told her sister that she hated her, but Marcela's voice was nearly as tear-soaked. "Don't make it worse. We'll just tell Captain Reilly."

Marcela and Mrs. Espino won in the end, and they called the police. Captain Reilly met them in the fluorescent-lit police station with his uniform only slightly rumpled, his blue eyes sharp and wary. Marcela's hand was on Paz's shoulder, tight.

"Go ahead," Mr. Espino said. He looked very carefully at Paz, as if silently begging for something. She didn't know what. "Tell Captain Reilly what happened, sweetie."

She knew well and good what happened. She almost started with "So Emily Novak called Chuck a bad word today," but she knew that wasn't going to help her case. She had to be smart about this. All she wanted was to be scared, but she had to "play the game," which hurt like a dislocated arm.

"I went out to the mill and I told Chuck to come, so we could give him a card, so he could be in the crew," she said, practically vibrating. It all came out at once, a tumble of words. "And I went through the mill and nothing happened—I got to the roof—but when Chuck came in, he . . ." She swallowed, narrowed her eyes. The mill had felt weird when she'd passed through. Too dark, too quiet. She should have noticed sooner, but there could still be time to put it right. She stomped her muddy shoe. "Something *got him,* Captain Reilly. I heard it! I heard the floor break and he fell and when I went and looked in there was an *eye* and I—"

"Chuck Warren fell," Mr. Espino said, his hand on Paz's other shoulder. It shut her up suddenly. "We didn't know she was out there, and we all know that mill was an accident waiting to—"

"It wasn't an accident!" Paz tried to say. "If you just listen, then we can—"

"I'll need to question her about it, to get more details," the captain said, eyeing Paz. He was a tall man, trimly muscled, not imposing, just average, but his face was drained grey too. Nothing like this had *ever* happened in Bridlington, and he'd been the one to make sure. "And I don't want to hear any lies this time. Get your story straight, Espino." He called every kid by their last name, but she never liked how he said hers.

Mrs. Espino's shoulders tightened. She opened her mouth to say something, tell the captain off for calling her daughter a liar.

It wasn't like Paz was some stranger—she was an eleven-year-old little girl that Captain Reilly had known all her life, and saying a monster ate Chuck meant she'd been traumatized, surely. But she felt the words gripped in her throat and shoved back down.

"Maybe we can still save him!" Paz said, hoping against everything that he hadn't been swallowed whole. She didn't like Captain Reilly at all, but if there was ever a time in the movie where the hero united with the crooked cop, it was before they killed the monster and saved the sidekick. "Captain—"

"This is the incident with the Meyers all over again," Captain Reilly said. His voice was a hiss, his face pinched and more worried than angry, already starting to drip with sweat. "And now you've trespassed a second time, and someone could be very, *very* hurt."

Paz recoiled, as if from a snake. "Yes, but—"

"You've got a bad case of lockjaw, Espino," Captain Reilly snapped, pointing his finger and shaking, too. "Learn to apologize or I will personally pry your teeth off this story with some time behind bars."

Paz's voice cracked. "I wasn't lying then and I'm not—"

"Paz," Marcela whispered, while the captain picked up the phone to get people to the mill and prep the Warrens for the worst. "Just shut up. Please just shut up."

Cruisers went out, and Chuck was found and confirmed to be dead, and the police recovered his body without seeing a single monster in the mill basement. Paz learned something horrifying from that: the monster was *smart*. It knew who to attack, and who to leave, and how to remain unseen.

And then the sobbing Warrens came from the mill to the station. They wailed about how Paz was an awful influence, always had been. Trespassing on the Meyers' property and lying about them, loitering around the town, schoolyard skirmishes, slashed tires, stolen library books, broken toys.

"I didn't do any of it," Paz said, shaking now. She felt farther and farther from her body, and every step away made her feel smaller, compressed. She was an easy target when a classmate lost their book, broke someone else's toy, wanted to slash tires but didn't want to get caught. Ever since the Meyer incident, ever since they'd heard that Espino girls locked their jaws like dogs.

Marcela was silent beside her.

"'Cela, tell them I didn't do it."

Marcela was silent while the adults shouted back and forth above Paz's head. Mrs. Warren wailed some more, and Mr. Warren said, "How do we know she didn't hurt Chuckie? Didn't drag him out there as some sort of . . . awful *prank*? Look at her!"

"What the hell do you mean by that?" Mr. Espino snapped.

Mrs. Warren turned up the waterworks.

Paz felt ready to shatter. Worse than the monster, there were the adults who weren't listening to her, and her sister standing silent. She felt so impossibly small that she thought she would slip into the Grand Canyon grouting between the floor tiles. Paz felt every cell of her body rumbling like a train getting closer, and it blurred the adults into fluorescent-lit silhouettes. It was one thing for there to be a monster, but it was another thing for no one to believe her.

Paz had never been violent, but every bough breaks.

"LISTEN TO ME!" she screamed, and she ripped herself away from Marcela's stiff hand to kick Mr. Warren as hard as she could with her muddy shoe. She kicked him again and again, to the horror of her family, until Captain Reilly grabbed her around the middle and hauled her off.

"IT WAS A MONSTER!" Paz howled, so hard her voice scraped. She was ballistic, a fury of small fists and gnashing teeth. "Don't act like you care about Chuck now! You didn't even notice he was gone!"

Captain Reilly thunked her back down, and she fumed at him, tears rushing acid-hot down her cheeks.

"Espino," he said. Not unkindly, or viciously; in fact, his voice was so level that it was infuriating, as if none of this affected him at all. They'd confirmed Chuck was dead, and now he just needed to manage the fallout. "If you keep on lying, more people are going to get hurt, and this will last a lot longer next time."

She readied to yell again. Only when the door clanked closed did Paz realize she'd been taken to the other side of the office, into the sectioned-off solitude of Bridlington's rarely used holding cell. That shut the rest of the room up for just a second. Even Marcela—still invisible—tensed her knees.

Captain Reilly said nothing, because he figured his actions spoke for themselves.

Mrs. Espino opened her mouth, her husband too, but Captain Reilly herded them into the hall along with the vindicated Warrens, and in the end, no one said anything about Paz.

The door shut all the sound out, so there was only the buzzing of the lights.

"A monster," Paz murmured, her lips numb against each other. Her eyes found the blurry shape of her sister standing silent against the wall. "Marcela, you believe me, right?"

"You've really done it now," Marcela whispered. Her voice was low and her eyes were blank. "If Mom and Dad get any heat from this, it's your fault."

It sure would be, but worse was coming, and Paz could feel it even if no one listened. She held it all inside of her like a blast charge, knowing the end would be bloody, and knowing it was preventable. That was the worst part, that in that cell at eleven years old, she knew.

That night, so many towns away, Asher Gordon dreamed the first semblance of his plan: graduating, taking Bird, buying some shitty used car, and leaving for good. The cosmic collision had already been set in motion, and it would be catastrophic.

LOUDMOUTH

A sher Gordon, fugitive and renegade with the support of what he assumed was just any ordinary pack of kids, grabbed a gas station sandwich, a newspaper, and a bottle of water. He kept his stance loose, smiling a bit and tapping his toes to the jingly convenience store music. He was "too blessed to be stressed," as he would have put it.

Asher sauntered up to the counter with his purchases. The clerk was frowning, pimpled, and reeking of Axe body spray. He was taller than Asher (most people were, he knew bitterly) but was clearly fourteen at the most.

Asher dropped his goods on the spread of lottery tickets. "Pump two," he said, with his easy smile. Small town life was chipper and kind, and he played along blissfully. "How's your day going . . ." He looked at the clerk's nametag. "Braaaaden?"

The boy stared blankly at him. "Brady," he said, flatly.

"Asher," Asher said cordially. His new name felt all right, a little rough but already softening, like new jeans.

Brady crinkled his nose, and though Asher couldn't see the

bat they kept behind the counter for "emergencies," or Brady's toe touching it, he felt a heavy uncertainty float around the empty Mac's, along with the smell of burnt coffee. Brady flicked his eyes up to the bulbous black camera above Asher's head, and Asher definitely noticed that.

"I don't recognize you," Brady said.

"I'm new here," Asher offered, jerking his thumb over his shoulder.

"Obviously," Brady said. "We don't get many visitors."

"I figured—"

"Mostly people shopping," Brady said, putting everything in a bag. He watched Asher closer. "You like . . . shopping?"

That felt . . . loaded. That felt like trying to say something without saying it, and with nothing you could point a finger at. Asher wanted to be sharp in his return, but it came out crackly. "Not really," he said. He was already doing a full-body scan of himself, trying to find loose threads. Black hoodie, straight-legged jeans, boring green Converse, a haircut he'd seen on a million guys his age.

He caught an image of himself in the mirror behind the counter, and something about his reflection set off every pain receptor in his body. He straightened his posture, grabbed dark sunglasses off the rack and tossed them to Brady, then pocketed his hands again.

"These too," he said, trying to pitch his voice down.

Brady was still eyeing Asher hard, but he scanned the sunglasses and tossed them in the plastic bag. Asher reached for it, and Brady pulled it back.

"That's $68.58," he said. He seemed stiff and strange, like looking at him too long might reveal some cardboard flatness. Like the town beyond this store was only a painted backdrop.

Asher was sweating buckets, and the price made him woozy all over again. He wanted that water and those sunglasses. The kid in the mirror looked scared out of his mind, his eyes wide and lost. No, no. He wasn't going to turn tail at the first sign of trouble. He was better than this, more adept, ready for anything. Renegade and fugitive. Paz had told him to just mind his business, so he would.

He forked over seventy dollars in tens and fives, from a white envelope of cash that he knew probably looked suspicious as hell. "Keep the change," he said, trying to deflect with another smile.

Brady opened his mouth like there'd be more, something that would strip Asher bare and leave him exposed for Bridlington to feast on, but then he closed it. He bent his face into a very prize-winning smile that was (unbeknownst to Asher) a genetic trait from his mother's side, which made it a Reilly trait.

"Blessed day," Brady said, probably not kindly. His eyes shone dully.

Jesus freak, Asher thought, with the earned resignation of someone who has survived K to 12 Catholic school. *And with your spirit*, he wanted to joke, but he didn't want to poke at any of this. He didn't want his words to tear through it like the soft skin of a rotten fruit. "Thanks," he said, taking his bag to promptly leave the fluorescent hell of the Mac's.

He stepped into the sunshine and the thick, hot air, trying to experience it as a reprieve. A car rolled down Main Street, and he could have sworn all four people inside stared at him. It sent shivers all the way through him. He thought of those old kiddy safety spells: the bad things can't get me if I'm under the covers; the bad things can't get me if I'm going *up* the stairs from the basement; the bad things can't get me if the sun is shining. And yet, even the sun felt wrong up there, like it could be unscrewed and broken on the pavement into razor shards.

Bird trotted over and nudged his nose into Asher's leg, so Asher let a cold hand hang down to pet him between his ears. Asher stood alone on the sidewalk, tilting his head up and filling his chest as much as he was able.

His dog, his shitty car, and this envelope of dwindling cash were everything he had in the world. He hadn't expected how much gas and provisions would cost, or his clothes, or breakfast, or lunch. Fugitive though he was, he wasn't a bank robber, and though he had a debit card, he'd seen enough cop dramas to know that using it was a rookie mistake for a man on the run. None of his IDs said "Asher Gordon."

Had the next moment never happened, Asher would never have slipped on those overpriced sunglasses, and he would have ended up dead in a Harville alley with blue lips and emptied pockets, Bird huddled against his chest. But Captain Reilly had made the seemingly neutral decision to walk to the Mac's for his free coffee, so when Asher looked up, he saw a man surveying his car. Had it been just any man, Asher might have assumed he was impressed that a shitbox like that was still on the road, but Asher sure knew a cap and badge when he saw them. And after waiting so long to get his license, he only had his learner's permit. Not illegal to drive, but without an adult in sight to sit passenger with him, he was toast.

Asher choked back a whine and fished the sunglasses out of the shopping bag. He wormed off the tag and slid them up his nose.

The dark shadows fell over his soft eyes and turned everything different and dark, like premature dusk. Something about it reminded him that he was the cool guy from the cardboard-set movie. *And hey, thanks Brady,* he thought, because that was a good rehearsal before the final take.

Asher Gordon was an actor. It would save his life, for a while at least.

Asher twisted his panicked frown into a smile, straightened the lines of his posture, hooked the thumbs of his often gesticulating hands into his belt loops, and he and Bird trotted over to the cop.

"Afternoon, officer," Asher called, while the cop was standing in front of the car, writing down the plate number that sure wouldn't pull up "Asher Gordon" if he ran it. "Can I help you?"

The cop turned, already smiling. He didn't look like the sort of hardball cop Asher thought would grill him to hell and back. More like someone's Little League coach who took everyone out for milkshakes after the game. "This your car . . . son?" he asked.

Asher noted the pause before the last word and widened his stance, nodding. *License and registration. License and registration.* "Yes, sir," he said. He thought about the casual way Brady had stood and emulated the joyless rigidity.

"Where you headed?" the cop asked, tucking the notebook

into his pocket. He seemed casual enough, but Bird was hugging Asher's ankles now, and Asher felt a rushing sound building in his head. There must have been a smudge on his glasses—something seemed to move across the cop, like a shifting of clouds, despite the pure blue overhead.

"Around," Asher said, though he instantly regretted it when the cop raised a "that won't do" eyebrow. Asher got on that quick. "It's my year off, sir, so I'm getting some traveling in before I go into . . ." He had no university aspirations, and probably looked like it. Was "the police academy" too obvious a suck-up? "The reserves," he finished. "Army."

Hoo-rah, he thought, and was glad he hadn't said that out loud.

"Good man," the cop said. He wagged a finger, and Asher knew he'd gotten the key into the lock. All suspicion was gone; his head began to clear of that rushing. "I've been trying to get more guys your age to consider it, but they all just wanna sit on their asses instead, waiting for the other guy to put in the effort." He laughed and nudged his elbow into Asher's arm. Asher laughed because his whole future was hanging in the balance.

"Yeah," he said, plainly.

"Well, I'll leave you to it," the cop said.

Just like that. Asher slowly, warily let all the built-up air out of his chest.

"Are you staying in town long?"

"I don't think so," Asher said, which was just good planning ahead. He was sure that a year from then, he would be so lodged in this town that even when it was clear he had no desire to wear camo and do push-ups and get yelled at, everyone in Bridlington would love him already and forget about the little white lie from his first hour. "I'll probably be gone by dinner."

It sure was a plan.

"Well, for now, I'm Captain Caleb Reilly," the officer said with his bright smile, and he stuck out his hand. Asher stepped forward and shook it. Bird's nervous panting turned into a thin whine. "Welcome to Bridlington, son."

The last word had more confidence in it. "Asher Gordon," he said, and it fit that time. *Yup, that's me*, Asher thought.

"Good to meet you, Asher," Captain Reilly said. He looked down to Bird, and Asher was sure he saw a hint of unease in the good captain's eyes. "And this is?"

"Bird," Asher said, letting go. "He's friendly."

Bird gave a very convincing smile.

The captain smiled back. "Good day to you too, Bird," he said. Then he tipped his cap like a guy in a movie and turned to walk off into the Mac's. The door clinked shut behind him and Asher caught his own reflection, where his nervous grimace looked like a chilling smile in the uneven glass. That smudge wafted strangely around him like a growing smoke.

Asher got in his car, dropped his forehead into the steering wheel, and let out the tortured groan he'd been holding in since stepping out.

PAZ

The morning before Asher came into town, Paz had already been spending a long time pacing, thinking, screaming, plotting, trying to figure out how one kills a monster that no one believes in. But by noon that day, she felt like she'd cracked it, or was at least coming up on some decision. She went trotting back from the now boarded-up mill with the sun burning hot and no breeze to move it. She hiked up the gorge and through the fence. Her trusty little BMX bike (which she had seen in a Canadian Tire flyer and *begged* for) was leaned against the chain-link, glittering, with the streamers blowing faintly and the playing card bone-white and blood-red.

She plucked the card from her spokes.

Paz kicked her way farther into the undergrowth, looking through the ferns and branches with the smell of greenery and water and soil thick and fresh. It was all very tough to move, but she found what she was looking for, half sunken into the mud.

Paz Espino found Chuck's long-lost bike, something no one else had thought to look for. The back tire looked almost like a grave marker, bent upward with the sun shifting over it. She was morosely quiet and focused, with the rapt attention of a child working magic in the summer sun. Paz took the clothespin and playing card and fastened them carefully on Chuck's back wheel. Put it on wrong and it would fall out or rip.

Childhood pacts . . . stronger than diamond, or distance, or death. There was nothing more haunting than that. Paz hadn't really been invited to Chuck's funeral, but this was her own solemn ritual.

She'd get the monster, she thought, standing alone in the forest as it hummed around her and the light shone warm against her chilled skin. She'd kill it, and then everyone would know she was right, and no more kids would die. It wasn't just *a* plan, but *the* plan, the only one available. Once the monster was dead for everyone to see, it'd be damn hard to ignore.

She pedaled as fast as she could into town. When she spotted Ben and Ellie's half-broken bikes outside the curio shop, a star necklace looped on the handlebars of one, she stopped and looked through the big fish tank. Through all the swirling, she saw brother and sister inside the shop, sipping one big slushy between the two of them and stepping on the back of the owner's shoes over and over. It was more brazen than they usually were, but Paz respected it. She grinned when the owner turned to snap at them and everyone in the store stared. Ellie and Ben hid behind a row of comics and bumped fists, doing nothing to hide their giggling.

The two skipped out the door, and Paz smiled and hugged both twig-thin siblings.

"Where were you?" Ellie asked. She punched Paz's shoulder and then readjusted her sling. "We haven't seen you since . . ." Her energy died suddenly. None of them really wanted to say it.

Paz shrugged, looking down at her spread feet and sticking her tongue in her cheek. "I was thinking things over," she said, nodding slowly. "You remember the monster?"

"Yeah," the two of them said, drawing a step closer. She'd told them about it the morning after Chuck's death, under the motel jungle gym, and both they and Sammy had believed her. They'd always known something was wrong here, and now they knew what it was.

"Did you figure out how to kill it?" Ellie asked.

Paz looked up, serious. "Oh yeah," she said, with no smile. She looked off down the street one way then the other. It wasn't safe in the open; she still wasn't sure if they'd be overheard by the people walking, even if passersby were keeping their eyes locked much higher than three eleven-year-olds. "Let's get Sammy, then we'll talk."

The three rode along Main Street, the playing cards rattling loudly and attracting a few glances or curled lips. But everyone who heard them turned back to chattering with their friends or browsing outdoor racks of clothes, minding their Bridlington business. Paz caught her name in a conversation she passed just north of Main Street—parents of Marcela's boyfriend's friend, which was the sort of roundabout way everyone knew everyone in such a small town—and the three children slowed to eavesdrop. They followed close behind, putting their feet on the sidewalk and stepping their bikes forward.

"I still don't understand how it happened," the woman said, a tote bag on her arm. "Marcela is so lovely. And then to have Paz so . . ."

"Beautiful," Paz whispered to her crew, flicking one braid behind her shoulder. Ellie snickered and pretended to swoon. Ben pretended to snap photos like a paparazzo.

"Her parents should have gotten her help the second she started running her mouth about the Meyers. She was just looking for attention," the man said. Ben and Ellie breathed out slowly. "The Espinos never had a good handle on that kid. I'm not surprised at all."

Paz sniffed, more indignant than upset. She wanted to kick their sustainable canvas shopping bag as far as it would go, but she knew better. The gossipers walked on, leaving Paz and her friends to stare after them. Paz sat low on her seat, jaded to what the town said about her. The silly old gossip would stop when they killed the monster.

"Do you think Batman could beat up a Level X Charizard?" Ben suddenly asked, and that sent them back into roaring good spirits while they rode off to get Sammy. The conversation evolved into whether this was a world with Poké Centers or a world with Lazarus Pits. Paz rode with no hands, Ben hopped off curbs, and Ellie bragged that she was doing the whole thing one-handed so she was cooler than both of them. Ben claimed he got his bike to wheelie when no one was looking. He hadn't, but Ellie and Paz believed him anyway.

By the time they arrived on Sammy's street, Paz felt better than she had since Chuck's death. She wished she'd called on her friends sooner; it all felt sunnier, easier to handle. The monster felt killable, and the town saveable.

They picked up the fourth member of their rattling crew with cheers and hugs, and Paz knew the final stand was starting. The ground was writhing under her feet, even the houses were tensing, but she wasn't afraid.

She felt the thing beneath the town whispering, and she dared it to come out and play.

ESPINO GIRLS

Marcela Espino was having a very lovely time sitting in the coffee shop. It was one of those modern, cutesy little places, with flowers painted on the walls, hissing espresso machines, chalkboards with fun doodles, and one Caleb Reilly, Junior, sitting across from her. Usually she spent the summers working at the motel, but her father had found some other sad sack to take care of maintenance. So she got to spend more time with Caleb while he sat as the youngest member of the town council or as the assistant coach of the junior hockey team, or for dinner with his parents.

At that moment, he was sitting across from her with the straw of his iced tea stuck in the corner of his mouth, plunking his thumbs into his phone screen and looking very focused. She knew he was planning a party at Quinn Bright's house, so they could all fulfill the innate teenage need to disappoint your parents in a controlled fashion. Caleb Reilly knew Bridlington, could track his family history all the way back to the days when the mill was more than a ghost story. This to say he understood how the town worked. He was very businesslike about Bridlington, very grown-up, unlike most of the boys their age, and she loved him for it.

Marcela smiled to herself and leaned forward to rest her chin on the heels of her hands. "Caleb," she said.

He looked up at her. He had a bit of a puppy-dog stare, if that puppy dog had eyes the color of glaciers, neatly cropped sandy hair, and the smooth suggestion of a growing tan. The pink light through the painted window carved at the solid lines of his jaw and his broad shoulders under his dad's old academy T-shirt. He was straight out of *Tiger Beat* magazine, or a pulpy teen romance, and boy did she know it. Jackpot, baby.

"Hmm?" he asked, quirking up the corner of his mouth.

"Nothing, just wanted to see your face," she said over the "OHHHH!" sound of some guys at another table watching something on a phone. She barely flinched.

"You're such a nerd," Caleb told her, but he was smiling.

The coffee shop was decently packed with people around their age. One of Caleb's hockey teammates (the goalie, Marcela knew) made a whipcrack sound when he saw Caleb grinning.

"Screw off, Adam!" Caleb called, spinning in his chair to throw one arm over the back.

One of the baristas (who Marcela definitely had all four years of math with and could still definitely not remember the name of) rolled her eyes and gave Marcela a seemingly under-standing look, mouthing the word "men" with her pretty glossed lips. Marcela mirrored the eyeroll exactly, shook her head with her perfectly looping curls glinting in the sunlight, and then turned a dainty profile to look out the window and appear as if she was better than boyish squabbles.

Marcela was not vain: she was calculated. She loved Caleb when she heard him tell Adam that just because he couldn't keep a girlfriend didn't mean he had to bash Caleb for loving his. She knew there were timelines where she was not so pretty as she was, and they were grim.

And so she had one thought, clear and exact: *I'm lucky.* It was set up like a wall in her head. It kept back the screaming, and the reaching hands, and the stalking threat she knew was there because hadn't her sister said there was a monster? And couldn't she feel it sometimes, a strange itch lurking under the tiles beneath her feet, or an echo in the bubbling of the machines? Couldn't she hear it in the laughter of the room which, when you really thought about it, sounded like screaming? And if you really looked, you could see everyone's teeth.

She let it all flow from her head like spilled nail polish. There was a sound in there like Blue River during a storm, or the hushing rattle of cornstalks, but it faded quieter and quieter. Monsters can't get you when the sun is out. Everyone knew that. And Caleb Reilly was his own sort of sun.

Still, she caught the eye of two middle-aged people in a booth across the room, who quickly looked away. It made curdling fear trickle down through her stomach, more real than monsters. She strained to hear what they were saying, if they were saying anything. Was she only imagining that she heard the name "Paz" slip from that old man's crusty lips?

"Hey," Caleb said softly. His hand landed on hers and she

jerked her head over to him with pursed lips. While his voice was kind, his face was set as stone. "You drifted off, Mar," he said, with a careful tilt of his head and furrow of his brow. "You all right?"

"I thought I heard . . ." She blinked back a growing pain behind her forehead. "Nothing," she decided. She looked out the cracked-open window at the mundane pleasantness of the town she grew up in, all brightly painted and quaint. The sounds of birds and slow cars drifted in.

There was no sense worrying. Things were going to be okay. Caleb would be back from police training in two years, there'd be a huge wedding, she'd be the pretty pretty princess that every girl dreams of being, then they'd get a dog that they'd unironically call a "fur baby" until they eventually produced two kids named dumb shit like Caleb III and Blaklynianna, and she'd bake pies for the church bake sales with all the other wine moms until she drifted off into the light surrounded by a huge family of Bridlington carbon copies.

She wanted it so desperately, she worried she'd sink her teeth too far, her jaw would lock, and all the blood would drain.

The door jingled open, and the whole coffee shop seemed to straighten up. Not out of fear or anything, but to arrogantly prove they were respectful. Marcela was, and did.

"Afternoon, Captain," Adam called from his table of hockey bros.

Captain Reilly stepped in and lifted his hand with as much dramatic labor as he could manage. He nodded kindly to the barista, who put his scone on the end of the bar before he could even order it, and stuck a ten in the tip jar. "Don't try and kiss my ass, Persad," he said with a Reilly-man smile. "Get a haircut."

Most of the coffee shop snickered, except Marcela, who figured she was too old to snicker like some child. Adam took his loss and laughed in good fun (but kept a careful, gauging glance, like a few others in town) because it was just jolly good fun with good old Captain Reilly.

The good captain wheeled toward their table. Marcela tightened her knees, did a mental scan for flyaways and loose threads. Caleb reached for her and they locked eyes—they let their hands sit obviously allied in the middle of the table. Caleb's skin felt warm despite the AC working overtime; Marcela could feel the delirious heat pressing into her thudding temples.

"We keeping out of trouble?" Captain Reilly asked, grabbing Caleb's shoulder in a tight claw. They looked identical. "Someone was messing around in the mill this morning."

At the mention of the mill, both Marcela and Caleb tightened their hands, barely visible. Caleb stared straight up at his father. His father stared at Marcela and seemed to be watching every pore of her face, waiting for some sort of tic. His mouth was smiling, but his eyes were focused.

"Wasn't you two, right?"

Marcela calculated and then took her hand from Caleb's to sweep back her hair. "Seems pretty juvenile," she said, and she couldn't help nervously touching her cheek, right over where her back teeth grated together. It felt for a second as if her fingers would break through waterlogged flesh to touch rotten molars.

"Yeah," Caleb agreed, hauling her back like a lifeline. Past the captain, Marcela could see two tween girls staring them down from another table, watching with the avid bloodthirst of vultures, so still they didn't seem to breathe. "We've been here the whole time, Chief."

Captain Reilly nodded. He still looked at Marcela, who had nothing to hide and reminded herself of that. But there was something about Captain Reilly that could always make her feel like she was somehow keeping a secret, like she'd unknowingly stolen something, or might accidentally blurt out a horrible lie. It felt like pressure boiling up in her, squealing higher and higher, like the steam machines.

"Good man," he finally said. He winked at Marcela, squeezed Caleb's shoulder, and left the store in the jingling of the bells over the door. The eyes of the tween girls tracked him laboriously before they went back to their cake pops and phone screens.

Marcela watched Caleb, whose eyes sparkled after his father ducking into the parked cruiser. Someone had been in the old mill. Not her, she assured herself, as if she might have somehow done it and forgotten. She'd been here with Caleb all morning and into the afternoon now, an alibi to give to Captain Reilly and to herself. Everyone had seen her here with him. The coffee shop threatened to spiral down but she wouldn't let it.

Caleb was looking at her now, smiling and reaching for her hand again. She stared at him, told herself to smile, did so, and let his huge hand close over hers. She imagined it crushing her fingers, splintering bones like toothpicks so they speared through her flesh. She imagined being a blue-faced corpse in a river somewhere, her hair stringy against her face, holes in her skin from where the scaley creatures nibbled.

And because he didn't, and she wasn't, she loved him. She loved him so much.

///\/\/\/\/\/\/\/\/\/\/\/\/\/\/\//\

When Captain Reilly strode to his cruiser with his little pastry bag, he walked right past Paz Espino. She felt vindicated by how easily he'd missed her and her crew, who were appraising the movie posters on the theater just next to them. Captain Reilly was speaking into his radio, not quite loudly enough for anyone else to hear.

"It at least wasn't Espino—Caleb was with her," he reported.

Paz chewed the straw of her slushy.

"Let's chalk it up to someone who didn't know any better. And tell Rick to fix the boards when he can."

"Roger."

Paz narrowed her eyes and wondered what would have happened if Marcela hadn't had an alibi. She was sure if the captain saw Paz sitting there, he'd pin it on her. She double-dog-quadruple-to-the-googleplex-million *dared* him to try that shit. She knew Captain Reilly would be no help in a monster hunt, and this confirmed it. He was just as shitty as always.

There were better people in this town that she thought she could try to talk some sense into.

The cruiser pulled away. The other three loudly declared this would be the summer they snuck into an R-rated movie, even if *Purge: Election Year* sounded like something Ben would watch from behind his hands. Paz hoisted herself up onto the parking meter and watched Marcela haul her chair around next to Caleb's, and lean her cheek on his shoulder to watch his phone. They looked real cute, Paz thought bitterly, framed in the window like something out of an Archie comic.

She wasn't going to let the fairy tale last.

"Marcela," she said through the open window, and she saw Marcela stiffen. She turned her head just barely, saw Paz sitting there waving her muddy little hand, smiling her toothy little grin, and her lips pressed tight together. Paz watched as Marcela drew in a very slow, very measured breath through her nose.

Marcela definitely knew trouble when she saw it, and trouble looked like her eleven-year-old sister smiling like she had a plan. But Paz knew Marcela could ignore a hurricane if she tried hard enough, and so she could ignore even this. Disappointingly, Marcela went back to her drink and her boyfriend, keeping her hands steady and her alibi tight.

Paz had expected this, but felt slighted nonetheless.

BEETLE

Beetle Hoang once wanted nothing more than to catch bugs. In the Greater Harville Area—of which the metropolis of Harville and piddly Bridlington were a part, as if they were anywhere alike—there are approximately 780 types of insects. When Beetle was seven, he used the library printer to produce a dichotomous key including every single one (to the charmed exhaustion of Mrs. Espino, the librarian) and kept the pages in a thick green binder. The town had pretended not to stare at the Hoang kid lumbering through fields with his too-big glasses and too-big Inuyasha shirt and choppy black hair, hauling the binder he could barely get his arms around with a mason jar clinking on his belt and a red marker behind his ear to check off the bug when he found it. His teachers would describe him as "very sweet" if they weren't calling him "really odd," but never in public, because that was rude.

Nonetheless, he would sit in the field or in the forest and record with gentle care the location and existence of every tiny creature he came upon. They were neutral things, so small and unknowing, with intricate lives you only saw if you looked under rocks or way down beneath the long grass. Beetle Hoang, before he turned twelve, believed in the small things.

At a fresh eighteen, he didn't care about the ants he crushed under his shoe while he painted the side of the motel, because he believed in getting the hell out of Dodge by whatever goddamn means necessary. His glasses were gold-framed and hexagon-shaped, his hair was four shades of pastel and softly permed, and though he wasn't wearing his Inuyasha shirt, he still did own it somewhere in his room. The Bug Book was half abandoned in his backpack, even though he only had a hundred more bugs to find. While he still liked bugs (obvious from his name, which he thought was a nice forewarning of exactly what you were heading into with him), he had no time to think about anything else when he was just a month of paychecks away from getting out of town once and for all.

"Are you going to be home?" Beetle asked, with his phone jammed between his ear and his shoulder. He slapped another coat of paint on the side of the motel, powering through the sour smell.

"Someone else called in sick," his mother said. Her end of the call was filled with utensils clinking and a sizzling grill, and his with the sounds of the jangling motel playground off to his right and the screaming laughter of the kids there, which made him cringe. He clenched his jaw to stop from shouting at them to shut the hell up. "I think you're on your own tonight, Beetle."

He huffed. "*Fine.*" Beetle finished one section, kicked the paint can sideways, and felt his skin simmering under his shorts and soft button-up shirt.

"I was thinking," he started to say, pausing when he heard his mother call out an order. He took the opportunity to look over his shoulder and confirm that the adults milling in the parking lot weren't looking at him. The fewer people who knew he was home after six years of Bridlington-less bliss, the better.

"Yes?" she said, back on the call. "You were thinking . . ."

"I know we said I'd live at home, but student housing has another spot that opens next week—"

"So early."

He tightened his jaw. It *was* early, but he was desperate to go back. Harville didn't have any stupid motels to paint or people you had to see every day. It had big-city things like a university, sure, but also Shoppers Drug Marts and H&Ms and Vietnamese restaurants and a hospital. Before he could think better, he said, "Yeah, but I miss home, you know?" and then instantly regretted it.

She paused. "I see," she said, despite certainly not seeing at all. She didn't argue with him, though he sometimes wished she would so he'd feel less like he was punching at someone with their arms behind their back.

"I have a lot of money saved—you can keep your car." He did worry about her walking home at night. He checked over his shoulder, to the small forest across the way and then up and down the road. The rumble in the air faded to something quieter when he looked for it, as if to mock him.

"We'll talk about it when I'm home," she said.

That was *always* the response. He fumed, sweating and blinking in the searing sunlight beaming off the wall. He wanted to tell her she was never home, but then he would have felt guilty because she was helping with his tuition. He wished she understood that he would be willing to put himself in ten thousand lifetimes of student debt just to get away before his scent was picked up.

Because being back in Bridlington forced him to remember shaking in the dark, waiting to die alone. And he wanted to get far away, not just from those memories but from the danger still lurking beneath this town.

"Beetle," his mother said, slowly. He blinked, hard, trying to keep his body from filling up with sloshy anger. He smeared more paint on the wall, so violently some splattered back and narrowly missed his glasses. His back teeth were grating and his shoulders felt so tight he thought the blades would snap against each other. His mother was incessant. "If you just talked to some of your old class—"

He didn't want to hear it again. "I don't need friends if I'm leaving soon," he said, hard. Aside from being accosted by Caleb on an empty street the night he came home (Caleb had backed him nearly into an alley to shake his hand and tell him how great and "grown-up" he looked, which felt more like a cornering threat), he had only seen Marcela. They'd looked at each other, swallowed stiffly, and gone their separate ways.

They shared the knowledge of Paz's monster—Beetle intimately and Marcela peripherally. Some hurt could be saved if they talked about it, but they had reputations to uphold.

Beetle shuffled a little farther, almost to the end of the wall. He shook his head, grinding the heel of his shoe into the ground.

He had mentally reared back his arm, and here was the punch. "You know what happened to Chuck," he said. The town thought it was an accidental fall, and Beetle knew it most certainly wasn't, but in the end it didn't matter because dead was dead. When he was Chuck's age, he'd nearly gone the same way. And oh could he let her know it. He switched to Vietnamese, as ill-practiced as he was, so there would be no way around the truth. "Má ơi. Có thể đó là con."

It was correct, but it was low.

He swore he could hear his mother pause, with the breath knocked from her. For a brief second, he wanted to take it back, tell her that she couldn't have known about any of it. What happened to Beetle wasn't her fault, and neither was Chuck. These things are nobody's fault. But he couldn't say that; it'd run his argument out. And he was desperate.

"If you want to leave, I'm not stopping you," she told him, almost sharply. He waited for the "but," for something he could yell at. There wasn't one.

The silence held.

"Fine," he said, feeling like a child who had to have the last word. He hung up the phone and was tempted to chuck it across the parking lot. He wanted to punch the stupid wall but he had to paint it, and he knew that, because he needed the money to get the hell out of Bridlington before he really did end up like Chuck Warren. Mrs. Warren had seen him the day he came home, swept her eyes from his pastel hair to his checkerboard Vans to the plastic bracelet he had yet to cut off, and immediately stumbled into her house, closing the door just in time to enclose most of her sobbing. Because you didn't make other people see you cry in Bridlington: you let them mind their goddamn business. All he did was remind people of the worst parts of this town, and he knew that couldn't stand.

He painted the wall and wanted to hate his mother. But he didn't hate her at all, and he knew he had no reason to, either. Because when Mrs. Warren had sobbed and Beetle had felt so unloved, Beetle's mother had taken him inside, the house all warm just as he remembered it. She'd spent the entire day before making bún bò huế between two shifts at the diner. He'd been such a baby about spicy food when he left, and so she'd made two small pots, one spiced for her and one milder for him. He'd felt small and young and vulnerable, and strangely all right with it.

He'd hugged his mom as tightly as he could in their sunlit kitchen with the air all thick and spiced, and she'd told him how happy she was that he was home. She said nothing about the Warrens. He wanted to beg her to. But he knew the unofficial town rules about moving on with life. He wanted to say, "Mom, you know how Paz Espino said she saw a monster? I did too. It's what made me have to leave like I did, so I know it's real. And I know it's still out there. And I know it's not over."

But he wasn't going to be the next town liar. Harville had saved him the first time, and it would save him again. Beetle finally finished painting the wall and nodded slowly at it. *There*, he wanted to say. *Now let go of me.*

He knelt on the boiling pavement to hammer the lid back on the paint can. He didn't even register the approaching sound at first (it was background noise, like insect drone or traffic), so by the time Beetle understood the flutter and rattle of a playing card jammed in the spokes of a BMX wheel, the bike's tasseled shadow already loomed over him.

He froze where he crouched.

No, he thought. *No no* no.

Two feet touched down onto the gravelly pavement, and with them the smell of cherry slushies.

"You run fast in those?" a voice asked.

He looked up without thinking.

Suddenly, he felt heat sparking and roaring in his stomach. It was compacted, broiling and turning like how stars are formed. The same searing anger he'd felt when Mrs. Warren couldn't look at him without crying. Every synapse shouting, *Why the hell can't this town just LET ME LEAVE?*

But however livid he was inside, the anger couldn't break through a chitin-shell of fear that kept him stuck in a crouch. He knew what this kid was a harbinger of. He hadn't breathed a word of the monster to anyone, but Paz Espino was notoriously keen, and he should have known she'd find him. She was sitting on her bike and leaning on the handlebars. It had been quite a few years, but she still looked so much like Marcela, and so much like the little kid he'd known before he left.

"You run fast in those?" she asked again, tilting her head to indicate his checkerboard Vans. Silhouetted in the sun, his eyes not yet adjusted, he couldn't read her features. "They give you superpowers?"

"No," he muttered, a sick growl. He had to finish up with the paint and just get his money, but he couldn't take his eyes off the shadows of hers, and he couldn't get his stomach to calm. He wanted desperately for this moment to stop, as if he could wind back the tape or else melt into the pavement until it was over.

"There's a monster under the town," Paz said. His vision was adjusting, enough to see her Super Mario T-shirt, her cargo shorts, her chalk-dyed braids. She looked like any other eleven-year-old, except she wasn't. "I want to kill it."

A graveyard-cold rush of air swept through him, sealing up every bit of magma, parching him to icy ash and the nothingness-gap of dead space. He was so cold he thought he might die right there. Just keel over. "Chuck fell," he lied. He could play this off, stay out of it like he intended. "Because you called him out there. I know the whole story, Paz. I know the truth."

"From who?" she asked. Her silhouette was becoming clearer—there was something almost amused about her smile. "Your mom? Who got it from someone who got it from someone who got it from Caleb who got it from his dad. Sound about right?"

It was, which made him even more apocalyptically angry. He knew what *really* happened, or could at least guess. Because it was no doubt hauntingly similar to the shit he'd gone through.

"No matter who I got it from," he said, swallowing bile, "monsters aren't real."

"Now I *know* you know that's not true," she said with a swinging rhythm and her finger waving like she was conducting an orchestra. "I know you know about the monster, Hoang. I think you figured it out before the rest of us, and I know it's still after you, and I know *you* know it too."

Had she seen how he kept close watch over his shoulder, how he made sure he was never alone? Had she seen the way he sprinted home each night after work? Did she note how his Bug Book had gone unopened, how his only focus was leaving, and that left no room for old hobbies, or friends?

"The monster is bigger than the mill and Chuck. And I need a big kid to help me get it. You got big," Paz said. She leaned, her bike creaking, the playing card stark on the wheel, bone-white and blood-red. "I'm not letting more kids die for this."

That was the Paz he remembered, who'd practically been born with her neck stuck out for the next kid. For the weedy foster children, the freaks, the quiet ones. Across the parking lot, Beetle saw the hazy, heat-warped figures of Paz's three friends, like waning specters or zombies dragging themselves closer. They stared him down, and he knew they would follow Paz into anything. And even if he knew she was right, even if he stretched his arms and legs in the well-lit parking lot every night before his race home, outrunning something hungry to finish what it had started, he knew Paz trying to kill the monster would only anger it in the end.

"Paz, lay off it," he said, and looked back down to his paint can to show this was final. "You can't kill this thing. I'm not dying for it."

He felt her grim smile. "Then you'll die because of it."

No. He refused. He'd have to be caught to be killed, and he wouldn't let it happen ever again.

A car came swinging too quickly into the parking lot. It hauled itself into the space in front of Beetle. Beetle looked up, sweat dripping down his gold-brown face, but Paz was already gone. Instead, a beat-up car sat where she'd been, and there was no sign of her.

For a split second, he wished the car had hit her. It was a guilty thought he immediately regretted. Still, he knew that there was no escaping the monster until you were out of its clutches, no escaping Bridlington until it was in your rearview mirror for good, and no escaping Paz.

Scaredy-cat? Maybe, but he wasn't dead under the mill.

The car door swung open and a dog leapt out to bound right into him. Beetle Hoang nearly punched its teeth from its smiling jaw.

BRIDLINGTON

Despite the heat and sun, Chuck's funeral descended on the town like a dark shadow. Technically, Paz wasn't not-invited. In small towns like Bridlington, weddings or funerals or baby showers or really anything at the tiny Anglican church were open events. But Paz didn't want to be part of the congregation.

She pedaled her bike up Main Street before the funeral was scheduled to start, leaving behind the shops and putting serious effort into climbing the lonely, tree-bordered road. At the top of the hill, the pavement pooled into a parking lot and the side of the stone church stood as tall and blunt as its own tombstone. She took a hard left, through the open gate and into the graveyard spilling out. She got off her bike and walked it toward the back, where the bushes shifted and moved, where anything could be hiding in the stretch of trees before it opened into farmland. Holding her clammy bike handles and staring off into the crisscrosses of trees, she dared something to come get her.

If you're gonna come and eat me, Paz thought like a numb radio recording, *you can get it over with now. I'm probably very tasty. All cold, like a popsicle.* It was thought not with arrogance but with resignation. Paz could do a good job of pretending she was confident, but she wasn't. She really wasn't.

She plopped herself down with a view of the front doors, beyond the ocean of graves.

The Warrens arrived not long after, Mrs. Warren red-eyed and trying not to sob again, Mr. Warren stoic. They stood on the doorstep to receive the crowd; Paz's family was the first to wander out from the parking lot and up the stone steps. Paz watched her own father shake Mr. Warren's hand, Marcela beside him in her neat black dress and tidy makeup. The church was too far away for Paz to hear what was said, so she didn't know if they apologized for her. She almost wished the Warrens would shove them back down the steps, scream at them, tell them to get the hell away because they were as bad as their daughter.

There was something painful about the way they were waved through the wooden doors. From her side angle, through the stained-glass windows, she could see their shadows moving up the aisle to find their seats. Paz knew then it was because her family was pitied, because of her, and that accepting them was only polite.

The Meyers came as well, Mrs. Meyer fussing with Ellie's recently relaxed hair and Ben being reminded not to drag his feet and scuff up his good shoes. When they got to the doors, there was a silent acknowledgment between the Meyers and Warrens. Mrs. Meyer regarded Ben so softly and touched Ellie's cheek so kindly that Paz was nearly sick.

As the two were herded into the church, Sammy came running from the parking lot, casting a quick look over her shoulder.

Sammy was a pebble-shaped latchkey kid who generally hid behind a dark bowl cut, glasses, and books to pretend she couldn't hear Emily Novak calling her names. She and Paz had been friends since pre-K. On the day of the funeral, Sammy had borrowed a clip-on tie from Ben and paired it with a used-to-be-black-now-gray shirt from the secondhand store and a skirt she'd worn to last year's Christmas pageant. She was sniffling and almost crying by the time she got to the Warrens. Mrs. Warren crouched to hug her, which Paz hadn't seen her do for any other kids.

Paz started to feel too cold for this, too tired of watching all the theatrics.

Sammy looked out over Mrs. Warren's shoulder, her owl eyes catching Paz standing under the shadow of the tree all the way at the back of the graveyard. Sammy lifted her hand to wave. Not to beckon Paz forward—they both knew it wasn't that—but as if to say someone had seen her there.

I'm gonna go, Sammy, Paz thought. *Tell Chuck goodbye for me, please?*

She wanted to believe Sammy heard her. But then Mr. Novak and Emily and Brady came around the corner. Emily called "Hi, Sammy! Cute tie!" in a way that probably meant "Hey, Sammy! Weird fashion sense, you little freak!" and Sammy let go of Mrs. Warren. By the time she turned to find Paz, Paz had already gone east through the trees parallel to Main Street to avoid the rest of the quiet procession.

Because Bridlington was small, and nearly everyone was at Chuck's funeral, Main Street was a ghost town when Paz went racing down. There was no one on the sidewalks, but she felt the workers inside the storefronts watching her as she passed. She could still hear her name and the echo of conversations behind the closed doors of Bridlington. She knew it was just in her head, but part of her felt like the soil and stone beneath her was speaking.

I always knew she was trouble.

Do you see the way she dresses?

Main Street followed a subtle decline toward the mill but she pedaled anyway, desperate to go so fast she might lose control and crash and split her head like a watermelon. But she knew she wouldn't be so lucky. The air whipped past her like hands trying to catch on. Let them. Let them scratch her into ribbons. But they didn't.

I heard her teacher say she had detention every day for a month and it still didn't stop her from causing trouble. It's that mouth of hers. Reilly's right: she can't let anything go.

She zipped past all the stores and then past the quiet motel and the *BE BACK SOON* sign on the office door.

The Espinos are a nice family. It's such a shame Paz is so hard to control. It's only a matter of time before someone gets hurt.

Paz felt like her head was stuffed up with hornets, buzzing and swarming and stinging. The sky was too wide and blank above her, the air too quiet. She felt like at any moment she might disappear off the black road, be plucked away like nothing. Like something could come barreling out from behind the

Mac's as she passed it, slam into her, drag her away, and who would know? Who would care? Would she?

Her head was still rushing while she poured and paid for a green slushy with all the rapt attention of a man ordering two fingers of whiskey. The fluorescent lights burned and all the colors and smells felt like an assault. She let the cashier keep all the change from ten dollars of her chore money—she didn't care. None of it mattered.

She thought she might have been crying, but when she found herself sitting on the side of the Blue River bridge, legs dangling down from the edge, she touched under her eyes and found them dry. She thought she *should* be crying, but maybe she was all out of that. She looked into the trembling water below and felt like maybe she wanted to slip off the bridge and plunge down, to be swept away forever. Because the town was swarming with whispered things, ignoring her and leaving her stranded.

She sipped her slushy and stared out at the mill.

Come out and fight me, then, she thought. For a moment, she swore she saw one of the boards over the windows buckle outward, and something shift beneath the black gap of the stair access. But there was nothing more, and so she stared until her eyes went dry and unfocused, and still she didn't stop.

//\\\/\\\/\\\/\\\/\\\/\\\

Sammy thought there would never be a more awful day than that funeral. She had to sit far too long, and she was so stiff her bones ached, begging for it to be over. She didn't go to the church very often (her family was technically Buddhist, but the only temple was too far away to go to except at New Year's), and she found it all at once too big and too cramped, like the stuffed-up curio store, and too dark and too light, like an overexposed photograph. Thankfully, Ellie burst into loud tears halfway through, which gave the three of them a good excuse to "get some air, loves," as Mrs. Meyer put it while patting Ellie's hair flat.

They left through the church's side door, trudged down into the cemetery, and wound between the tombstones until Ellie stopped crying. Ben was blue and quiet. Sammy dragged her eyes across the dates on the stones, reading names no one ever repeated after their own funerals . . . names left unremembered. They wandered right to the back, found the unfilled grave where Chuck would go, and Ben promptly puked into the grass next to the dark trees and creaking branches.

Sammy stared. "You okay, Benny?" she asked carefully.

Ellie mopped an arm over her still-wet eyes. "Nice going, *loser*," she said, hiccuping back another sob. "At least you didn't puke *in* the grave."

Ben looked up so reproachfully that Ellie almost laughed, which got them in slightly better spirits. Sammy watched a fat yellow-banded bumblebee bump along around them. She knew it wouldn't sting them, even if Ben was shaking out his hands. They only stung if they had to. *Kind of like Paz*, she thought.

A branch cracked when a bird took flight, and all three children jumped. Ellie moved closer to Sammy, hanging on her sleeve, and they stepped toward Ben, who gave another dry-heave. They were alone out there at the back of the cemetery near the trees. Sammy felt a prickle move through her slowly, resting cold in her stomach.

A shrill scream speared through the regular forest sounds. The three of them jumped again, hearts hammering and limbs tangling to keep them all together.

"What was that?" Sammy hissed. The sky was so painfully blue above, like it didn't care that all the blood had drained from Sammy's face and left her ice cold.

"I don't—" Ellie started to say.

It came again: a long, echoing wail. Sammy's heart slammed. The world beyond the cemetery seemed to spin, like they were in the eye of something.

"I-it's the gate," Ben stammered, holding Sammy's other arm now and pointing to the gate into the parking lot. Fine, gates creak, but they watched in numb horror as it eased open without anyone touching it, sending that painful metallic scream shivering through them.

"No thank you," Ellie muttered.

"I-it's just gravity," said Ben, his voice going shrill. "It's fine, it's—"

Thunk!

Ben screeched. They all jumped, realized the sound wasn't coming from the gate or from the woods behind them, and turned to see four people trailing down from the church's side door and weaving between tombstones like Plinko tokens.

Suddenly, all fear of that gate was replaced by a more immediate threat.

"Damn." Ellie sighed. She wiped the last of the tears from her eyes. "Just what we need, huh?"

Sammy mumbled in agreement.

Caleb Reilly was marching toward them, towing both his always-reliable best friend Reece Kalchik and his Novak cousins. This would hurt even more than if the monster ripped them limb from limb, Sammy thought.

The mob approached in the blinding daylight. "I'm sorry about your friend," Caleb started, very dutifully, with all his citizenship pins shining. Sammy was surprised he didn't just wear all the medals stacked up. "I know you were close, and it's always a tragedy when the community loses someone."

"Why d'you think we were close?" Ellie asked. They'd only hung out with Chuck once, on the last day of school.

Caleb looked at them a little harder, as if realizing he might have misstepped with a not very "mind your business"-y assumption.

Brady Novak hadn't yet learned all his manners. "Cause you're all kinda weird."

Caleb cuffed the back of Brady's head. Reece snorted.

"We're sorry it happened," Caleb said, to a very prim nod from Emily on his left. "You tell Paz I said the same thing." That's when the grin came out. Just small, a little tug. Caleb wasn't so careless as to leave physical marks. "It's sad she still believes in monsters. I hope she sets herself straight, or she might be spending more time in that jail cell."

Ellie narrowed her eyes, so did Ben, but neither said anything. They knew who not to pick a fight with.

So did Sammy, but her mouth opened anyway. "If Paz says there's a monster," she said, sure of herself in a way she so rarely was, "then I believe her. Something killed Chuck."

"Oh," Emily said. Her eyes lit up, vicious and excited, like she'd just been waiting for this sort of opportunity. "Gonna defend your girlfriend, you freaky little—" The word meant a break in your armor, and Sammy was so shocked she couldn't say anything back. A cold wave washed through her, then a hot shock of shame. Her lips fumbled open, slammed shut, and twisted, and she looked to Caleb like he would say something. If he liked Marcela so much, and Paz liked Sammy, then shouldn't he? Weren't they all connected somehow in such a small town?

He saw the stunned look on Sammy's face and barely managed to stop a laugh. "Oh, come on," he said. Brady was howling already. Reece looked away like he might have heard something. "It was a joke."

"You're a dick, Caleb," Ellie said. When Reece shot her a warning glare, Ben stepped in front of his sister, like he'd be any match.

"Don't come over here pretending you care about us," Sammy said, keeping her head up despite her red-hot face and a feeling of deep hopelessness that this moment might never end. In a way, it wouldn't. "You don't get to talk about Paz when your dad is the whole reason the town hates her. Maybe if you told your dad to stop, then—"

Sammy saw Emily decide her next move. Sammy had been told that bullies had been bullied before by someone else, and so Sammy should feel sorry for them. She knew that wasn't why Emily was like this.

She did it because she was the minister's daughter and the police captain's niece, and she could get away with it.

Emily stepped forward, all prim and blond and sweet, and shoved Sammy backwards.

Sammy didn't even remember falling. One moment she was standing with her friends, and then she was staring up in winded horror, the world hazy and soil-smelling and looking like a whole lot of black-brown with only one rectangle of white. Everything rang for a moment, and in that ringing, Sammy swore she could hear something laughing. Not people, but a *something*, some shivering feeling rumbling under her, a cosmic wrong.

Her shocked lungs gasped for air, and the regular noise of the world rushed in over the other sound before she could make sense of it. She realized that rectangle was the sky. And she was in a child-sized grave meant for Chuck, with the world ready to collapse in on top of her.

Sammy tried to scream, but her throat choked. She stared up at Ben's and Ellie's shocked faces, and Emily leaning over and smiling smugly in her neat dress. Sammy heard Brady laughing like this was the funniest Saturday morning cartoon in history. She tried to scramble up but her eyes were too wide and she couldn't remember how to breathe. She heard Caleb snapping for Reece to shut Brady the hell up. Now he sounded rattled, like he knew this was a step too far.

From where she could do nothing but croak out something

that almost sounded like "Help," Sammy heard Captain Reilly's distant voice. "Caleb, bring everyone back now."

"Y-yes, sir," Caleb called, a million miles skyward from where she was. Then she heard him mutter, "No one'll believe that it was Emily, so just get her out of there and stay quiet about it."

No one would believe them over Caleb or Emily or even Brady and Reece. No one believed Paz, so why would they believe her friends?

Sammy knew it. That the town was rotten and infested. The world was made of big things and little things, and Sammy felt like the littlest thing alive. She believed in Paz's monster, but she didn't know how they could save themselves from something so inevitable, or how four children could get away in a town like this.

BAD DOG OWNER

"Bird!" Asher shouted, but Bird only knew how to "Stay." "Bird!" was not "Stay." Bird had bounded practically on top of someone Asher hadn't even seen over the hood of his car, and it took Asher grabbing his dog around the haunches and hauling him back to get him off.

"I'm so sorry," he said, fast, trying to placate. "I'm so, so sorry—he's friendly—he just wants to play—"

"Why isn't he on a *leash*?" the person shouted, scrambling back into a maintenance cart. Asher detected the faintest hint of an accent, staccato and crystalline. Their face was pinched and starting to turn red. "He could have killed me!"

Overstatement. "He's friendly," Asher tried to say again.

"As hell!"

Asher's mind was getting all swimmy. The day was far too hot to be trying to carry a very warm dog, and Bird possessed a magical ability to become heavier when held. Plus all the wiggling and tail-smacking sure wasn't helpful. Asher dropped him, hissed at him to "*Stay,*" and turned back.

He adjusted his sunglasses. Time to be a good citizen. "I'm sorry, and I'll make sure it doesn't happen again," Asher said. Bird was panting against the back of his knee, turning his jeans even more soggy. The mutt had better hope this person didn't report this or anything. Then they'd both be in the doghouse, har-dee-har. "Did he hurt you?"

"That's really not the issue," the person grumbled, which meant the answer was "No, but I'd like to continue complaining." Asher tried to size the person up. Though they were still crouched against the cart, they seemed like they'd be taller than him, just like everyone else was. They were built somewhere between stocky and round, with sturdy arms and pecs that suggested they were the owner of that maintenance cart. Their hair was four different shades of pastel hanging in a loosely permed cloud. They were like no one Asher had ever seen before, and his brain promptly shut down.

"If he comes at me again, I'm not gonna be nice," the person snapped.

Asher didn't think they were nice to begin with but knew better than to say it—Bridlington was teaching him quickly. "You work here, right?" he asked.

The person huffed and stood up against the wall of the motel, groaning when they took their hand away and it came back white. Asher only then noticed the paint was fresh, and was grateful that, at the very least, Bird hadn't managed to get any on him.

"Yeah, I work here," the person said, and added a contextless "for now" that Asher hoped he wasn't meant to understand. The person swiped up the paint can angrily and clunked it into the cart. "I'm the maintenance guy."

Maintenance *guy*. Boy? Asher had zero idea how to navigate this person's gender, and also zero inclination to ask for pronouns and look like a person who knew what a pronoun even was.

"Maintenance guy *for now*," Asher said without thinking. Trying to be clever earned him a glare that said to cut the comedy act. Tough crowd.

He touched his sunglasses nervously, where the bridge felt like it was bruising into his sweat-greased nose. "I'm Asher," he said. He nudged his leg back into his dog. "This is Bird."

"And I'm not really interested," the guy said. Their face was getting all pinched again, smeared with a bit of paint. They looked down at their cart. "Listen, buddy, I've got a million things to do today and your dog attacked me—"

Asher's face hardened. "You said he didn't hurt you."

"We don't accept pets," they said. That wasn't even personal. That was hard facts.

How the hell was he going to get a place to stay if the only motel in town didn't accept pets? How the hell was he going to set up long enough to—well, he'd need a job eventually, right? And you needed an address to get a job, *right*? His head was a flurry of half-baked plans. He skated the line between surviving and dying penniless in Harville or, worse, going back home to his parents. He was screwed. He was so screwed.

But he was an actor. And, moment by moment, this was going to get easier. Asher took a slow, compressed breath and put on a small-town smile.

"Thank you for this lovely talk," Asher said with Stepford precision. It was coated in sarcasm, but not obvious enough to be called out. The key to Bridlington was to force derision through cheerfully clenched teeth. "Have a truly blessed day."

Asher turned on his heel and trotted for the main building of the motel. Bird plodded after him, staring up with a smile.

"You're gonna get eaten alive," the guy called after him. "We don't do strangers here."

Asher stuck a thumbs-up in the air and walked on. He heard the maintenance guy scoff, and then the cart squeak away in the other direction.

Asher looked down at his smiling dog. "Are you having a blessed day yet, Contraband?"

Bird wagged his tail so hard he almost smacked himself in the face. Asher smiled, only half forced.

Okay, Bridlington, he thought with his new straight-lined gait. *Keep doing your worst.*

//∧∨/∧∨/∧∨/∧∨/∧∨/∧∨/∧∨/∧

By the end of the night, Bridlington would leave Asher completely broke and out of options. The motel office was closed when he got there, so he waited around until an impressively mustached man arrived (Paz's father, he guessed, though his eyes lacked the keen glow of Paz's), but one look at the exhaustion on his face said Asher should just bow out of this one. He explored Bridlington—from up and down Main Street, from the northern cul-de-sacs to the southern farmland—but saw no "Help Wanted" signs. He checked the newspaper he bought and a barrage of apps to find that rental housing here was not only slim, but hugely unaffordable.

A guy could get frozen by too much choice, you know, so at least this made things straightforward.

Asher knew his Runaway 101: he forked over fifty-five dollars at the gym so he'd have a place to shower (shutting up and minding his business avoided any hassle with "Reece" at the desk), and then parked in the Dairy Queen lot to eat his suspiciously warm gas station sandwich, giving Bird the lunch meat. They watched the sky turn fire-red over the roof of the DQ, glinting on all the cute little families at their cute umbrellaed tables.

The white envelope on the dashboard stared at him. Asher swiped it up and rifled through his cash. There was almost a hundred dollars left, which was almost a hundred options while he figured out how to get some sort of income. He could probably keep going another month *at least* with just that. He didn't need shelter—his car was a good enough room—and the monthly gym fee was small-town reasonable.

"Short rations," he told Bird, who was sniffing furiously, surely tempted by the smell of grease from the DQ. "No complaining, soldier."

Bird huffed and Asher's stomach grumbled, but they'd both have to wait until morning. It was getting dark, and they needed to find somewhere quiet to hole up. The good news was, he'd already scoped out the entire town to find one of the most secluded spots.

Asher was hurtling toward that night's damning conclusion.

He slammed the car into drive and headed west on Main into the setting sun, past all the happy families heading home and the small shops flipping their signs so quaintly early in the evening. The shops faded off, replaced by trees. The road swerved a bit, black branches rustled together, and the air smelled more like sour farmland. As the sky eased from indigo to black, the first few stars popping awake and chasing back the sun's heat, Asher crawled to the end of the road.

There, the town's stone church reared up to his left. There were no lights on in the windows or even in the adjoined parking lot. He pulled in, counted his chickens about there being no cars there, and tucked into the farthest corner beneath the reaching branches. He'd be decently hidden until morning.

Asher turned the engine off, let darkness fold over him, and felt safer.

Bird, on the other hand, was tapping his claws on the faux-leather seat and spinning in anxious circles.

"What, Contraband?" Asher asked.

Bird whined and tip-tapped.

Asher sighed. "Walk?"

Bird yipped happily.

To be safe, Asher put the envelope in his kangaroo pocket, and then he and Bird went spilling out. He shut the door with that same too-loud *thunk*.

Silence. The sky was far too wide, like a mouth between the trees that would swallow Asher up. He could hardly see anything with his sunglasses on, and he felt alone. Not in a "comfy solitude" way, but in an "I could be the last person alive" sort of way, where he wouldn't even know if the town down the hill snuffed out all at once.

Asher pulled his hood up and held on to the drawstrings. "*Quick* walk."

Bird was currently sniffing at some small animal in the bushes that Asher couldn't see, so Asher tapped the dog's haunches with his toe to get his snuffling attention and then started off.

There was a small path that carved alongside the church, into the cemetery. The gate was unlatched and creaking steadily back and forth, back and forth, as the breeze teased it open and gravity teased it shut. It was a little maddening, and Asher was glad to fasten it behind them.

With the moon nearly full that night, the graveyard sprawling ahead of him was silver and blue. It was bigger than he'd expected; Bridlington wasn't big, but it was old. He kept his back to the church's side wall and his hands in his pocket, cradling the envelope.

"Creepy," Asher said, because talking out loud felt safer. He wasn't all too frightened of ghosts, but he *was* all too frightened of a guard or somebody catching them. Still, with how quiet the graveyard was, Asher doubted anyone was around.

He doubted wrong.

Bird sniffed a tombstone, momentarily froze as if he'd already forgotten what he was doing, and then zipped off to do the same to the next one. The stones were mottled with moss and lichen, half sunk into the earth, the dates so faded that Asher wasn't sure of the years on them. He figured they had to be as old as the town, which seemed to be quite old. He was almost sure one said "Reilly," and though the dark and wear made it hard to tell, he was correct. The trees corralling him in scraped each other in the wind, and there was a loud *pop* when a branch snapped off.

A squirrel, he had to think. *Must be.*

"Creepy," Asher said again. His skin felt like it was shrinking down around him. Better start heading back.

Bird suddenly jolted his head up and stared out toward the back of the cemetery in that horribly still trance every pet owner knows and fears, the moment where you remember you've lost the instinct to see the unseen and anything could be out there waiting.

"What're you . . ." Asher tried to ask, but the words died in his aching chest. Bird's nose twitched once, then one ear. He panted for a second but then shut his mouth and stood stiff-legged, focused past the gravestones and out to where the trees were nothing but blackness. Asher looked too, waiting for Bird to give up the creep-show.

Instead, Bird breathed out a quiet whine.

Okay, Asher thought. *We now conclude our "quick walk."*

"Let's go," he said. "Bird."

Bird didn't move. If anything, he stiffened further, and Asher swore he saw his muzzle crinkle like he might snarl, which Bird had *never* done.

"*Bird*," Asher said again. He thought his voice would go higher, but it went lower.

"*Asher*," Bird whispered, except it wasn't Bird, obviously.

Asher snapped his head back to where Bird was looking. The voice had come from across the cemetery, in the trees? Or did he even really hear his name? It was more vibration, strange and bubbly.

"H-h . . ." Asher couldn't make a sound come out. He felt like those worn, cold tombstones, rooted into the soft ground. He squinted; it never occurred to him to take off his sunglasses, and the smudge still on them made the darkness shift strangely. The crickets sang and the trees hummed. Bird's hissing whine crested into garbled chatter. Asher took a step closer to the church wall, never taking his eyes from the flat black of the trees. He heard nothing else and assumed it was the wind, or he was tired, or a million other maybes. "Come on, B—"

"ASHER!" the voice boomed.

Bird barked once like a gunshot. Asher yelped before tumbling backward, ripping his hands from his pocket to break his fall and scrambling against the rough stone of the church, with Bird racing over to stand in front of him like some sorry, medium-ish-large shield. Asher saw a shadow out at the end of the cemetery, the glow of a single eye, heard the click of claws and smelled rot.

The side door of the church slammed open beside him, and he clapped one hand over his mouth to muffle his lurch of surprise, grabbing Bird's collar with the other before he could go bounding off to make friends with the person he was certain must be the minister. She was standing up the short flight of stairs with a phone in one hand and was undoubtedly ready to call the cops . . . unless she saw him first and decided to beat his brains in herself with the baseball bat she was holding.

Asher forgot how to breathe. Bird panted once and then was silent, which was the least he could have done.

The minister gave the graveyard a scan, and only then did Asher notice that the shadow was gone. He swore he heard retreating laughter—the vibration of it, low and sinister—and he moaned softly against his hand as his knees turned to Jell-O.

The night got worse when he spotted something bone-white in the black-green grass. It took a moment of numb staring before he realized: the envelope had slid from his pocket and sat glowing like a beacon just ahead of the graves, far out of his reach and well within the minister's sight.

She pocketed the phone, placed the bat against the door-frame, and walked down not four feet in front of Asher to investigate this strange envelope. Asher watched with his ribs grinding against each other as she picked it up, rifled through what was nearly one hundred dollars, squinted carefully, and turned back to the church doors with the envelope held tightly in her hand.

Asher kept opening his mouth to say something, say it was his, that he needed that, and he was sorry for bringing his dumb barking dog. There were endings where the minister, Mrs. Novak, helped Asher up and he admitted that he only had a hundred dollars to his name. He'd be given a bus ticket to the big city and a half-promised room in a transitional home, where his odds were practically hopeless. He'd be lucky if anyone took a chance on him when there were a thousand other kids in the same situation. Bridlington may have been small, but that meant he was the only charity case.

So he thought.

The church door closed and Asher collapsed to sit in the grass. Bird licked his cheek carefully.

"I oughta wring your neck, mutt," Asher breathed. He wanted to believe it was a joke. And maybe if he could joke, he could pretend none of it happened. Somehow losing the envelope was scarier than whatever the hell that voice was.

At the thought, he gave one quick look to check if the shadow was back, saw it wasn't, and then he and Bird sprinted to the car. Asher knew he was stuck in Bridlington.

And something knew his name.

BIRD

His Boy fell asleep in the reclined front seat, breath whistling and creaking from his compressed lungs. Bird was too restless to sleep, and he hung his nose out the cracked window. They had pulled in along Blue River on the town side, at a tiny lookout way up in the north past the houses and nearly in the countryside. His Boy had taken a bit to nod off, smelling electric and terrified even in sleep. Bird thought the whole town smelled funny, especially the river tumbling just ahead of him. It was sour, like the Dead Place that yelled, like things had died violently there over decades and decades and decades. Bird suspected something had gone wrong in this town, but he couldn't place it.

Something whispered to him, speaking in a voice so low that it was a feeling more than a sound. It came from the other side of the river, past that hole in the fence, along the muddy bank and under the bridge, into the mill he could barely see, from deep within the hole where Chuck Warren died. Down in the dark and spiraling tunnels where the cement dripped and the water wailed and things moved. Something in there was saying his name.

His Boy twitched in his sleep and gave an unhappy moan.

Bird whined, half a desperate sigh, and lay across his Boy's stomach for good measure. He rested his chin on the other window to keep watch over the incoming road with his watery black eyes.

The monster would be back, Bird thought. He could smell how it killed in every corner of town.

He would protect his Boy.

DRIFTER

Asher's first five days in Bridlington were spent living in a state of anxiety that no average seventeen-year-old should ever experience, but which was common for the average unhoused seventeen-year-old. He would not call himself "unhoused" so much as "sleeping rough," though, which seemed less depressing. If he barely ate anything more than stolen Clif Bars from the gym or stale café pastries fished from the bag the closers threw out, and if Bird was made to feed himself off the much grosser diner scraps, well, that was what the world had come to. Surely, there would be better things around the corner very soon.

The gym was his only saving grace. He was glad he'd forked over that cash early so he could escape the heat by taking wildly uncomfortable and tense showers while Bird waited in the car's thrown shadow. No one at the gym seemed to care to talk to him beyond civilities, and he knew exactly when to stroke the teenage trainers' egos by asking what they recommended for a workout, even if everything immediately made him dizzy or sent pain to light up his cramped rib cage like burning neon. He faked an "old injury" and flashed his "hell yeah, bro, I work out" face enough to make up for this, and for being a guy with an eye . . . sensitivity . . . thing that meant he had to wear sunglasses inside. Had he not managed to keep this up, he would have (at best) been ostracized and watched too carefully for what would come next, or (at worst) crawled into his car with six broken ribs and a smashed nose and his eyes swollen shut because he got too comfy with the wrong person. But he did, and he wasn't, and he didn't, so he coasted for a few days waiting for providence to strike.

And did it ever strike. Five days in, Asher leaned against the wall of the gym right next to the desk, pretending to check his pulse while actually eyeing the iPhone charger. He was waiting until Reece the desk jockey was so engrossed in his *Men's Health* magazine that he wouldn't notice Asher's Indiana-Jones-and-the-boulder-button-swap where he weaseled Reece's phone out and his phone in just long enough for a decent charge. He had done this maneuver many times and thought himself very clever.

(Unbeknownst to him, Reece knew he did this, but considered it way too awkward to intercept such strange behavior.)

And then, fate. Or perfect design. The gym door opened and Asher, exhausted and a bit light-headed, felt the universe finally shift in his favor.

A decidedly *huge* guy walked in through the plate-glass door and strode toward Reece at the desk. By Asher's calculations this guy was a serious behemoth, and he looked like he should have some sort of choir entourage and cartoonish dazzling light rays coming off him. The guy scanned the gym as if assessing, and Asher again proceeded to check his slightly elevated pulse. The whole energy of the gym changed: Reece looked up from his magazine, which he didn't even do that one time Asher nearly brained himself on the handle of the elliptical; the one other employee looked at the new guy for quite some time before she went back to cleaning the elliptical Asher had nearly brained himself on the handle of; and some middle-aged lady on the treadmill smiled and said, "Oh, Caleb, I thought you were your father."

It clicked: Captain Caleb Reilly had a son, who frankly looked almost exactly like him. It was almost too good to be true.

"Afternoon, Mrs. Devereaux," he said, with a smile of so many very-white teeth. He was all casual, smooth like running water.

When Caleb finally finished talking to Mrs. Devereaux by telling her that he was really looking forward to some Heritage Day thing when she was going to make some pie that was allegedly very good, he turned back to Reece and lowered his voice.

"Did you get it?" Caleb asked, quick on the draw. "Quinn's dad left this morning. She says you can drop it off whenever."

Reece folded up his magazine with a sure nod and they exchanged details. Asher didn't know what "it" was at first, but he used his handy-dandy context clues: "it" was definitely booze, there was clearly going to be a party, and Caleb Reilly, Junior, was going to be there. If anyone could hook Asher up with a job, or at least some sort of option other than starving in his car, it was this guy. The last five days had been rough, but they'd look kind compared to what was coming if Asher didn't figure out a plan, and soon. He knew how to be invisible, but what he needed was to be safe.

He had no idea where Quinn lived, and making his eavesdropping obvious was probably not a good call. He could do this.

Asher sped out the door and into the street. Even if his jeans-and-hoodie wardrobe selection was brutal in the day's muggy humidity, things were finally looking up. He strode to his car like the cool guy in a movie, sunglasses and straight gait to match.

Bird followed, bristling a bit because something in the air felt wrong, and because he was hungry too.

///\\\///\\\///\\\///\\\///\\\///\\\

Asher swung his car into the motel parking lot, Bird whining beside him and tapping his claws against the seat.

"Dude," Asher said, five parts annoyed to one part concerned. He turned off the car and looked over to his dog, who stared back at him with those huge, watery eyes. "What gives?"

Bird, of course, had no answer aside from nervously licking his nose. Asher realized that Bird was looking a little thinner already, his fur losing some shine. He put his hand on Bird's back to calm them both.

"Almost there," he said, as if he knew what was to come.

Asher got out of the car into the hazy heat and trotted toward the back lawn with his hands in his jean pockets and Bird slinking around behind him. He found exactly who he was looking for.

The maintenance guy was near the toolshed, hauling out the lawnmower. Asher headed that way, hardly aware how much his posture had changed in five days, how much more purposeful and blunt his stride was. It had been a subtle transformation, more reaction than action. He had a killer headache and it sank into his nauseous stomach, but he could hold it together. This wasn't the bottom of the world just yet.

Asher got close enough to hear the maintenance guy call the lawnmower several words in a language he did not understand.

"Afternoon," Asher said, smiling with so many very-white teeth. He was all casual, smooth like running water.

The guy flinched and whirled around with a long, fat knife in their hand.

Asher stopped breathing. The lawn felt huge. Then he noticed the blade was a trowel from the guy's toolbelt, and he twitched out a nervous smile. He was jumpy for all the wrong reasons. He played it cool. "Don't garden me to death." Okay, he *thought* he played it cool.

The maintenance guy sneered, and then looked up and away from Asher, narrowing their eyes as if focusing, or as if they were in a teen coming-of-age movie where they were about to say something like "Anywhere is better than here."

"What the hell are you doing back here?" they asked instead. "I thought you'd leave town."

Asher kept his hands in his pockets. "I think the question you should be asking, good si—" He stopped himself. Titles were dumb anyway, just part of the faux niceties, but it didn't work if he had no idea how to gender this person.

And they seemed to know and revel in it. They crossed their arms and raised their eyebrows. Their patterned shirt was open over what would have looked to anyone else like some cross between a sports bra and half a tank top, but Asher recognized it for what it was. He felt his stomach churning.

"Go on," they said, waving one hand encouragingly. "'The question you should be asking, good . . .'"

Asher's jaw tightened. He had never punched someone, but he thought that might be an interesting hobby to get into. He did *not* come here to play mind games with some gender non-conforming jerk-off. He had a party to go to so he wouldn't starve to death.

"I think the question you should be asking yourself, my friend . . ." he went with, ignoring the person's amused snort. He would have gone catatonic if someone had that much trouble pinpointing his gender, but there was no time to think about that. ". . . is how the hell you can *stop* me being back here?"

The person tilted their head and the mockery turned to very clear exhaustion. Asher wanted to believe they had been charmed.

"What do you want, Asher?"

Oh ho ho! Asher thought, victorious. *You remember my name. How kind.* He cut straight to the point, like Caleb. "Where does Quinn live?"

"Why should I tell you?"

"Because I will go away if you do." Asher could have flipped two finger-guns, been his usual, possibly-lovably-goofy self. But he didn't, and maybe he was better for it.

The reaction was almost instantaneous. The guy pointed the trowel over the lawn, across a large section of high grass, to a farmhouse up the road. "Quinn's house. Are we done here? Because I really don't get paid to stand around and talk to you."

Yes, they were. "Thank you," Asher said kindly.

"Beetle Hoang," they said, clearly not content with the power imbalance of being forced to know Asher's name. Or else just finished with yanking his leash, because they also said, "He/him."

Asher's polite facade cracked for a second. "Your name's Beetle?"

"Your dog's named Bird."

Oh, Bird. Asher looked down beside him and Bird was staring off at the main road. His nose quivered once and then stilled.

"Touché," Asher said, and promptly followed it with, "Thank you for being of such great assistance."

Beetle gave him a hard look and turned half away like he was trying to protect his core for a fight. "You're really staying here, aren't you."

"Uh-yup."

"Just . . ." Beetle seemed to think it over, and then said, "Be *careful*." He looked like he was pulling something out of his throat and it physically pained him. "Try to stay in the open, and make sure people know where you are."

Asher blinked. "Or what?" he asked. He tried to make it a cocky, too-cool dare, but he was getting the same feeling he had about Paz's game: something was up, and no one was telling him jack shit.

"Accidents happen," Beetle said, which would have seemed like an after-school-special about fire safety if it wasn't so horrifyingly cryptic, bordering on threatening. "If someone cares about where you are, they can find you." Beetle looked longer at him, swept his eyes over Asher, and said, "And . . . if you come by the diner—and this is *so* far off the record, like, if you tell a single goddamn person about this, I'll kill you—"

"Garden me to death," Asher said, and felt a little of his old smile returning before he fixed his sunglasses.

Beetle sneered. "I was gonna say, if you go to the diner and you say I sent you, you could get some food."

Asher almost reeled back, like one of those rescue dogs who freaks out whenever anyone goes to pet it. "Why?"

"Don't overthink it," Beetle snapped. "Maybe I don't want you turning up dead after I talked to you, huh?" He crossed his arms and stared hard at Asher like he was trying to say more than what he was. "Too many dead kids in this town already, all right?"

Asher knew nothing, hadn't even walked through the cemetery fully since that horrible first night. If he had, or if he'd asked more, it would have sent him sprinting right out of Bridlington, so it was a good thing he was practiced in keeping his answers short. "Okay," he said. This felt more "feed a man a fish," whereas Caleb could "teach a man to fish." "While you're in the business of being helpful—"

"I'm not."

"—what do you know about Caleb Reilly?"

Beetle's posture immediately stiffened so sharp Asher thought he'd get punched, but instead Beetle took a step back and put all of that anger into wrenching the lawnmower cord so hard the rusted old engine roared to revenant life.

"He's a dick," Beetle said plainly over the rumbling. "He'd bury you alive if he thought you were bad for this town."

Asher had no idea how to respond to that, because he didn't think he was bad for this town, not at all. And if Beetle was right that he needed people to watch his back, then who better than the good captain's behemoth, sun-god-looking, man-as-all-hell son?

Caleb would care, Asher thought, and then turned to start walking up to Quinn's house. He had gotten halfway across the lawn when he heard Beetle say, "Uh, your *dog*?"

Asher was so used to Bird keeping at his heels that he hadn't even realized he didn't follow. He looked back, and Bird was still sitting down, staring off toward the road and the mill. Too still, like a statue.

"Bird," Asher called.

Bird didn't move. Like that night in the graveyard.

"Yo!" Asher called. "*Bird!*"

Nothing.

Asher felt something jolt through him; it came up from the ground and grabbed at his legs like hands. The feeling leached through him until it got to his face, where it smothered him, where it clawed his jaw open and wormed into his mouth and down his throat to choke him from the inside out. His face felt hot and muggy and wrong, and his eyes flashed.

"BIRD!" he shouted. "NOW!"

Bird jumped so high and so quickly that he practically somersaulted in the air, landing in a scramble of paws. Asher turned and pointed himself up the road to Quinn's, and heard Bird come galloping after him. He didn't turn back to look. He just pulled his hood up and stuck his hands deep in the pocket. By the time Bird caught up to him, Asher was still simmering, and felt suffocated and strange.

Bird whined and nosed the back of his leg. Asher resisted the urge to kick.

"Stay close," he said more softly, like an apology, and maybe because cryptic warnings that made him feel watched were *not* what he needed when he was oh so close to making it work but also oh so close to starving. He wouldn't take pity handouts: that didn't feel very grown-up. He just had to get in with the right crowd. "We've only got one shot to make this guy like me."

It was just easier to mesh with Bridlington and mind his business.

MARCELA

Marcela zipped her makeup clutch closed, unplugged her straightening and curling irons, turned off the light to a bathroom strewn with magazines and a mirror half covered in the white remains of stickers, and sped toward the suite door. She'd been trying not to spend too much time at the motel, to avoid her truly wonderful yet always exhausted parents who would read something wrong on her face. Caleb had been letting her stay at his place, in the spare room that was practically her second home. His mother adored her and taught her how to make peach pies and do other nice Bridlington things. His father was, well, Captain Reilly, and Marcela thought he trusted her more every day.

She left her room quickly, looking around like a hunted animal. The day wasn't as hot as some of the others, but painfully humid; she touched her hair without thinking. The westward-sinking sun had just gone down behind the small swath of forest across the road, sending premature darkness over the parking lot. She heard a lawnmower groaning from the back lawn, which meant she wouldn't have to look at Beetle Hoang. That had been their routine since he'd come home. Everyone knew Hoang had been sent away for talking about monsters, same thing Paz was still on about. Nope nope nope. Not her business.

She stepped forward but was stopped in her tracks by something far worse than Hoang. She heard someone clear their little throat from the direction of the white plastic chair beside her parents' door, and she froze at zero degrees Kelvin, some dangerous future bearing down on her. She shut her eyes tight and tried to make her thoughts flow away like nail polish.

"No," she said. "No way. This isn't happening."

"*Marcelaaaaa*," Paz said, half a whine and half a song, but all brat. "Avoiding me is *ruuuude*. I need you for *somethiiiiing*."

Marcela was not going to indulge that one bit. Maybe there had been a day when she would have done anything Paz asked of her, would have gotten in on schemes, but this was a world after the mill became a killing floor. This was a world that Marcela knew was haunted and couldn't face.

"You look gross," Paz said. It nearly tempted Marcela into turning around, because she was sure her rug rat sister could look no better. But nope. No part in this. "Wanna help me kill a monster, 'Cela?"

Not after everything. Not after the mill and the hell they had gone through over that. Marcela begged her parents not to hear any of this. "There's no way you still believe in that, Paz," she said, and felt insane.

But in the premature dark, the shadows thrown off the trees

covering her entire walk up to Quinn's, she almost believed in monsters. She should have known Paz wouldn't let it go.

"If there's no monster . . ." Paz began—it was a double-dog-quadruple-to-the-googleplex-million *dare*—"then start walking, 'Cela."

It all could have stopped right there if she'd turned around, the same way it could have stopped the night Chuck Warren died if she hadn't just rolled over and kept messaging Caleb when she heard Paz leave.

"If you think I look gross, Paz," Marcela whispered, "it's your fault for forcing me to take up the slack."

There was no response, but she felt her sister's small, cold hand brush hers. Something snapped in the trees across from them, and Marcela took off running for Quinn's so fast she didn't breathe. She left her sister in the company of the motel and blazed down the long, empty road.

The shadows felt like ice-cold waves, drowning her and pulling out every warm memory. She tried not to let her imagination run with Paz, but she heard the thin forest rattling on her right side and considered all sorts of things that might jump out to get her. If not a great big monster with teeth and one glowing eye, then an ax-murderer, or a regular murderer for that matter. Wasn't she seventeen and pretty and a little unmissable, and wasn't that always how a bad story started?

"*Marcela.*" She heard her name over the sound of her footsteps pounding the road, the tubes and bottles in her bag chattering together like teeth. "*Run, doggy, run run run.*"

She sprinted faster. Her shadow on the pavement looked

nothing like her but everything like someone who could survive. The key was to never stop running.

The Bright house got closer, and Marcela saw Quinn lounging on the front porch with one glass of lemonade and one glass of iced tea, condensation dripping down them. Quinn looked up and beamed from under the latticework shadows of the porch. Marcela could have cheered or maybe burst into tears. She knew she was only a few different choices from a world where no one was waiting for her besides something in the forest. From an end where she died cold and alone. She knew it viscerally, like she had seen it happen already in a dream.

"Who's this stunning babe come to bless lil' ol' me with her presence?" Quinn asked, in a voice half sarcastic and half familiar and homey.

When Marcela came to a stop at the foot of the stairs, the monster-thoughts faded back into the dark. She tried to catch her breath, to ease the shock from her legs, and struck a pose with one hand on her hip and her chin tilted up. "Oh, me?" she asked, waving one hand dramatically and clearing away her damp hair. It was already beginning to frizz, but she didn't have time to wince over it.

They both laughed, Marcela bounded up the porch to grab her iced tea, and the two of them walked giggling into Quinn's house.

There was no such thing as monsters. Chuck died from a fall. Caleb loved her and she loved him.

BRIDLINGTON

Some time after Chuck's funeral, Paz arrived on Sammy's street when the sun was just brushing the tops of the houses. She was aware of the guy across the road eyeing her, and she had been aware how the general store clerk watched her as she passed the outdoor racks, but she didn't care about any of it. By morning, she'd prove them all wrong. Monster killers got taken seriously. They were good people, or trying to be. She didn't want to be a hero; she just needed to stop being called the villain.

She dumped her bike and walked up Sammy's driveway with her hands in her pockets, chin down, long chalk-dyed braids thunking into her shoulders. She shambled up the porch steps and drew back her shoe to kick the door—her way of knocking. Her toe had rapped that faded spot a hundred times before, and she hoped it would a hundred times again.

It wouldn't. There are choices you make that you don't realize will be your last. In that moment, Paz was almost aware of it. Before she could dissolve into panic, the door swung open and her best friend hovered in the doorway wearing a nervous but determined smile . . . and her Power Rangers sneakers.

"You run fast in those?" Paz asked. It was the most she could manage when she was trying to keep her face set and cover up how cold and heavy she felt inside.

"Real fast," Sammy said. She grabbed her house-key lanyard off the ring and closed and locked the door behind her. "We're going to get that monster tonight," Sammy said.

Paz tried to say something. She tried to look brave. Instead, she watched Sammy break apart behind the tears filling her eyes.

Sammy hugged Paz, so quick she couldn't dodge away from it. After a moment (Paz couldn't say what she felt about being touched, if it was surprise or anger or disgust or deep, desperate longing), she wrapped her arms around Sammy and held on tight. Paz hid her face in Sammy's soft shoulder, tears falling hot and slow.

She had to ask, just in case. "Do you think I'm a liar, Sammy?" she said in a small, wet voice.

"*No*," Sammy said.

"Are you scared?" Paz whispered.

"I don't wanna be."

Paz almost wished they had all been scaredy-cats. That Chuck hadn't been brave enough to meet at the mill. That they hadn't been brave enough to put cards on their spokes and not just be what everyone told them to be. That they had been cowardly little fraidy-cat babies like Marcela on Caleb's arm. But Paz wasn't sure that would have helped any of them in the end.

"I wish we didn't have to be the brave ones."

"That'd be nice," Sammy whispered. She held tighter. "I think you're all my best friends," she said instead. "Is that okay?"

It was more than okay. Hell or high water. Diamond, or distance, or death.

Eventually, Paz got on her bike and pedaled, and Sammy jumped onto the pegs on the back. They rode off toward their meeting point at the bridge with a rattle of Paz's playing card, close to dark.

A dozen people watched them go, and would say they regretted it.

MARCELA

After drinking their beverages, and Quinn forcing Marcela to take a cookie she'd baked, and then a second and then a third, and doing the necessary praising of Caleb (which Quinn liked to keep short), Quinn started up about her brother, who was off in another city with his new girlfriend.

"She's dragged his backwoods ass to brunch," Quinn was saying, continuing to rave. "She got Jack Bright to go to *brunch*. He owns a *blazer*. He cut out red meat to stop *climate change*." And on and on.

Quinn had her arm looped through Marcela's and was tugging her up to her room. Marcela had known Quinn since their infancy and they'd always been close, but their relationship had shifted to cookie-cutter "popular girl and bubbly best friend" around the same time Marcela befriended a young but not-so-different Caleb Reilly. Quinn was all sweetness and kindness, with seashell-shaped ears and strawberry-blond hair, currently pulled back except for a single strand falling down the side of her face and into the slope of her neck.

"One day, 'Cela," she said, opening the door to her room, "we'll get fancy brunch in a fancy city."

"I'll visit you in Harville," Marcela promised, even though her stomach felt low and sloshy at the idea of having to travel so far. Quinn was going to university, Caleb was going to the police academy, and she was staying home in a town she didn't overly enjoy, without Quinn's company. And Caleb's, she thought quickly.

"Hmm," Quinn said. She turned her smile on Marcela, poking at her sides. "But would you cut out red meat for me, 'Cela? Would you would you would you?"

They both howled with laughter. Marcela would have said she'd do anything for Quinn, including giving up a good burger, but it didn't matter—it was just jokes. Quinn was just jokes, nothing serious. Not like Caleb.

Marcela swung into the chair in front of the huge pink vanity. Quinn flopped onto her bed and fumbled for her speaker to turn on the sound. Marcela was partial to Hayley Kiyoko but felt distant even as she swayed, nodding while Quinn talked avidly about how Jack went to a drag show, a goddamn *drag show*, with *drag queens*. Marcela pulled her curls back into a ponytail and watched through the mirror as Quinn pulled off the red polo she had to wear for her job at the grocery store.

"You know they're thinking about getting a dog?" Quinn said.

"Who?" Marcela asked, darting her eyes back to her own reflection. Hair secured, she reached for the eyeshadow.

"Jack and his girlfriend. Keep up." Quinn audibly shivered,

and Marcela did her very best to look dead ahead. "I told him that if the thing is bigger than a cat, I won't go near it."

Marcela nodded slowly. She knew where the conversation was headed. "They don't have those dogs anymore, right?" she asked, quiet, low. "The Meyers?"

"I think they ran away? It was a while ago," Quinn said. "That's what they get for not tying them up. I'm not sorry."

Marcela tilted her head up a little higher, fluttering her lashes, analyzing the lines of her jaw and cheeks before grabbing her palette to soften them. The transformation was slow and exact. "Good riddance," she said. "Probably dead by now." Vicious things though they were, Marcela doubted they could survive in the wild.

"Well, I sleep better knowing they're not out there." Marcela kept her eyes ahead but heard Quinn slip off her bed and creep up behind her. "Stalking their prey. Getting closer and closer . . ."

In the brief moment without Quinn talking, Marcela could hear birds through the open window, and if she listened, the memory of the hush of cornstalks and distant barking, or the rushing of Blue River as if it was calling her, beckoning her out toward the mill and toward the schemes of a little girl with a face too similar to her own. She could picture Paz standing on the rocks in front of the mill, with the rain rattling down into the water with a sound like fireworks, or gunshots? No, it wasn't raining, but the image refused to dissipate, like it had melted, thick and sticky, into her head.

Dull claws closed around Marcela's shoulder. She shrieked and jumped up, whirling around with wide eyes. The chair slammed back into the vanity and all the little bottles tipped and clattered.

"Dammit, Quinn!" she shouted, more from fright than anger.

Quinn backed off just a step, hands up in front of her chest—Marcela didn't look. "Yikes. Sorry, 'Cela," she said. Her eyebrows furrowed together. "I didn't know you were still jumpy about the dogs."

"I'm not," Marcela said, blinking hard. Quinn was only half a step away from her, perfumed, with that one strand of loose hair. "Sorry, I—"

"Caleb said you've been off," Quinn said.

It had been a rough five days, where it felt like clouds were gathering and lightning was preparing itself to burn everything down. Marcela shook her head and dabbed the backs of her hands against her forehead.

"I'm just . . ." She couldn't think of what to do with her hands, with her eyes, when Quinn was right there in front of her in only her jeans and a pink bra. "Maybe the dogs are spooking me a bit," she admitted.

"Well, they're gone," Quinn said, hands on her hips and her smile attempting to be easy. "No more nightmares, okay? Jack says they're looking at Schnoodles anyway."

Marcela laughed at that. "What the hell is a Schnoodle?"

"I dunno," Quinn said, throwing her hands up and going back to her bed. "But it's not a King Shepherd, so good for them."

Marcela tore herself away and went back to her makeup, pulling mascara through her lashes in a vacant routine. She said nothing more about it, leaving Quinn to flip through her phone. They both remembered that day with the dogs, the Meyers, and Captain Reilly.

In Marcela's memory, it had gone like this:

Back in her elementary school days, Marcela was rarely seen without her younger sister following after her, and so it only made sense that the two were walking up the road past Quinn's house in nearly matching grass-stained jeans and ratty sneakers. Paz was glumly holding a store-bought pie and Marcela had adopted the same somber demeanor.

They were trudging past the Bright house just as Quinn opened the door, hurled the words "You're such a *dickhead*, Jack" over her shoulder, and stormed out with her jump rope. She dropped it immediately when she saw Marcela and Paz standing in the leaf-strewn road.

Quinn stomped over in her pink dress and denim coat. "Jack won't let us watch anything but wrestling," she said, and crinkled her nose back at the house as if he'd see. But there were more interesting things than that, clearly; she squinted at the box in Paz's hands. "Why do you have a pie?"

Marcela rolled her eyes, and Paz puffed out her cheeks, looking only slightly guilty.

"Apology pie," Marcela said. That was how you got favor back from the town: kick up the church involvement and send a pie to the offended parties. There would be many more pies sent between that day and Chuck's death.

"For what?" Quinn asked, joining their trudge without request or invitation.

Paz crinkled her freckled nose. "Captain Reilly told the Meyers that I started a bad rumor about them," she said, kicking at the leaves and rocks and refusing to look either of the other girls in the eye.

"What'd you say?" Quinn asked, but Paz only shook her head. "'Cela?"

Marcela shrugged, feeling bad about it. "I'd tell you if I knew."

They trotted up the road, past the cornfield between Quinn's property and the Meyers', and stopped at the mailbox.

"Hurry up," Marcela said. There were better ways to spend a Saturday. Paz grumbled but set off solo to the front porch, while Marcela and Quinn started a very avid thumb war. Quinn was twisting Marcela's arm to win, and Marcela was red-cheeked and letting her.

That's when they heard the screaming. It tore through the still sound of rushing cornstalks and calling birds: a high-pitched, all-systems-go, bawling distress call. Marcela caught one moment of similar panic on Quinn's pale face, and then she twisted their thumb war around to grab Quinn's hand, and both went sprinting up the angel-ornament-adorned path to the front of the Meyers' farmhouse. Everything was laid out, with just one moment to try and decipher what had happened.

Mr. Meyer was standing on the porch with the pie covering the front of his flannel shirt, frozen in that half-second between confusion and absolute rage. Paz was screaming shrill, incoherent accusations. For just a moment, Marcela was sure she saw Ben Meyer standing in the doorway behind his foster father, saw his tear-streaked, numb-blue face, but then he was gone. And along the side of the house, throwing up leaves and dust beneath their huge paws, the family's three King Shepherds were bounding from their kennels. Time seemed to freeze in that moment—the dogs were as tall as Paz, spined with bristling fur and sharp eyes and so so many very white teeth in those pointed jaws. Horror sunk through Marcela like a gut punch.

She tightened her grip on Quinn's hand and raced to grab Paz's too. She felt like she was running in a dream, each step taking a millennium, Paz never seeming to get closer, the dogs bearing down on the three of them now. She could smell their horrible breath by the time she managed to get her hand on Paz's arm and yank her away from the jaws of the biggest Shepherd, who was shimmering white with cold blue eyes, just like the Reilly men.

The three girls raced into the cornfield with the stalks cutting sharp against their cheeks. The barking followed them. They ran straight for Quinn's house, Paz stumbling in the rear. Marcela pulled her with a grip so tight that she left bruises. All around them, the corn snarled and snapped like a thousand dogs closing in, blotting out the October sky.

This is how we die, Marcela remembered thinking. *This is how I die, because of Paz not knowing how to apologize properly.* And yet she wasn't mad at Paz but at the dogs. No, at the Meyers. She knew whose fault this was.

They burst free from the cornfield onto the flat lawn of the Bright property and didn't stop sprinting until they were on the porch. Quinn scrambled for the door, ready to yank it open. Marcela was hugging Paz against her chest (to hold her in comfort or hold her to restrain her, Marcela couldn't remember), and watched the quivering stalks with terrified, rapt attention.

She swore she could still hear the growling and snapping, but there were no eyes or teeth coming for them anymore. The corn swayed innocently.

Paz's hands tightened on the back of Marcela's shirt. If Marcela was about to be mad that Paz almost got them killed, it faded when her sister's small, still-shocked voice asked, "'Cela, can we go to the Mac's?"

Marcela sat in Quinn's room so many years later and remembered how they'd trooped off and tried to forget it had happened, but Paz was uncharacteristically quiet the entire time, like she was contemplating something much larger than herself. The three of them pooled their change, hot from their pockets, and bought one big slushy. Paz tried to pour a green one, but Marcela kicked her sister's ankles until she let Quinn get the blue one that she liked. Quinn kissed her cheek for that, and Marcela blushed and pretended it was from running. The three sat on the out-of-season saltbox, a good place to be in Bridlington on a young Saturday even with the autumn chill. They drank the slushy to the dregs and made faces with their blue tongues. The dog chase might have become just a harrowing playground story.

Until Captain Reilly found them sitting there.

He had his hands on his hips in a very fatherly manner, and his cap threw a shadow over his icy eyes when he said, "Ladies, I've just gotten a call about trespassing on the Meyers' farm." He tilted his head to Quinn and jerked his chin back to the road. "Bright, you head on home. Espinos, can we have a chat?"

Instantly, Marcela understood that Mr. Meyer hadn't mentioned Quinn. Quinn slid nervously from the box and her warm fingers drifted from Marcela's to leave them prickling in the October breeze. Marcela closed her hand into a careful fist and watched Quinn leave as fall leaves rattled past. Watched that retreating pink dress and ballet flats and strawberry-blond braid until they were out of sight.

By the time Marcela turned back, Paz had stamped her foot down on the pavement so hard her Pokémon shoe lit up.

"They're not good!" Paz was screaming, which Marcela thought was horribly vague. But sometimes, looking back, she wondered if it was simply all Paz could think to say. She was working herself up again, her words hard to decipher. "They're bad people, Captain Reilly. They're not good—they're monsters!"

"I have no idea how you've come up with this, but I've known the Meyers since *I* was your age, and they've never been anything less than kind," Captain Reilly said, even-toned.

"Captain Reilly—"

"You're really dedicated to this fib, aren't you?" he asked. "Lying is just getting you in more trouble."

"I'm not—"

He narrowed his eyes, shook his head, and pointed his finger. "You're acting like a little dog, Espino. Unlock the jaw, drop the bone, and let it go before you ruin a good family's good name." And what was worse was that when he said it so sternly Paz couldn't argue, Captain Reilly snapped his gaze up to Marcela, too. And what was even worse than that, Marcela's lips wrenched themselves open by instinct alone and she heard herself say, "I don't know what she's talking about." And she didn't. She wouldn't.

Paz's red-rimmed, glassy, betrayed eyes were stained into Marcela's memory, but she didn't know what that day was about. She knew only being driven home in the cruiser and delivered to their father, and how she asked for a boutique dress on Sunday and befriended Caleb on Monday, and how things became different. Paz went left to Chuck and the mill; Marcela went right to the Reillys and her nice, neat face.

In Quinn's room, after a new lifetime of separation from her sister, boots with a heel waiting with the other clothes she kept here for such occasions, Marcela knew two things: Paz was a liar who couldn't let anything go, and Caleb was one of the only things that convinced the town that Marcela wasn't her sister. Because if he loved her, his father could too, and the town would as well. If Caleb thought her deserving, then surely she was, because he wouldn't love someone like Paz who threw pies and made trouble and led little Chuckie Warren to his demise.

"To Jack and his Schnoodle," Marcela said, raising her mascara and hoping that was the end of it. Quinn was still wearing only her bra, and Marcela kept her eyes glued to her own lips.

"Hear hear," Quinn said, and tugged a T-shirt on.

As if the universe had heard them talking about dogs of various sizes and levels of aggression, Marcela was torn away from the mirror by the sharp bark of one that sounded a lot nicer than the Meyers' Shepherds. She and Quinn moved to the lace-curtained window to open it. Rainforest-lush summer air wafted in, smelling like grass and aphids, chasing back the foggy scent of Quinn's perfume. Quinn's arm pressed warm to Marcela's while they looked out across the cement patio and the field.

The Reillys' truck was parked by the edge of the tall grass, and Caleb had his shirt off and was splitting some of the logs he'd brought. Some young-looking teen Marcela didn't recognize was setting up the pit with a beer bottle next to him and a dog dancing around behind: a feathery something-or-other that looked like it was smiling, definitely not small and possibly not even medium-sized, but certainly not mean-looking. Marcela didn't recognize the boy from school or as a sibling of anyone she went to school with, and he didn't look familiar enough to be a cousin.

It was intriguing, but not damning. If Caleb seemed to trust him enough to let him handle the fire, then what did she care? Because she loved Caleb and he loved her.

There was no escaping the perfect life she had made for herself.

"Hey!" Quinn called, and both the boys looked up. Caleb winked at Marcela, and the new kid flicked his chin, fiery sunset glinting across his sunglasses. "Who's the new guy?"

"Asher," the kid called, and waved with a frankly Caleb-looking smile. He was lanky, short, and white, with either a sunburn or oncoming heat stroke; straight-legged jeans and a black Under Armour hoodie sure was a choice for this time of year.

"Hi, Asher," Quinn said, propping her chin on her hand. "Your dog looks nice, and I'm not really a dog person, so that's a huge compliment."

"His name's Bird," Asher said, and Bird barked in recognition that this was in fact his name and he almost knew that, though he wasn't sure what to do with the information. He almost knocked over Asher's beer, so Asher dove to catch it and let the skeleton of the unlit bonfire fall. He swore at the dog, more of an "I'm disappointed in you for acting so childish in front of company" tone than anything hurtful. Caleb snickered.

"He's kinda cute," Quinn said to Marcela, in a bland, charitable way.

"Looks greasy," Marcela said, feeling a tingling numbness in her jaw where her back teeth touched.

"Grease can be good," Quinn said. "That's why I won't be giving up red meat."

Marcela huffed out half a laugh but could muster nothing more. "Then you can take the scrawny kid."

"That's not my type," she said, in a way that dared Marcela to ask for clarification, and went off to her closet to find her shoes.

Marcela tried to peel herself from the window but couldn't seem to. Something about that Asher guy seemed cursed, or maybe she was cursed, or maybe this whole night was.

Paz, she thought, *I've figured this damn town out.*

Don't you dare screw me over now.

CALEB REILLY,
BUT SMALLER

Asher Gordon thought Caleb Reilly was just about the coolest person he had ever met in his entire life, which was unfortunate. Asher had floated around Quinn's house until Caleb pulled up in his truck, floated around a little longer while Caleb texted some people, and floated around even longer while Caleb started unloading the firewood, because Asher was waiting for his perfect time to strike.

And *then* he had walked up to Caleb and offered to help. Bird was good and stuck by his side, which he was grateful for. He'd expected Caleb to grill him a bit and had readied himself. But Caleb just wagged a finger at him, squinted an eye half closed, and said, "Asher, right? Reece's friend?"

Asher was surprised Reece even knew who he was, then assumed "friend" was probably a nice way of saying "a guy Reece knows."

"I go to the gym," Asher said, well aware he possessed the spindly frame of someone who didn't go to the gym with much success. "Reece is there. He seems chill."

Caleb seemed to like that response and nodded.

"Where are you from?" he asked, waving Asher over to help unload the truck. Caleb picked up a huge orange net bag of logs. Asher pulled out some sticks of kindling. "We don't get many visitors in town."

"I'm on a road trip," he said. "Or I was, but I kinda like this place."

"Where are you staying, then?" Caleb asked him.

"Motel," he lied. Even with five days of practicing, he was almost surprised how easily he slipped into the deception behind his sunglasses.

Caleb paused and tilted his head. His eyes were horribly blue. "You met Hoang yet?" he asked, in a way that seemed to mean "Are you two friends?"

Asher took a second to realize he meant Beetle; he'd butchered the last name. "Talked once," Asher said, trying to gauge what he was supposed to say from the micro-movements of Caleb's tanned face.

Caleb nodded a bit. "Kind of a . . . recluse," he decided on.

Asher made a sound between a hum and a laugh.

Caleb went easily back to unloading the wood, casual again, like the flick of a light switch. Asher noted that hairpin trigger: there was a thin line between "intriguing new vagabond" and "dangerous untouchable."

"That should be good for firewood for now," Caleb said,

dusting off his hands. "We can leave the rest in the truck until we need it. You drink?"

Asher turned back from the tiny pile on the cement deck and saw Caleb was motioning to a case of beer in the truck's flatbed.

This felt like a trap. "Not legally," Asher said. "Not old enough."

Caleb pulled a bottle out and popped the cap off with a tool on his keys. "It's fine," he said, holding the bottle out to Asher. "Nothing too rowdy here, I make sure of it. Just chill."

Chill was good, and this Caleb guy really did seem to have a handle on the town. Asher was making good choices, he thought. He trotted over and took the bottle, his fingers brushing Caleb's just casually and not weird or anything.

"Thanks," Asher said. He motioned to the police sticker on the back of the truck, next to one for the Liberal Party. "Police won't bust us up?"

Caleb shook his head and grabbed a bottle for himself. "My dad's the captain. He doesn't want to know, so he doesn't." He was still smiling, one thousand and ten percent genuine, by Asher's meager calculations. His eyes were all sparkling and his posture had straightened up and puffed out. "Bigger things out there for him to worry about. He's the only thing stopping this town from going off the deep end."

Asher couldn't imagine what "big things" happened here, so he assumed it was just bragging. He found it so incredibly strange to brag about your father that he almost frowned, but kept on smiling. "Good for him."

Caleb clicked his tongue once, took a quick glance at a window of the house up above them. "This town is a good place, with good people," he said, with more of that contextless, ominous secrecy that Asher really didn't like about Bridlington, though he was much more beggar than chooser. "Some people think otherwise and cause trouble where there isn't any. Hoang was one of them awhile back, but was sort of . . ." Caleb trailed off and spun a finger near his temple.

Asher didn't want to ask more about that. He wanted them to just stop talking about Beetle—it felt cruel, or oddly exposing.

"That's why I wanted to know if you were friends," Caleb said. "You might have heard some things."

Here it was: the grilling. Under Caleb's frankly lupine stare, Asher felt hunted. The sun was still up and he wanted to believe that things would be okay, but everything was flattening at the edges again. "I've heard nothing bad," he lied. Bird had gone sniffing off to the edge of the cement deck and was staring into the trees that blocked the Mac's from view. Asher felt his heart lurch like something had tugged it.

"Hoang was always a little different, but that's just not how we are here. It's nothing personal, some people just don't fit with the climate," Caleb said, staring harder.

Asher kept his bottle hugged neatly against his chest, his stance solid, mask up and worn so well you'd swear it fit. Yet half his mind was focused on Bird taking one slow step off the deck, ears twitching and eyes fixed into the darkness past the sun-warmed grass.

"And when people don't help the town—" Caleb was still saying, while Asher fought to keep his cool.

Asher, he swore he heard. *Here, boy.*

"—the town doesn't help them," Caleb finished, while sweat beaded down Asher's stinging temples. "You get that?"

Keep it together. Asher took a careful sip. He wasn't sure he liked the taste. He could have said so, been honest, gone down with his morals intact. "And if people fit in and help the town," he said instead—Bird whined pitifully, stiff-jointed like he'd bolt—"the town helps them."

Caleb stared like he meant to nod but forgot. "Exactly."

Asher took a good hearty swig, fixed his sunglasses, and swallowed. "Cheers to your dad, then," Asher said, and Caleb's smile widened at that.

"Yeah, cheers," he said. He smacked his palm to the police sticker and drank too.

"Bird," Asher called, just as Bird had begun to press down like he might spring away. "Come say hi."

Bird shook himself off vehemently, gave the woods one more side-eyed glance, and then came trotting over. He seemed to instantly forget whatever it was and happily allowed Caleb to jostle his head around and rile him up into barking.

From then on, Caleb seemed to trust Asher pretty well. He pointed up to the window of the house and said the Latina-looking girl with the moody lips was his girlfriend. She seemed familiar, but Asher just decided to add a "She's hot," which sent Caleb into details about their picture-perfect relationship. Asher nodded along. He got tipsy enough to make all the appropriate "wow"s and "damn"s and found the exact right point to add in a "You're so lucky, man." Bird hugged at his ankles until Quinn started to put out some snacks. Asher took another sip of beer to forget how hungry he was.

Marcela came down, kissed Caleb, and Asher tipped his bottle to her.

She stared at him, just a second too long. It was subtle—he didn't think anyone else caught it—but Asher felt himself run a little cold. This close, he realized why she seemed familiar: there was no doubt in his mind that this keen-eyed girl was Paz's older sister.

Apparently, both could see right through him.

***

Asher spent the rest of the party shadowing Caleb, who had yet to put his shirt back on and was huge. The sun had gone down completely. Asher watched Caleb chuck back two bottles and shotgun a can, all lit up with the firelight and the headlights of more cars pulling into the field. Reece From The Gym (who had wanted to add Asher on Snapchat, so Asher had dipped behind the snack table to frantically make an account) cut a can open for him and Asher shotgunned it, with limited success.

"Attaboy!" Caleb roared, clapping him on the back. Asher almost keeled over into the fire, but Caleb grabbed his shoulder and shook him roughly. Had Asher been there a week earlier, his face would have burned red, but he was instead filled with bro-ish triumph he had learned from the gym. It was all finally working out. Caleb tossed him another can—they cracked them open and toasted. Asher's head was all swimmy.

"You ever been hunting?" Reece asked him. He was tall and his eyes were orange-and-green with fire and Asher thought you could maybe call him attractive.

"All the time," Asher said, tilting his chin up. Quinn had picked the music on the speakers, which meant it was country, which the majority would like. Asher couldn't really hear it much over a thrumming roar growing in his head. "Dude, we gotta . . ." He felt a little sick, and drank more. His phone was being passed around so everyone could get his username. He was proud of more-sober Asher for factory resetting it before he left home, and slowly building up all the usual apps and accounts—Snapchat had been a blunder (it was still new-ish and he didn't quite "get it" yet), but he'd covered that base. "We gotta go sometime."

"Yeah!" Reece said, and Caleb laughed and was calling his cousin to say to get down here and meet the new guy and okay, fine, bring the kid too for a bit, and Asher thought about how he was gonna go hunting with "The Guys" and felt hazy with happiness. He was Asher Gordon, and he was exactly like Caleb Reilly. He smelled like smoke and his head was blurry with beer and this was a good summer—a *great* summer. He took a swig of Fireball and coughed and Caleb thumped him on the back, so he did it again and Caleb touched him again, too.

Caleb Reilly was six-foot-one, roughly two hundred pounds, and had what you could call *experience* with alcohol. Enough to maybe shake your finger at him when he was caught, tell him it wasn't "adult behavior," that you "expected more of him," and he wasn't "some kid with a playing card in the spokes of his bike." Asher didn't know any of this and kept trying to match him shot for shot and swig for swig.

He chugged back another can, let another hockey guy drag him to another group of people, and introduced himself with slurred words and a dopey grin. Reaffirmed a few times that he was actually seventeen despite his young face.

"Almost eighteen," he told some girl. He couldn't remember how old he really was. It took him a moment to realize the round, blurry shape he was talking to was Quinn. He and two hockey guys had stumbled over to the parked cars where a stone-cold-sober Marcela was sitting in the back of Caleb's pickup truck with Quinn and another girl behind. With his buzz and his sunglasses still on, Asher thought Marcela looked like a total buzzkill party-killer Grumpy McGrumperson. "I'm practically legal," he hiccuped.

"You should slow down, Asher," Quinn said, a dutiful hostess. "Go eat something."

"I'm so sober," he said, with a too-wide grin. "I'm having . . . I'm having so much fun."

Marcela eyed him.

The other girl had leaned over the wall of the truck bed to make out with Reece. Asher felt a little jealous it wasn't him but couldn't be bothered long. He whirled around and watched Caleb's smile and Caleb's I-Work-Out arms and listened to his gruff voice, and he looked up at the sparks and the smoke and the stars and hoped he'd remember it all in the morning.

Asher Gordon, Bridlington-made.

He drank another beer and stumbled back onto the cement deck.

Quinn slid away to check the snacks, that girl and Reece wandered off, and Bird breathed out slow from behind Marcela.

"You and me both," she said, and wondered what he was hearing with those constantly twitching ears.

BEETLE

Knowing there was a party at Quinn Bright's, and seeing Caleb's truck pass by the motel earlier on the way there, Beetle was extra anxious to be home before dark. When twilight split the sky into a thousand colors, he strode from the lawn and past the playground, where he spotted what he swore was a sword-tail cricket sitting right in the middle of the nearest swing. It was so perfect he would have called it chilling, like someone was live-baiting a trap made only for him. His Bug Book was still in his backpack, and the mason jar for collecting, and the fat marker for checking off bugs he'd found.

He could keep walking, be on his block by the time the sun set, be within screaming distance of help.

And yet, the cricket.

"No," he said to himself. Another car went rushing down the road to Quinn's. The sky was getting darker, the shadows drawing out slow and treacherous. "*No.*"

It wasn't worth it. Who cares about childhood promises to yourself to find nearly eight hundred bugs? Let it go. Forget this shit. Grow up.

He could have kept walking and maybe junked the Bug Book in a dumpster on the way. He resented ever being that small child who lived here. He resented being charitable to that dumbass Asher.

But Beetle, with all of the kindness of a boy who grew up surrounded by fields, opened his backpack, knelt on the pea gravel, and ceremoniously scooped the cricket into the mason jar. Beetle laid down the jar and hauled out the book. He skimmed the dichotomous key as he had done years ago, tracing the branch-offs. He lost himself in them for a moment.

"Sword-tail cricket," he finally confirmed. He checked off the picture and wrote *motel swing-set—07/08/2016* beside, but there was no joy in it. It felt like paying off debts to his younger self so it would leave him alone. In a stupor, he watched the horrible little thing throw itself against the glass, again and again and again. It jumped and hit the lid with a *tock*, fell dazed into the dead grass, and tried to dig out the bottom. He watched so closely that it felt like he was in the jar too, feeling every painful throe. It felt revolting to watch, and yet he couldn't look away.

While Beetle watched the cricket slam into the glass and begged himself to not care, he felt Bridlington close tightly around him. The longer he stared, the smaller his own jar felt, until he could practically feel the cold on his arms.

He unscrewed the lid and dumped the cricket out onto the grass, breaking the spell. Beetle watched as it hopped away to join the chorus of chirping mingling with the soft tinkling of the wind chimes under the motel eaves.

The sky was almost entirely dark then, and the party across the fields was a dull croon of music with more headlights pulling in, silhouettes of already staggering people highlighted against the distant fire. Beetle wanted no part of it. He scrambled to sweep his Bug Book and the jar and the marker into his tattered backpack, yanked it shut, and rushed to his feet.

Beetle took a quick scan of the well-lit but empty parking lot and the gauntlet of road before it hit the intersection of the lonely highway. Even that was still a sprint from where Main Street truly started, or the winding streets of houses where people would be. It was the same run as always.

He swore he heard Paz's voice: "Can you run fast in those?"

Checkerboard Vans weren't Sammy's Power Rangers sneakers, and they definitely weren't made for running, but he was sure as hell going to try.

Beetle took off at a mad sprint, faster than the average eighteen-year-old, despite what was hardly a runner's build. He might have done well in high school track if all the races had taken place in empty Bridlington at night. He ran alongside the gutter of the road with the dark trees looming just across the street beside him, the branches reaching out for him, calling him to those depths. In the intersection ahead, the blinking-yellow stared out at him, a slow wink like a taunt, washing the street in and out, in and out, in and out.

And then came the usual feeling, the one that stalked him every time he left the relative safety of the motel: something was chasing him. He ran faster, the intersection seemingly farther and farther away. He heard crashing in the forest beside him and caught a flash of light through the trees, like an eye. Despite burning muscles, he was suddenly washed in cold sweat.

Laughter rang out (the party, he thought, just the party), but it sounded too strange and echoing to be real. It didn't feel real, and Beetle was *real*. He hadn't spent all those years with a plastic bracelet sitting in the uncomfortable chairs of group sessions not to know as much.

He broke into the intersection, lit up in a strobe of horrible yellow. Bridlington at night came in flashes. His Vans gritted against the gravel to turn up to the shops on Main, which might have felt at least a little safer than the half-backwoods of the motel. He knew they weren't. He knew no one but his mother would care when he disappeared, and she would take too long to notice his absence anyway.

Main wasn't safe. One glowing eye was rushing for him. It growled and puffed hot, rancid breath.

Beetle yelped and stumbled sideways, tripping into the shallow gutter along the road and landing hard. He heard the mason jar shatter in his bag. He scrambled back.

The thing with one eye snarled as it stopped beside him. It wasn't a toothy, supernatural monster, but it was no less dangerous.

The dirt bike rumbled, idling as the two riders flipped up the visors of their helmets: Brady Novak, with his sister sitting behind him. Brady was dressed in the all-camo of a farm kid who seemed to know no other pattern, and Emily was in shorts and a T-shirt that would protect against nothing—not road rash and not teeth. There was mud scraped up the body of the bike and flecked on the singular headlamp. With curdling horror, Beetle wondered if they were chasing him on purpose.

"Who the hell . . . ?" Brady started to say, leaning over to look harder at Beetle on the ground. He palmed the throttle so the bike growled louder.

The yellow light blinked above the Novaks, alternately turning them from sallow-skinned ghouls to monstrous shadows with hollow eyes under their helmets.

"What do you want?" Beetle managed to say. He didn't dare stand.

Emily leaned over so far her brother had to really set himself to keep the bike from tipping. Emily's thrice-daily playground destruction extended far beyond the blacktop, and there was no need for pleasantries now; no one would hear them. "Caleb said you were back, but he didn't say you looked like *that*."

He gritted his teeth. "Looked like what?" he asked, like it mattered.

Brady palmed the throttle again, silent but clearly smirking even behind his helmet. Emily put her chin up. "I guess we shouldn't be surprised that nuthouse Hoang turned into a—"

The next word (a very uncreative slur that just adds a "y" to a known fact, and still stings just as much) made Beetle run hot and unstoppable. No shame, all anger.

If what happened next was going to be his word against theirs, he was going to make it count. "You're a transphobic piece of shit, you know that?"

Emily's eyes narrowed and she shook her brother's shoulder. "Brady, you gonna let this freak talk to me like that?"

Beetle knew he'd done it. He slapped a hand against his

chest first before he fumbled in his pocket, looking for some means of defence.

Brady rocked the bike forward.

Beetle's shaking fingers hooked his keys.

Brady kicked out the peg.

Beetle's keys snagged as he tried to stand, and instead he crashed backward with his hand still stuck in his pocket.

Brady swung his leg up to get off the bike, intending to give Beetle Hoang a few good slugs for talking shit where no one could hear him scream.

The sound of unhurried footsteps, and a quiet humming approaching:

I wanna be the very best
Like no one ever was . . .

All three of them turned to look up the road towards the Mac's.

Oh no, Beetle thought, hot anger crystallizing into chitin-shelled fear.

Paz Espino, wearing her ordinary Super Mario shirt and cargo shorts, was walking in their direction with a last-call slushy between both hands.

"Is that . . ." Emily squinted at the waning figure stepping in and out of the street lamps, untouched by the blinking glow of the overhead bulb.

Beetle saw Paz tilt her head like some horror movie kid, smiling lips bloodied from the slushy—bone-white and blood red—waiting for the moment of recognition.

Sometimes being Bridlington's most notorious trouble-maker had its perks, even if it was mostly lies.

"Hell no," Brady said.

Paz stepped from the light and was suddenly missing in the shadows.

"*Hell* no," Brady said again, and slammed his visor down.

"Don't be such a chickenshit, Brady—" Emily started to say, straining to catch another look, but then the bike was racing off for the party as fast as it could go.

Beetle, breathless, watched the retreating red light. He knew that could have been so much worse.

"Heya," a voice suddenly said behind him. Paz was crouched with the slushy between her feet.

Beetle swallowed, staring down the motel road. He wanted to pull his anger back out, but instead he just felt tired.

"Why do you want me to help, Paz?" he asked her, because he assumed this was about that monster hunt.

"I need someone strong," she said. She was so small next to him.

The wind brushed gently on Beetle's numb face. "Please," he choked out. His eyes were prickly and he felt sweat popping up above his round top lip. He needed to say it. It was too late, but the story of the monster was clawing through him. Every horrible memory. Every terrified moment. "You need to let it go. You can't kill this thing."

She slurped her slushy down to the bottom where it gurgled awfully, like a sick dog. Paz's voice was very low and very flat. "Someone has to try."

"You could just leave, Paz," he said. "Find somewhere better than here."

"And if the monster is there, too?"

Beetle wondered if it was. He had to hope it wasn't true. There had to be a way out.

"Paz . . ." And then he said what he wished he had heard as a kid, what might have kept him chasing bugs instead of running from bullies and monsters alike. "People love you, or they will. The world is way bigger than Bridlington."

He turned to find her, but she was already gone.

"Paz?" Beetle said, louder. He didn't care what heard him. Even if he did fear monsters in other places too.

He stood up, stumbled into the middle of the road where anything could have found him, and whirled around under the blinking yellow light. He saw no sign of her.

Beetle didn't know what Paz was planning, but he knew it would end well for no one. He had options, collected after six years out of town. He could do nothing and get his paychecks and leave. He could mind his business. The monster wasn't just a thing with teeth—it got in your head, too. He felt it bubbling in his blood. It called him toward the mill, sang into his ear.

There were easy choices to make, but Beetle knew life wasn't easy.

MARCELA

Marcela had mingled a bit, taken some pictures, done the usual grandstanding of teenage popularity. The night had grown a bit colder, turning the humidity to a sinking chill, so she'd swiped a pink-and-black flannel shirt from Quinn. It was too short and too baggy, but it did the trick. She danced with Caleb until he got a little too drunk to form coherent sentences and wanted to hang out with the hockey team. He turned from her then, his hand slipping away while he fell into a wave of reaching fingers, leaving Marcela alone in the swarming crowd of people she didn't really care about.

In that gap, she swore she heard rushing water and giggling, faint, beyond the twanging music. If she paused just long enough, she might hear where it was coming from.

She went back to the truck at the edge of the party and pulled herself into the uncomfortable bed, dabbing the backs of her hands against her forehead to mop off a faint sheen of sweat. There was a small shuffling of paws, and then Bird's cold nose was sniff-sniff-sniffing at her cheek.

"Get out of here, mutt," she said, but it wasn't meant unkindly, and she made no move to shove him. She just didn't have time for it, really; she was scanning the crowd to make sure that Caleb wasn't face down on the pavement yet, that Hannah Evans wasn't trying to make a pass.

And that's when she heard the retching. It took her a moment to confirm it was real and not those hazy sounds on the edge of everything else. But that awful croaking was too close by and was punctuated by the unmistakable sounds of an entirely liquid diet hitting the grass.

Marcela looked to Bird first, who breathed out slowly in a mournful little whine. She gritted her teeth and shuffled past Bird to lean her folded arms on the side of the truck bed.

There was Asher, of course, puking up every ounce of approval. With the party still raging and howling with increasingly drunk laughter, she was sure she was the only one who'd heard him, and he was well hidden between the dark of the cars, only firelight on the edges. She could have easily ignored this, and wanted to. She wasn't the one who'd let him play two rounds of king's cup, and she wasn't Vicky Devereaux giving him another beer as an offering to dance with her, then kissing him. Marcela had noticed the way he chucked back the rest of his beer after she did, and noticed how it seemed to give him the gall to kiss her back and get his hands to move. Marcela had kissed Caleb then, as if reminded that she should.

No, she told herself. She was not going to start feeling sorry for him, or herself.

But still, she stared at Asher in the shadows, at the way he pressed his clammy forehead to the cold steel of the cab, the way his brow seemed furrowed under his sunglasses. Bird hung his head over, whining quietly, and stared down at Asher too.

"I resent being made to babysit," she said.

Asher turned sunglass-covered eyes on her.

"Babysit?" Asher asked with stumbling lips. He turned his head slightly to where Bird was leaning his head over the wall of the truck bed, and clued in. "Oh . . . sorry."

"Pathetic apology," she said.

"I told him to stay. He doesn't really run off."

He stared at her then. For a second, Marcela felt watched so closely it prickled, as if there were river beetles crawling over every inch of her skin. Asher twitched out an easy, very Caleb-like smile. It should have made her relax her shoulders and breathe out the stale air bubbling in her belly, but her face stayed pressed in a tight frown, nearly a sneer.

"I'm sorry I kept you from the party," Asher finally said. He tried to lean into the side of the truck but miscalculated how far away it was and ended up stumbling. Bird regarded him warily, tilting his head so one ear flopped over.

Marcela rolled her eyes and looked back to where Caleb was lurching but still standing. "The party isn't my thing," she said.

"Then why are you here?"

"Caleb," she said, which was a good reminder. "He likes it, I like him."

"Makes sense," Asher said. He was swaying like he'd just gotten off a carnival ride, and staring up at all the stars. It seemed a very innocent gesture, childlike, but it also made her sure he was no small-town boy used to seeing those ordinary specks. And then it made her remember that she didn't know anything about him, as if on purpose. When she scanned him with that buggy-skinned closeness, she could get no further than the black shield in front of his eyes.

"Are you *really* seventeen?" she asked. Maybe this Asher was an honest drunk. "Because I don't believe a word out of your mouth."

Asher Gordon grinned in a sick, languid way. Having now located how far away the side of the truck was, he leaned into it. He looked very, *very* unwell.

"I've got ID," he said, stepping closer to her with his shoulder dragging against the truck. He was still slurring a bit. "But it's in—" He stopped, and his chest jumped like he might puke again, but he didn't. "It's in my car."

"Where's home?"

"Oakdale."

"Never heard of it."

"Wish I were you."

They stared at each other. He seemed to be telling the truth, so she handed him a bottle of water from the back of Caleb's truck. He took it, moodily uncapped it, and downed a bit. Most of it missed his mouth and pattered into the grass.

Marcela heard Caleb joining the chorus of guys daring Brady Novak to jump his bike over the picnic table in the field, and Quinn laughing. Wrapped up under it all, the memory of smelling dry cornstalks and cheap blue-raspberry syrup— Paz and her schemes ached rotten and cold against the hinge of Marcela's jaw. Her eyes prickled, desperate for this night to be over.

"I'm not really real," Asher said. She had guessed right: he *was* an honest drunk. It was just the sort of strange half-truth that fit in with Bridlington. "But *shhhh*," he said. Bird nosed for him again and Asher pushed him away. Bird growled and wagged his tail, probably thinking they were playing. "Don't tell Caleb," Asher said. "He likes me."

She'd noted that, keenly. "Why are you telling me, then?"

He wagged a still-drunk finger at her. "I might be drunk," he said, and pinched his fingers almost-together, holding them up to her.

She raised an eyebrow. "Dick size?"

"No!" he almost shouted, and he frantically separated his fingers as far as they could go, which wasn't all that impressive either. Asher laughed a bit, bitterly. "Maybe. But that's how drunk I am. Just . . ." He pinched his fingers again. "That much."

"Clearly."

Caleb laughed from back on the deck. She noted the way Asher jerked his head to the sound like a dog on a leash, how his lips fell open just a bit.

Asher may have convinced Caleb that he was no threat to their good Bridlington sensibilities, but she wasn't sure how long he could keep it up. She found Caleb so easy to convince that sometimes she truly felt like an asshole for it, but Asher didn't have her practice. And really it shouldn't have mattered to her, she thought frantically. If the truncheon of civic duty came down to split Asher's skull, Marcela could just stand aside and let it all happen. Pretend she didn't care what happened to stick-outs like her sister, that it was just the business of running a nice little town. Nothing personal.

This didn't have to be her problem, and yet everything wrong in town always felt like her problem, because it was Caleb's.

"Where are you living now, well-endowed stowaway?" she asked him. She wanted it to sound a bit like a threat. "Because you should be getting back there."

His smile stayed slick and unwell. "Why?" he asked. "Wanna come with me?"

Marcela narrowed her eyes. "Where do you live, Asher?"

He tilted his head a bit. "Currently?" he said, and here was the kicker she should have known was coming. Here was the horrible, freakish conclusion from an overly honest drunk who was getting too comfortable. "In my car."

Bridlington had never had what Caleb would call a "home-less problem," and that was completely intentional. It wasn't to say there'd never been people who lost their homes, just to say they didn't stick around very long. "Does Caleb know?"

He seemed to realize he had misstepped, because she watched his eyebrows shoot up under his choppy bangs. He ducked his head sideways to check if Caleb might have heard.

"I'm sorry I'm bothering you," Asher managed to say. He ground his hand into his temple as if warding off a headache, but never let his sunglasses slide. "Don't tell him, all right?"

Not a chance in hell.

"He wouldn't like me if he knew," Asher kept saying, and she knew it was true. He was starting to work himself into a frenzy as Caleb lurched closer to them. Asher lowered his voice and looked like a snared animal. "I've got it made here. I just need a job and he can—he can't know, all right?"

Agreed. "I won't tell him," Marcela swore, and he stared up at her like some sad puppy-dog, like Paz used to.

And then Caleb came stumbling up to them between the cars. Stumbling was maybe giving him a little too much credit: every step was just stopping him from falling flat on his face.

"Asher," he said with a dopey grin. "Asher, come here. We're gonna mix Jägerbombs."

Marcela did *not* like the sound of that, though Asher put his smile back on.

"Cheers," he said, taking a suddenly steady step toward the fiery silhouette of Marcela's one and only Caleb Reilly, the truncheon of civic duty, destroyer of dogs. "I love . . . caffeine."

No way. He'd proved himself too honest for his own good. This was skating the line, and Marcela's blood was starting to expand in her veins, pulse louder and tighter in her temples.

"Caleb," she said, sliding down from the truck to gently touch Caleb's shoulder. "Leave the kid alone. He's wasted."

"I'm not," Asher said.

"It's fine," Caleb said, shoving her off. "He wants a drink." It was rougher than he'd intended, and she tripped. Her high heel plunged into the soft grass, and she would have fallen if she hadn't grasped the hand-grip on the back of the truck.

Caleb's eyes had that lupine attentiveness that made Marcela's blood flash-freeze.

She stared at them in dramatic tableau, at the way the

firelight gleamed across Caleb's sweat-slick side, and at the way Asher looked impossibly small against the side of the truck. The music shrieked like wailing spirits, there was scattershot laughter and the sound of Brady revving his engine in preparation for something. "He can handle a drink, Mar," Caleb said to her, and then he turned his stern face on Asher like a warning. The world seemed to silence to nothing but this: "He's not some sissy."

It was one of those playground slurs, one that had lost all meaning and thus should have lost its sting. But Marcela saw a vague flash of panic move across Asher's drunkenly red face, saw his lips fumble open, and she felt her stomach seize. *Caleb Reilly*, Marcela thought, *stop making it so damn hard to love you.*

"Caleb," she said. She was trying to yank her heel from the ground, but it felt like something had a hold of it. That made her blood beat even harder. "Leave him alone."

Asher's stunned lips snapped shut and his teeth grated. "I'm fine," he snapped, because clearly he had to get pissed at someone and it couldn't be Caleb, who had just stepped for him with huge hands that made huge fists.

"Attaboy," Caleb said with a friendly smile, a welcoming one. It was a dare, just a childish dare, no harm by it. "You ever been to Blue River, Asher?"

Her heel wouldn't budge, and if Caleb hurt this kid she might never love Caleb again, and what then? What would she have if not him? Asher was collapsed against the side of the truck, buckling under Caleb's leering. "N-no," he said, nearly a retch, but still smiling. Did he know how dangerous this was, or did he just not care? "But I'm game."

Marcela finally managed to yank her heel from the ground just as Caleb whooped and reached for the front of Asher's hoodie with a triumphant grin like a snarl.

A sudden monstrous sound, a flash of teeth and blood, and Caleb reeled back with scrapes down his hand. Bird had somersaulted forward out of the truck, landing paws-over-tail in front of Asher but scrambling up into a defensive crouch, head lowered and teeth bared, while Caleb pressed his back into the hatchback beside them, and the party still raged on because no one heard.

"Bird!" Asher shouted, but Marcela was already rushing over to them, keeping her weight solidly on her toes.

"Serves you right, Caleb Reilly," she said against the frantic pounding of her heart, but making her voice sympathetic and soft. Caleb just looked stunned, holding his barely bleeding hand where Bird's teeth had grazed it.

"What the hell?" Caleb muttered. He blinked and looked back to Asher, narrowing his eyes. "What the *hell* is up with your bitch? That thing needs a muzzle—"

"I'm taking them both to the motel," Marcela said, glaring at Asher, who was starting to sweat. He kept looking from Bird to Caleb, like he still wasn't sure what had just happened.

"Mar, that dog is—we don't even know this guy." He looked over to Asher and said again, more slowly, "We don't even know this guy."

"He's not driving out of here like he is," Marcela said. She was going to be practical, speak reason. Because if Asher ended up crashing his car because he tried to leave, or if a monster

142

dragged his guts across a field or drowned him in Blue River or hung him from a fence post, Marcela might never forgive Caleb, and that would be the worst thing. "Caleb, I'm taking him back. You sober up."

"Screw you," Caleb said, his nose crinkled up and his teeth flashing. She recoiled as if she'd been bitten. "I'm sober, Mar. Maybe you just need a drink—you're no fun."

He reached for her waist, his fingers snagged her shirt, but she ducked away.

"What—" Asher was trying to say, but she grabbed his too-warm wrist and yanked him after her into the tall grass between the Bright property and the motel. No more could go wrong that night. No more. Her head was pounding and her throat felt tight and sore like she might cry, but she wouldn't. She would make this all right.

"Just so we're clear," Marcela said as they waded into the dew-beaded grass. It came up to the high line of her denim shorts and to Asher's hip. Bird was nearly hidden apart from the top of his head. "This is not about saving your dumb ass, it's about mine."

"I was handling myself," he said. "*Bird* screwed it up." He tugged against her arm but was still a little too uncoordinated to pull free, and this was the grip that had raked her sister from the jaws of those King Shepherds. This was the grip that left bruises. "I can fix it. Just lemme go back!"

She hated hearing him grovel. It sheared against her like bone on bone.

"You're getting a room in the motel," Marcela said. "And you better hope Caleb is too drunk to remember details about

Bird biting him, or his dad'll give you a one-way escort out of town." At *best*, she knew.

That shut Asher up.

They got farther from the party. The firewood smoke was fading out, and with it came a bloody, rotten sort of smell. Marcela walked more stiffly, careful. Bird was weaving beside Asher, and he growled, but neither of them heard him with the grass swishing.

Marcela Espino didn't believe in monsters or things with teeth, but as she waded toward the motel, she had a brief thought that there might have been *something*. Something too endless about the sky, something too still about the air, something too eerie about the quiet night peppered with the sound of wind chimes calling her home from the tall grass where the crickets hummed. She could hear the swing-set creaking in the slow breeze, and she wanted to be relieved about getting closer to home. But everything felt wrong.

"Asher," she said, pulling him like she'd once pulled Paz. "This town is a shit show. It doesn't care about you, and no one's a good enough actor to *make* it care. So if you still want to go get yourself killed, have the decency to do it where no one can hear you, and don't do it when I'm anywhere close."

She hated Asher. And Paz. And herself.

"I'm not acting," he muttered. He sniffed, and that's when he must have smelled the blood on the breeze. Bird was growling louder; Marcela noticed then.

Marcela had just stepped from the tall grass when every-thing seemed to suddenly click into high-definition immediacy.

She heard heavy steps careening in their direction. Bird started leaping and barking so loudly the bloody smell shook out of the air, and Marcela swung her head sideways.

A dark figure was racing for them.

There would be deaths that night. Asher Gordon, maybe trying to salvage the last remnants of what he'd learned at Caleb's side, leapt in front of Marcela and reeled his fist back for a punch.

CALEB REILLY

Caleb Reilly was pissed at his girlfriend. Asher was just some scrawny kid he was toughening up. If his dumb dog were out of the picture, everything would be fine. Caleb hated dogs. And that night, he hated Marcela for getting in the way. He was too drunk to picture her face properly; he kept seeing one too similar to Paz's, with flashing white teeth.

He cracked another beer and drank it in one go. Emily had finally convinced Brady to take her home before he got too drunk for it. She'd be dead in the morning, and Caleb would be unable to recall most of that night's events.

Caleb remembered:

The bonfire was hot and huge, and he hadn't put his shirt back on yet. He felt like he was cooking in his skin, and that was okay.

The sky was very close, like looking at a sheet of paper with holes punched out. Caleb was contained, closed in. He was also *real*, like the whole town was cardboard except for him.

He remembered stumbling and grinning and knowing his

dad wouldn't catch him out there, because he didn't want to know about anything Caleb had ever done in his life besides good grades and hockey medals and civic awards, and so he wouldn't. And he remembered cracking another beer, shouting "Hell yeah!" and downing it. He remembered everyone cheering and great applause. Actually, it was only Reece, and it was half pity, but Caleb didn't realize in the moment.

He thought about his dad, as he often did when he was drunk. He felt the burbling mix of overwhelming pride and curdling unworthiness, and he grinned to himself. Because imperfect things could be made perfect. He could be perfect for his father, make the town perfect, too. And he would continue to be loved fiercely.

There was no mistaking that Captain Reilly loved his son; he'd never been shy about showing it. He taught Caleb to skate by taping butter knives to his teacup-sized baby shoes, because they didn't sell skates that small. It was the first thing Caleb remembered. It was the great shining sun over everything else that had ever happened.

Caleb had been the first outside party to hear about Chuck Warren, because he'd woken up when his father left the house and stayed awake until he came back. By the time Captain Reilly had sorted it all out, it was very nearly morning, and Caleb had been waiting up for him on the couch with the TV droning. Caleb, attentive and cold in the light of those other-worldly cartoons that only come on between midnight and sunrise, said, "What's up, Chief?" as he always did when his dad came home.

Captain Reilly laughed in a short way, shaking his head. "It's the Espino girl," he said, and Caleb knew he meant Paz. Because, since the Meyer incident, no one ever meant Marcela. Captain Reilly sealed the Reilly men's fate when he said: "She's like a dog: bites and doesn't let go. Should have seen us trying to pry her off her story."

Like a dog, Caleb thought at the bonfire. *Like a dog like the damn dog that bit me and not like a person how can you be a person if you're a dog?* And dogs that won't be trained get put down, yes?

The night Chuck Warren died, Captain Reilly had looked at his son, very solid. "Caleb?"

"Yeah, Dad?"

Caleb Reilly mouthed it again, swaying and sweating and staring at nothing.

"You don't believe in monsters, right?" Captain Reilly had asked. He had two fingers of whiskey, and he held the glass out to Caleb.

Caleb took it and laughed then, the bright, full laugh of a grown man. Caleb never had monsters under his bed. If he did, he would have told them his dad was the police captain, and would kill them.

"No way." The words were whiskey. "Anyone who thinks monsters are real is crazy."

Untrue, but Bridlington's monster was a slippery, awful creature, intangible and sick-smelling, impossible to stop. You couldn't kill the monster that roamed the town and mowed people down in its wake; you could only hold it at bay.

"Good man," his father said, and he poked a finger into Caleb's chest. His eyes were dim, but his smile was easy. "When you protect this town, it protects you, all right? You keep this place happy, and you'll have everything you want."

He was his father's son; he was loved, he would love right back. He was the thing that protected Marcela from herself, and the thing that protected the town from Paz, and would protect it again from this new Asher kid. Because he felt something strange in the air.

"Caleb," Reece suddenly said from behind. He put his hand on Caleb's shoulder, holding tightly and giving him a good little shake. "Slow it down, dude."

The party was still cardboard. Caleb would fix it. He would keep it all perfect and clean.

"I'm my dad," Caleb said. It fell off his lips like rain falls onto river water. He swayed, and Reece grabbed his arm to steady him. "Reece, I put down dogs, did you know that?"

"Shit, bud." Reece sighed. He waved to Adam Persad and Dylan Devereaux, and motioned to the case of water by the table. "You need to sober up—"

Caleb whirled around and his huge fist snapped up, locking into the front of Reece's Captain America shirt. Reece was yanked forward; he was tall and broad-shouldered but nowhere near as wide as Caleb.

"I put down dogs," Caleb snarled, like he was one.

Reece buckled forward, too close. His hands flew up to Caleb's, but there would be no prying him off. The smell of beer and whatever else clouded between them.

"They didn't run away. They died. I helped," Caleb said. His vision was wavy at the edges, smearing like paint.

"The Meyer dogs?" Reece asked, having heard about their disappearance from Quinn.

Caleb was too drunk to know how to spin up a proper response. He wanted Reece to ask further, not mind his business, let Caleb be the honest drunk and give all the details.

"I kill dogs, Reece," he could only say. "I'm my dad and we kill dogs."

It took two other guys to put their hands on Caleb's shoulders before he let his fist fall from Reece's shirt, leaving him standing stone-still in the middle of the patio while Caleb collapsed back into a folding chair.

Everyone at the party could feel the inevitable slipping over them like mist.

Because here's the secret: two things haunted Bridlington that night. The monster, and the creature. The monster was impossible to stop—Paz and her crew couldn't kill it as easily as they thought. But the creature would be a flesh-and-blood thing. It would be able to hurt, and die.

It hadn't even started its reign yet. But something was creeping around Quinn's house, staring down Caleb Reilly. Reece may not have known what Caleb meant when he said he was his father, and they killed dogs, but whatever was watching Caleb through the roses on the trellis knew damn well what that meant.

It wasn't entirely a surprise, but it was delicious confirmation.

BEETLE

Beetle ran toward the shadowy figure of Marcela because he cared about Paz, and maybe he cared about himself, too. Maybe he owed both those people some scraps before he got the hell out of Dodge, and that meant breaking the silent pact not to talk about Paz and her monster. Unfortunately, Marcela was not alone. Fortunately, whoever was with her was very bad at punching, and Beetle easily stepped aside to let whoever it was go stumbling past him. The broken glass in his backpack clinked and shifted.

"I need to talk to you," Beetle said to Marcela's shadow. There was only the thin light from the motel, which carved the edges of her face like a ghost. Beetle shivered and committed himself to adding the clincher. "About Paz. I need to talk to you about Paz and the monster and I don't care if you feel too guilty to talk about it."

Marcela curled her lip at him, stepping forward out of the high grass. "And what the hell do you know, Hoang?" she asked. He expected her to be angrier, or more dismissive. But she asked him in a low voice that suggested she knew more specifics than he thought.

Beetle swallowed. He looked around quickly (that person who'd tried to punch him was Asher, who had adopted a wide-legged slouch), scanning for any sign of Paz or anyone else in town. "Where's Caleb?" he asked.

"Marcela says we're not allowed to talk to him tonight," Asher said, half a snarl.

"I'm getting Asher a motel room," she said.

Beetle felt a drop of sweat down his back. "Why?"

She looked at him with the side-eye of someone else who knew something was wrong that night. Someone else who felt the ground moving strangely and smelled the blood in the mist seeping up from the still-warm soil. "I don't want him out tonight," she said. "Alone. So he needs a place."

Asher straightened his sunglasses. "Technically, I'm——" He "whipped," which is technically a dance move. Asher was an actor, not a dancer. "——hoooome-leeeess."

Beetle's face was flat and unamused, the sweat starting to dry. "I know, dumbass. Go sleep in your car."

Marcela spoke slowly. "It sounds like you and I both know why leaving him in his car might not be a good idea."

Beetle grumbled.

"Paz," Marcela said decisively, amid the humming of the bugs and the rush of a faint breeze through the trees and the distant thrum of the party.

One interloper was not going to ruin his decision to fix what he'd started. "Paz," Beetle relented.

"I feel sick," Asher added.

Marcela stalked back to the motel with Beetle behind her and Asher glumly bringing up the rear.

BIRD

Bird was doing his best to be a Good Boy, he really was. He would have followed his Boy or barked if he had seen the three of them clomping off without him. Would have told him to wait! Not to leave him alone!

Alone was a very bad thing to be in Bridlington, and Bird knew it.

But he'd been preoccupied. He was standing stiff-legged in the high grass and the low fog, barely able to see out to the road. He didn't need to see. Something was coming for him, the same thing that had been calling from just beyond the party, slowly getting closer. He felt it vibrating in his paws and could only just hear it when he twitched his ears and strained. Bird whined. The crickets chirped and the wind chimes rustled. The swing-set creaked a little louder, a little out of sync with the wind, but none of Bridlington noticed.

Bird's whine was very nearly audible, a quiet hiss. He reared up twice in the grass, prancing and weaving and spinning. His tail swished. Not because he was happy, but because he was terrified. He wanted his Boy and he wanted to get back in the car and go for a nice drive away from this bad town where he smelled every single death sitting sour where the spirit was sucked out of them, the ancient memory of things that happened beneath the paved streets. The monster had been there for hundreds of years, and Bird smelled it laid out like a crime scene. Even in the high grass where he dipped and spun, he smelled the rancid death.

He heard a high wail out there beyond the motel lawn. It sounded a little like the Boy. He thought of when the Boy had been smaller. When the Boy stole his older brother's clothes and wore them alone in his room in the dark with his long hair pulled under his beanie. When he turned slowly in the mirror and asked what Bird thought.

"*Come on, Bird,*" something said, a vibration and not a voice. It came up through the ground, bubbly. He felt it in his paws and fizzing in his brain. Moonlight shone through the grass onto Bird's dark, watery eyes.

He looked up at all of the stars. He panted twice, licked his nose, and then was still. He stepped from the high grass slowly. The motel lawn was silver in the moonlit mist.

"*Here, Bird. Come here. That's a Good Boy. It's time, Bird.*"

He hadn't been told to "Stay." His Boy had forgotten. Bird licked his nose again, but there was no panting smile.

Alone and un-missed was a dangerous thing to be.

Bird raced off like a caramel-sort-of-brown-with-a-little-white shot, feeling the bloody air chase him. He skidded into the road and sped past the Mac's with his paws pounding into the ground. He thought of watching his Boy cut his hair with silver Value Village scissors behind the first gas station they went to. He remembered his Boy smelling different with those sunglasses on. He thought of his Boy as he ran all the way across the bridge and down the off-road path where the bloody smell was joined by the green scent of pine and ferns. He got closer and closer to the rushing water.

"*That's a Good Boy*," something murmured in the muddy ground, while smells and leaves whipped past his festering-hot nose. "*Come here, Bird*." He could hear it now, not just feel it. Bird raced faster, his tongue lolling out of his mouth and the wind streaming through his bloody-feeling fur. He raced past where there were bikes buried in the undergrowth. He wriggled under the fence, tugging out some of his fur. He had an easier time getting through than the Meyers' Shepherds. He smelled them still, the scent years old by then, and frightened.

Bird slipped down the slope, tumbling with a sharp yelp before he landed back on his paws, and ran down the bank, splashing through the shallow edge of the river where countless people had drifted away from Bridlington, their scents soaked into the rocks. They were called drownings, accidents. No one could have stopped them, it was said.

Bird went under the bridge to the boarded-up mill and pranced outside of it to split the mist into wisps and puffs, whining high in his throat. His coat was strewn with mud and leaves. The blood in the air was caking into his fur and vibrating wrong. He heard things laughing. Felt hands at his paws. Felt something dripping onto him. He felt how Chuck Warren did when he died, except there really *were* laughing things, and there really *were* hands dragging over his fur with split nails. It was not Paz's monster, but what had come of it.

Bridlington was out of time.

BRIDLINGTON

Marcela and Beetle could talk all they wanted about Paz, but it was far too late.

A month after Chuck's death, which could have changed the town and didn't, nightfall fell flat and cold over sleepy Bridlington, and over three bikes bumping off the bridge and into the forest. Paz pumped the front brake, fishtailed with precision to point a hard left, and went tearing down toward the gorge. Sammy stood on the pegs behind her, with her hands gripping Paz's shoulders. If Emily Novak had seen that, she'd have had words, but none of them cared. Ben and Ellie zipped along behind, Ben tonguing experimentally at the newly empty spaces in his still raw gums. It wasn't going to matter much longer. They were going to be heroes.

They were going to the mill, to get into the monster's domain the only way they were sure to, and they would kill it, for Chuck and for themselves. Paz had given Marcela one more chance to make it right, told her this was monster night and she could still at least pretend she liked her sister. But in the end,

Marcela would rather hang out with *Caaaay-lebbb* than fight the monster his father ignored. It was no secret Caleb picked on Paz and her friends whenever he got the chance, let Emily get away with her name-calling, and never backed them up to his dad. If Marcela knew, and didn't help, did that make her just as bad?

Paz knew Emily Novak and Caleb Reilly, and even Brady Novak and Reece Kalchik, and every person who blamed her for their problems deserved more than detention or their parents telling them to stop being rude. She wasn't sure where that left everyone else. Would that all be solved when they killed the monster? Would that make her important enough to be listened to when she rolled out her list of people who had wronged her? Did taking out the crumbling teeth cure the infected jaw?

A thing that couldn't feed would starve, Paz knew. But because she knew no way of stopping monstrous people from being monstrous, she'd just have to prove them wrong.

They hit the bottom of the hiking trail. Ellie and Ben threw their bikes into the undergrowth, crushing the slushy cup that tumbled from Ellie's cupholder. Paz propped her bike against the fence. Sammy had already gone kicking around in the bushes to find the weapons they had been preparing: sticks sharpened with a knife Ellie stole from the kitchen, and which Ben was caught returning very dull. He'd tripped into the counter just after that, lost his front teeth, and was scheduled to see the dentist tomorrow after the hunt was done. He pushed the foliage aside to find an old BB gun he'd taken from the farm shed earlier, and Sammy's Nerf gun.

Paz slung her sharpened stick through one belt loop, Ben put the sling of the BB gun over his shoulder, Ellie took the Nerf gun, and Sammy grabbed the other stick. They all ducked through the fence and loped down to the side of the gorge where Blue River ran fast and foreboding. They raced just as inevitable along the side of the river, under the bridge.

They slowed as they approached the old mill, and the moon and all the stars watched. Ben and Ellie were silver and bronze in the moonlight. Ben's upper lip was a little puffy still, and a bruise just below Ellie's collar could be seen when her pink shirt shifted. Sammy looked pale.

The police tape wrapped around the mill fluttered languidly like the streamers on Paz's bike. It all looked awfully cold and quiet, unassuming, but Paz knew better. She offered her back, Ellie unzipped her backpack for her, and they all divvied up the flashlights.

Captain Reilly had put boards over the mill windows, and Paz would have been grateful for a big kid to help pry at them. The good news was that with her crew all cramming their fingers between the boards and tugging, they cracked one off, and silently crawled through the meager gap.

Paz came in last of all, into the sealed-off dark, with only one thin rectangle of moonlight following her. She felt awfully closed in, buried, and everything smelled like chalk and wet mud. Their flashlights peeled through the gloom, uncovering nothing but spray paint and broken bottles while they pressed tight against the wall.

Paz hadn't been sure if the monster would be in its lair or

out hunting. But the mill echoed with the sound of something breathing down in the pit. Blood drifted in the air, both a smell and a taste. Sammy gave a hissing moan. Ben gulped, and now it was Ellie who was shaking the sweat from her hand. Paz's skin crushed in on her, two sizes too small.

This was it. It was time to be as brave as everyone expected.

She stepped forward first, through the glass and grit, careful to be silent until she was close enough to stare into the great chasm. When she shone her flashlight down, she was relieved and terrified to find that no eye gleamed back at her this time. With the extra flashlights, the light touched the bottom.

There was blood on the cement floor—Chuck's blood, she realized—and a bunch of broken wood. But no monster in sight . . . yet.

"It's far," Sammy whispered, looking down. "Are we gonna jump?"

It was only a story or so. They could probably survive a fall like that, but Paz didn't want to account for possibly broken legs. "No," she said. She pulled a huge coil of rope from her backpack, one she had taken from the maintenance shed at the motel. Ellie had been in Girl Guides before she came to live in Bridlington, and her slung arm was almost back to full strength, so she got the rope fastened around one of the iron stairs.

Paz looked at her crew. "It's sleeping right now," she said, assumed. Only something sleeping could breathe so evenly—it was just a matter of finding where under Bridlington that sound was echoing up from. A thin film of sweat formed on her skin and she was crinkling her nose against the rancid smell, but Paz

Espino was not afraid that night. Not anymore. She had a sturdy stick and she had gotten that sucker damn sharp. "We might be able to kill it before it wakes up."

They all nodded, determined and ghostly yellow in the flashlight glow.

One by one, they grabbed the nylon rope and climbed down. Paz went first, sliding most of the way like it was the fireman's pole at the motel playground. The breathing got louder and louder, and the air thicker and thicker. She landed in a crunch of wood. Alone.

Paz turned away from the rope and whipped her flashlight beam around, hoping perhaps to see the monster and goad it into the reach of her stick. Instead, she saw only the cement basement of the mill, huge and dusty, the floor littered with old machinery that smelled of soaked iron, and rats shuffling in the dark corners. The thing's breathing came from somewhere distant, and Paz stood solemn and ready.

She heard Ben touch down behind her, and his light beamed around while he shook out his hands. "Checkpoint One," he joked. He caught Ellie, while Paz let the idea of a checkpoint flow through her head. What gear did they have on them? Did they stock up before the cave?

A backpack of snacks, and sidewalk chalk.

One slushy cup.

Three bikes with cards in the spokes.

Her, and her friends, and Chuck Warren in spirit.

Paz, in all her stubborn glory, noted it down. She had her finger on Start, and let the battle music play.

But when she turned around, she saw only two weedy-limbed twin shadows staring back at her, silver and bronze. Only Ben and Ellie had joined her.

"Sammy?" Paz asked them, to two shrugs. They all turned to point their flashlights up. They saw the rope and its fuzzy sheen of nylon and nodes of dust whirling about it, but with only three flashlights, they couldn't see all the way to the top of the pit. It was like they were staring up at a blank, black sky.

Paz opened her mouth, croaked out half a sound, and then heard things moving behind her in the gloom. Too small to be a monster, she assured herself, despite her skin tightening worse and worse, but it was a nice warning that they weren't alone down there, and couldn't hazard shouting for their final friend.

Come on, Sammy, Paz thought, tapping her feet to keep from standing too still, to keep from freezing again.

"Do you think the monster . . ." Ellie started to say, but none of them wanted to consider that the monster was so clever as to pick them off one by one from behind.

It was.

///\\\//\\\//\\\//\\\//\\\//\\\//\\\

Sammy was in fact still standing up there, fighting the trembling feeling in her bones that could shatter her away entirely. She had watched Paz disappear, and then Ben with his BB gun, and Ellie with the bright blue Nerf gun on her back. Sammy hadn't told her that the gun was missing quite a few foam bullets, and that you had to pump it exactly thirty-seven times or it would overfill and jam or it would underfill and just make a sad hissing sound.

That reality hit her all of a sudden, that the gun could jam. The reality that a foam bullet would be useless hadn't set in yet, but she realized in that moment they were fallible. Kids in movies never died—they came close sometimes, but they didn't *die*. This was real life. They could be crushed, like bugs.

She stared into the mill pit and started to breathe quicker. Her feet were numbing. The glow of her friends' flashlights was dim and far away. Even when she scrambled down onto her knees to look over the edge, she couldn't see them. She could hear nothing but her heartbeat.

There were four options in Bridlington:

You run, you freeze solid, you grovel, or you fight until your nails bleed.

Sammy heard the walls of Bridlington whispering, crawling toward her, and her eyes widened slowly as the pieces came together. It was far too much and too complicated for a child just shy of twelve to articulate, so Sammy didn't understand it in words so much as she felt it in a great rush of *fear*. She'd loved Paz too much to question her, but suddenly she knew they'd all been wrong.

"Oh no," Sammy wheezed. "Oh no, oh no, oh no."

She understood.

Chuck Warren died in a horrible accident, and Sammy knew it.

The simple fact was that Chuck Warren had been a lot bigger than Paz, and falling onto the wooden cap of the old drop chute had sent him straight through it. That cap now lay in splinters at Paz, Ellie, and Ben's feet.

The complicated fact was that, in a way, Chuck had still been killed by the monster.

The monster didn't eat Chuck, but it still lived and breathed in Bridlington. It swam on the lips of kids who spat names on the playground and the stern fingers of teachers when they said only "That's not very nice" or just looked away. The monster attacked Ben and Ellie with missing teeth and wrenched arms and parents who were *so lovely, so don't make up lies about them*. The monster was Caleb closing ranks with Emily and letting her get away with it, pretending it didn't matter when it *did*. It *hurt*. It dug its teeth into Chuck Warren, ignored by the neighborhood, and the latchkey kid who no one looked out for when they rode away at nightfall. It was the glassy eyes of the town that carried on like nothing was wrong, because it wasn't their neat suburban business.

The monster infected people like a sickness. Bridlington was not unique in its troubles. Sammy knew the monster had a million forms and a million names (apathy, ignorance, status quo) but she knew it was real, and she swore it was in her while she sat like a coward at the top of the mill, too scared to do anything. Too scared to go down into the grave and help them, too scared to tell them all that they were wrong, too scared to run and get help from someone she trusted. But who did she trust? Captain Reilly? The Espinos? Her own mother might not have time.

Sammy felt overwhelmingly defeated, like being buried alive and knowing there was already too much dirt on top to bother fighting the rest of it.

Who could have ever expected a different end, and who could have held out a hand to pull her from the path of it before she was struck down dead?

Sammy closed her eyes. Numbness crept tentatively from her bones, feeling its way through her body, sinking ice into every atom. It froze her entirely until she thought she might not be real anymore.

She wasn't, not really. Sammy (like Asher) was just a mask to keep up Bridlington appearances.

Her friends turned into the dark, and were swallowed by it.

MARCELA

Asher collapsed onto the cottage-quilted blanket of Paz's bed and promptly passed out cold. That was better, really, Marcela thought as she flicked on the lamp and chucked the wastebasket next to him in case he thought about puking all over the nice clean carpet. With Asher passed out, she and Beetle wouldn't have to mind their words. It was better for everyone if he didn't know about the full scope of Chuck Warren and the monster.

"Paz," Beetle said, narrowing his eyes. Marcela tensed at the name. Caleb could *never* hear about this talk. "Marcela, there is no way she didn't tell you that she's planning something tonight. She came to talk to me, and I'll bet she talked to you, too."

She moved to lean against her parents' door, to hear if they were awake. "I thought you went to Harville to stop talking nonsense," she said coolly, probing carefully.

He tightened his fists. "With a lot of respect to everyone there," he said, blinking hard, "they have no idea what's in this town. I know Paz is still going after her monster. It's no delusion—"

"All right, all right," Marcela said. She was sweating now and dabbed her hands against her forehead. This was all insane. "You know what, maybe this whole monster hunt is a good thing."

"How?" he squeaked. She thought he might burst into tears. He looked like he was carrying a thousand pounds on his shoulders. He kept tugging at something under his shirt. "Marcela, how the *hell* is this a good thing?" His voice had speared up slightly. She pointed a finger at him to lower his voice. One of her parents tossed in their sleep and went quiet again.

She'd been waiting so long to talk about Paz, but no one would let her. Caleb would dismiss it, her parents were tired of it, she didn't want to ruin Quinn with it. And now, finally, here was Beetle. Maybe he was a scowling little freak who needed to get out of town before he could cause trouble for her, but that meant he could take all her secrets to Harville with him, far, far away from anything she cared about.

"There's no monster that killed Chuck Warren," she said. "Caleb's been in there with his dad and there's nothing in that mill—"

"I *know.*"

"So then why are you all worked up?" she asked him. "It's not like anyone can get hurt if there's no actual monster."

"Doesn't it bother you that she's still after one in the first place?" Beetle said. "We let her go to that mill before—"

"She. Snuck. Out," Marcela said, stepping closer to him. She was tired of this argument—what good did it do anyone now? "Maybe this way she gets the proof she needs to just shut up and move on. Isn't that what you want for all of us?"

Marcela wanted to believe that was best for Paz. She really did.

Beetle looked away, deflated. She didn't think he agreed with leaving Paz alone, but he couldn't fight it.

"Yeah," Marcela breathed. She wanted to keep her Reilly girl face on, and did. "That's what I thought."

BRADY NOVAK

The night of the party, Emily Novak was the first victim of the creature. Not the monster. Emily had been part of the intangible monster so long that she simply considered it to be part of her ever-sunny personality. Brady would agree that the monster gave his sister a dark sense of humor that often included slurs, but that wasn't a crime or anything, they'd both say. "She's just trying to get a rise out of you," teachers said. "Sticks and stones."

The siblings had left the party when Caleb started to get messy-drunk, and by midnight they were on their front porch, sitting on either side in big wicker chairs while warm light shone through their glass front door. They lived on the south side of Bridlington, on the last farm property. Past their huge front lawn, they could see the backyards of a meandering cul-de-sac, with the church steeple sticking up from the distant mist like a lighthouse. Everything was still and quaint, the air a monotonous cricket hum.

Emily and Brady were both pretending to be on their phones,

attempting to forget the night's events. They knew nothing about accosting that Hoang freak, they knew nothing about Caleb's propensity for drunkenness, and they knew *not a single thing* about Paz Espino. They stuck to their Facebook feeds and mindless Vine scrolling.

It all happened so fast that Brady was never quite sure what he saw. One moment he was sitting, staring at the scroll, thinking vaguely about work and the way it smelled, and the next there was a snarl: an angry, awful sound from far too close.

He looked up and saw the pale panic on his sister's face when something reared up onto the porch and sunk its white teeth into her arm. Brady heard bones snap. They both shrieked, and the air rang with the metallic-sweet stench of split muscle and pulsing blood. The creature was a shaggy mess of soaked fur and stick-out bones, and its eyes were cherry-slushy red.

The creature dragged Emily Novak off her porch and then under it while she clawed at the grass. She screamed for her brother, but his name ended abruptly with a wet *snap* that echoed out through their property.

Brady listened in blank horror, still stuck in his wicker chair with his phone clutched tight to his chest. He heard the wet tearing of the creature under the porch making a mess of its first meal. The air seemed flash-frozen around him, gluing him in his seat. He waited to die next. The house far across from their property had children's play equipment in the chain-linked backyard, and lights on in one of the rooms. They must have heard the scream and struggle. He begged them to call the police, call animal control, call *someone*.

He saw a shadow sprint out from under the porch and head for the road.

As horrified tears rolled slowly down his cheeks, he heard a new sound: a strange flutter and rattle that he couldn't quite place.

He sat for several minutes, staring at the light on in the other house, waiting for either his sister to reappear or the police to speed up the lane and pull into the driveway beside him.

They didn't, because though that house had heard the screaming, they knew nothing bad ever happened in Bridlington. They carried on with their board game while Brady sobbed silently.

BRIDLINGTON

This part of the story is not for the sort of people who cry when the dog dies, but it must be told.

Sammy waited for Ben and Paz and Ellie in the dark mill. And she waited. And she waited some more. She waited until every cricket stopped. And she waited as the light trickling into the cement coffin turned to gray-pink dawn. And she waited as the pink turned to yellow-white daylight and brought suffocating heat, and then damp-orange sunset, and then gray-blue, storm-clouded dusk. She was cold and tired and hungry and thirsty and scared. In her mind, she begged someone to come find her.

//\\//\\//\\//\\//\\//\\//\\//\\

That morning, when Ellie and Ben's foster parents found their beds empty, they didn't call around to ask if anyone had seen them. They didn't bother to look themselves. They figured "those two" had run off. Foster kids, you know. Troubled.

The monster was behind their eyes, in their useless hands, swarming in their heads.

The monster was in the town, too, drifting through the air. Ellie and Ben were ghostly children who haunted the curio shop daily to watch the big fish tank, and the owner there had noticed their absence. He thought to call the Meyers and ask about them. But then he thought about Ellie's sprained arm and decided it was none of his business.

At that very moment, Ellie and Ben and Paz were deep under the town, having slipped through a pulper-tank drainage tunnel in the mill basement. They weren't reckless kids; they marked every turn with sidewalk chalk. They ate packed snacks while they silently climbed through tunnels and looked for the flesh-and-blood monster, following the sound of breathing. Sometimes they got close, right under it they thought, and they'd freeze to listen. They were always beneath it, so they looked for a way up. They were only eleven.

They were only eleven.

Ben's mouth ached awfully and he was getting tired. Ellie was too, though she wouldn't admit it. Paz was relentless and unshakable, she'd say.

She turned to them both in the dark and held out the hand that didn't have her flashlight.

"Give me the gun," she said. Water dripped down on them, like something slobbering. Tree branches drifted past their ankles from the storm drains like grasping hands. The wet metal pipes smelled like blood. The breathing sound echoed around them. "Head back."

"No," Ben said, holding the strap tight.

"We're gonna kill the monster, Paz," Ellie said. "We said we would and . . ." She looked over her shoulder, her hair limp with sewer water. She was wondering if she even wanted to go back to the Meyer house but couldn't admit it out loud. She was lucky to be out of the group home and have foster parents, people said, and she wouldn't go anywhere without Ben.

Paz's face fell for half a second, invisible in the low light of the flashlights. Paz Espino wasn't scared. But she was *unsure*, which felt worse. They were almost one day in by the count of her Agumon watch, which meant it would probably take Ellie and Ben a while to get back even if they followed the chalk markings.

"I'll kill it," Paz said to both of them. "And when I do, we're going to Captain Reilly first. And we'll tell him about . . ." She looked at Ellie's arm, but didn't want to say it.

"Okay, Paz," Ellie said.

Ben sniffed and shook out his hands, nodding along. He handed over the gun.

Paz watched him and Ellie walk hand in hand back down the tunnel. They were suddenly swallowed up by shadows, as if they'd stepped into a separate reality, leaving Paz the sole survivor of some great cataclysm.

She took a slow breath of the soaked, rotten air and turned around to continue her hunt. The breathing was coming from behind and above, so she trekked forward to find another way to double back. She swore they'd been this way already, but they must have missed a ladder.

Ellie and Ben followed the markings. But the walls were wet, and the chalk was melting away. Far above in the living world, clouds were closing in.

Around that time, the Espinos went to Captain Reilly with Marcela in guilty, silent tow and told him Paz had been missing all day.

"She's probably just off with her friends," he said. He messed with some papers on his desk while Mrs. Espino sat in the chair across from him and tried not to cry. Her husband was stoic. Marcela was in the hallway, staring at her hands. She was thinking about the monster under the mill. She knew Paz wouldn't give it up.

"She always comes home," Mr. Espino said, flat and already exhausted. "Or she leaves a note, or calls me from her friend's house. Paz is responsible."

"I'll do a little sweep," Captain Reilly said, but he seemed unbothered. "It's more than likely she's at the Hoang house. Have you called there yet?"

They had, but the line rang out. "You're not hearing me," Mr. Espino said with a shaking voice. "She would have called us if she went over there."

The captain shook his head. "I understand the worry—"

"This needs more than a 'little sweep,'" Mrs. Espino snapped. Her eyes widened when she realized she really had just raised her voice to the good captain. She tried to smooth it, but there was no use. "She could have been taken—"

"By who?" Captain Reilly said, smiling slightly as if to a kid throwing a fuss. "I've been at the bridge all day. I would have stopped anyone suspicious." He took a breath to calm the room. The monster slipped from his lungs and billowed up like smoke: "I think it's probably all a small misunderstanding." He laughed. "You know how kids are, especially Paz."

176

The insinuation that he knew Paz at all felt like a red-hot knife twisting right through the hinge of Mrs. Espino's jaw. Her eyes flashed, and before she could think better of speaking out of line, she said, "So if it was your son?"

Captain Reilly started, and then furrowed his heavy brow. "I think it's impossible to compare—"

It was Mr. Espino who got to his feet with his chair squealing on the tiles. He pointed a very stern finger, which Captain Reilly had never been on the receiving end of. The monster was waging a war on the Espinos that day, and they were fighting back.

"My daughter is *not* a criminal, and we are *not* bad parents," he said. "She's an eleven-year-old girl who is dealing with quite a bit of extra hassle from this town. The number of times my daughter has been harassed would horrify you, *Reilly*, but there's nothing done about it because the whole town has decided it's easier to say she's a delinquent when she's usually just saying what needs saying. Paz, Sammy Hoang, and Ellie Johnson and Ben Levi deal with more than your son ever has or ever will for a number of reasons. And this town ignores it every time."

His voice cracked. His lips quivered like he couldn't believe what he had just said, but he doubled down. "Find my daughter or . . ." Mr. Espino felt the grave soil settling, like Sammy. There was no "or."

"Thomas," Captain Reilly said, his eyes sharp and lupine. "Let's trust the system."

At that time, Marcela Espino slid out of her chair in the hallway. She checked her Bratz watch and it was almost 8:00 p.m. She knew where Paz was. Not just the mill—she knew she was under the town, under her very feet. Call it what you will; some people would say twin telepathy. Marcela was older by six minutes, but since that incident with the Meyers a year ago, she had treated it like six years.

No more.

Eleven-year-old Marcela ran out of the station and straight to Caleb Reilly's house with her pink dress fluttering behind her. The clouds were matted and thick overhead. She ran so hard and so fast that she fell once and scraped both knees awfully. She was getting blisters in her ballet flats. Marcela Espino, who dreamed of being anything but like Paz, raced over her twin sister's head. Both knew it.

She pounded on the Reillys' door and was gently let in by Mrs. Reilly. Marcela ran to find Caleb playing video games and drinking organic juice that the general store custom-ordered for special little boys such as he.

"Marcela?" he asked, pausing *Call of Duty* and looking at her bloody knees and wild eyes. He thought she looked like Paz, and dread bored into his bones. "What happened?"

Around that time, Sammy Hoang got up from where she sat in the mill. She trudged along Blue River while the rain started to *plick*, and then up the muddy side of the gorge. She picked up Paz's bike and pedaled very slowly home, so slowly that the bike almost tipped, spilling her into the road. The card in the spokes made a slow *plomf, plomf, plomf* sound. The crickets were silent in the rain, but Sammy could still hear them laughing at her. Calling her a freak, and a word that rhymed with "bike," and a word that meant "you wear boy clothes a lot, but who the hell are you trying to fool?" She was a scaredy-cat, a huge one.

Ms. Hoang was driving around town in a state of near-panic, but was managing to keep it level. She had worked late the previous night and hadn't checked on Sammy when she came home, hadn't even noticed she was gone until midday and then had simply assumed she had slipped out to play with Paz. It wasn't a large town, and she figured someone would call if Sammy was in trouble. Wouldn't she do the same?

Then she had remembered Chuck at the beginning of the summer, bloody-red under the stoplight. And because of that, the fear of being an awful mother, she didn't tell a single soul about her missing child and instead got in her car to search.

She found Sammy just past the motel as the first rumble of thunder rolled over Bridlington. Sammy said nothing about what had happened, but indicated that she was with the others, and then they had gone off on their own and she didn't know where they were now. It was mostly true. But when asked where they *had* been, she didn't say. She couldn't. She was sure she'd get in trouble like Paz did after she told the captain about Ben's cigarette burns. Or get in trouble like Paz did after Chuck died. Or get in trouble like Paz did just by standing around, being so easy to blame for everything from missing chips in the Mac's to broken windows in the coffee shop. She knew Caleb was right that day in the grave: no one would believe her.

Ms. Hoang called the Espinos when Sammy was home but could give them no real answers. Sammy slept for a long, long time.

Around the time Sammy arrived home, Marcela and Caleb were racing for the mill, and the rain was turning vicious. They went over the bridge and ran down toward the gorge, the drainage pipes chuffing angrily with the city runoff. Caleb Reilly was the spitting image of his father, with sandy-brown hair and cool blue eyes. Yes, he was at that point much shorter, with ears he had yet to grow into, but he was his father's right-hand citizen.

It was a good town, and Marcela was a nice girl, but when they went scrambling down the side of the gorge, he saw mud muck up her legs right to the hem of her dress and over her bloody knees. She kicked off her ballet flats to stop the blisters. In a flash of lightning, he saw the whites of her maddened eyes, saw her hair tangled and soaked behind her. When she panted from running, Caleb saw her teeth. He often forgot they were twins, but suddenly it was Bridlington's most notorious liar running beside him.

Espino girls bite and never let go, Caleb thought as they hit the bottom of the gorge, and the sky opened to drop buckets and buckets and sheets and sheets of water. Espino girls are dogs—Caleb had heard it said. Blue River roared like a waterfall, or like something breathing, loud and awful. The two children barely had enough room to run along the side without being swept into the current. They went under the bridge, where Marcela was lucky not to cut her feet, and slid to a stop in front of the old mill.

Marcela was crying angry, frustrated tears. The thing about twins was they could be so similar and yet still different. There were things Marcela Espino wanted (to wear jeans, and play softball, and cut her hair, and be friends with Quinn forever) but she didn't want to go through a mostly boarded window into the dark. She didn't want to look down into a pit and know her sister was in there, know she hadn't been fast enough. She was only eleven.

"I can't go in there," she sobbed. The rain shattered against the surface of the river, the thunder rumbled, and the air cracked with lightning, closer. In the flash, she was pale and gaunt. She fell onto the rocky ground, in the mud and rushing water, and covered her eyes. Marcela sobbed along the side of Blue River and wished Paz weren't so *Paz*. She wished Paz had just learned to like being someone else. Got in the current and learned to swim, not—

"Drown," she whispered to herself, and knew the end before it was written.

Caleb stood stone-still beside her with water dripping from him. He stared down with stunned fascination, like an infant discovering its hands. Marcela was sobbing, and broken, and tired. She was no snarling dog. She needed his help. She was eleven and he'd been twelve for three months and was a grown-up already, and he could fix this like his father fixed the town.

"I'll go look for her," he said. He swallowed and put his cold hand on Marcela's shoulder. She would think about that for a long, long time. She would think about that when they were older and that hand was on her waist at prom, or every time it held her own in the café. She had been a snot-nosed little coward, but he loved her anyway, and would protect her if the town wanted to gossip about her family.

Caleb Reilly went into the mill, shutting himself off from the pounding rain. The silence was a delicate thing, like dust or spiderwebs. It stuck to the water on his Junior League jersey. He had grabbed his father's big police flashlight, so he unclipped it from the belt loop of his jeans and shone it around from over his shoulder. His brain was a radio reel, like a recording of his father's voice on repeat: *Stop right there! Police! Put your hands up!*

He cast the light around, fearless, and saw the rope tied to the stairs. The fact remains that Ellie and Ben would never make it back to that rope to begin with, nor Paz. Really, all it did was serve to mark the path. It could have been some closure, though. Perhaps they would have been mourned, and perhaps a lesson could have been learned.

Police, Caleb thought, with his eyes wide. Marcela was outside, and she was counting on him to fix all of this. A crack of lightning. The rattling of the rain like playing cards in spokes. *Captain Reilly, reporting for duty, sir yes sir.* It played like a sick loop in his head. *Captain Reilly, Captain Caleb Reilly.*

"Paz is a dog," Caleb whispered. It would echo in that cavern, bounce around for years. Paz Espino felt something cold wash over her while she still lived, though she wouldn't know the truth of that night until Caleb vomited up the words at Asher's flagship party. "She bites and never lets go."

"You're not like them, Caleb," his father had told him after Chuck Warren died, putting his heavy hand on the back of Caleb's neck. He was a few sips into his whiskey. "You're my good boy, yeah? Making your dad proud?"

He would spend the next six years proving it again and again and again.

Caleb pulled the rope up and hid it under the stairs, as if Paz and her crew were never there.

A week later, on a sunny afternoon, Caleb explained what had happened, and Captain Reilly shouted at him for what felt like hours, reminded him of it for what felt like years, but still knew his son hadn't killed those children, and it was too late to condemn another person to the legacy of Paz Espino. So they boarded up the mill together, sealing the secret of the rope into dusty gloom. That was the monster: it was Caleb's decision in that mill, but more than that, it was a grown man who believed his family took precedence. The whole incident was marked a runaway case, treated with pity and false hope, and stayed that way.

Caleb pulled himself back out the window and found Marcela still collapsed on the rocks, heaving out sobs. He walked over to her, crouched down, and put his cold hands on the sides of her face.

"She wasn't in there," he said, earnest and blank-faced, chilled by the rain. "Let's leave it to my dad—I'm sure he'll find her."

Marcela said nothing, because she already knew Paz was done for. She felt it. She flung herself forward and clung onto Caleb, Blue River screaming at them both. She gripped the back of his shirt and cried and cried.

"I c-c-could have s-s-saved her," she sobbed.

"It's over now," Caleb said, which wasn't true either. He rubbed her back. "I won't tell anyone what you did."

She thought he meant that she didn't go in to look for her sister, that she'd always been a coward.

But he was looking down at her muddy feet, was holding her soaked in his arms. He meant he wouldn't tell that she had looked so fierce, and wild, and person-like. Caleb Reilly liked Marcela when she wasn't person-like, because he wanted everything to be okay, and his dad taught him that people aren't perfect.

People are dogs.

THE GOOD CAPTAIN

It was three in the morning the night Emily Novak, twenty, died. Captain Reilly was walking to the motel from the Bright house, down the nearly pitch-black road by the scarce light of the moon that was slowly clouding over. His feet struck the ground, sharp and brisk and purposeful. As always, he knew of no reason to fear walking Bridlington alone at night, especially with a service pistol at his hip.

The last three hours had been a bit of a flurry, but not a panic. Captain Reilly would never let it become so wild as that, even despite seeing his niece massacred by what was surely a wild animal. He shoved it into the back of his skull, compacted like dynamite. There were higher callings, he had reminded himself: he had to protect the rest of Bridlington.

The night patrol questioned his nephew in vivid detail while Captain Reilly called the coroner down from Harville, called in the day shift so they could have all hands on deck, and promised his sobbing sister he'd do everything he could to find out just what happened. Before the night patrol took Brady to the station, Captain Reilly heard that there had been a party at Quinn's, and his son was there with some new kid.

Captain Reilly clued in immediately. "Was this the boy from the Mac's?" he asked his nephew, a firm hand on the back of Brady's boiling neck, half wrenching him. "With the sunglasses, Brady. Think hard."

Brady gulped like a fish and wiped his eyes and nodded profusely. "Y-yes. Asher. Caleb said he was . . . said he was a good guy."

Brady hadn't seen Bird in the truck, or in the Mac's that first day, but the good captain made sure he had every town liability catalogued. He should have known the kid was trouble. He should have smelled it off him. He'd make it right.

Captain Reilly swung into his cruiser and he called Caleb as he drove. Reece Kalchik picked up, and Captain Reilly asked if Asher Gordon had stayed at the party.

"I don't know," he said. The captain could hear him stumbling a bit. "I wasn't around the fire."

"Kalchik," Captain Reilly said, slow. If his windows had been rolled down, he might have heard something following him. Several somethings. And the click of claws. "If I find out you knew anything, then that's interfering with police business."

Reece paused. He was aware of Asher stealing Clif Bars, charging his phone, and using the showers a little too often at the gym for someone who had been staying at the motel. Nothing too egregious. But if Reece got caught protecting some random kid, then dating Quinn in junior year might not be enough to cover his ass. He had his own part to play.

"He was here," he confessed. "He told Caleb he was staying at the motel, but I think he lives in his car, and I know he talks with Beetle Hoang."

Ms. Hoang was a kind, quiet lady who owned the diner. She'd been mixed up in the Espino-Meyer runaway case a few years back, and the Hoang kid took a trip to the nuthouse shortly after. But he and Caleb had been certain that the Hoang kid would leave in the fall and cause no more grief. Evidently not, if the kid was fine with talking to dangerous vagrants.

"So Gordon was there," Captain Reilly said, and bristled slightly when he asked, "Did you see the dog?"

"I didn't," Reece said, then paused and admitted, "but I heard it bit Caleb. Not badly or—"

The captain wasn't listening now. The mutt had gotten at his son. It made him *livid*, but he kept it down. Not his son. Not his goddamn son. "Thank you, Reece," Captain Reilly said, past the enraged static kept behind the dam of his gritting teeth. "Is Gordon still there?"

"Marcela was going to get him set up at the motel for the night."

And now Marcela was involved too. "I'll take a formal statement when I get there, and drive you home," the captain said as he turned onto Quinn's lonely farm-lane street, the quietest stretch in Bridlington. He heard a dog bark distantly and saw something sprint across his rearview mirror in the gold-and-blue shadows, but it was gone too quickly to tell what it was.

By the time the captain pulled into Quinn's long driveway (dark aside from a single, searing safety light over the garage doors), the field was empty and the party was clearly over. The light felt unbearably hot, like it could blister his skin, burn up his eyes. He breathed out and stepped from the cruiser into the thick night air that parted around him like marsh water. He swung the door shut.

Thunk.

(*Thunk thunk thunk*)

The safety light buzzed so loudly it seemed to be growling.

Quinn had to be threatened with detainment, but she finally spilled that Gordon's "really sweet and friendly" dog had in fact bitten Caleb, and the boy *and* dog had left with none other than Marcela Espino. It was a grim confirmation of what he'd always suspected: she was so much like her sister.

The captain found his only son on the back deck, where his head was dropped into his arms at the picnic table. Captain Reilly looked at him then, hunched so he might have seemed small, and felt the clashing titans of disappointment and love collide in his head. Caleb reeked of beer and sweat, and was fever-hot even in the dreary, cold mist.

There'd be a talk in the morning, he thought. The important part was the scratch of teeth over Caleb's hand and the way it fired up a kiln in Captain Reilly's stomach, one that lit his eyes up lethal and reminded him that there were things to do. He wanted his son kept safe, and far from this until he could be trusted again.

He shut Caleb into the back seat of the cruiser, and then the good captain started his walk to the motel, down the empty road. The dog would be animal control's business, but Asher

Gordon? Once the cuffs were on, he'd call for another cruiser and take that son of a bitch in. He was liable for Emily's murder (a dog was a weapon, he knew, and murder-versus-manslaughter was not yet determined) and that meant jail time. A fine for vagrancy on top of that, loitering charges too if he was lucky, and Caleb's assault as well.

If that didn't scare Espino straight, then nothing would, and maybe she'd be better off hitching a ride to Harville with Hoang.

He noticed the bushes on his left rustle slightly, then nothing but the sound of bugs and his feet crunching the gravelly pavement. Something prickled up the back of his neck. He touched there nervously, thinking it was a bug perhaps, but then goosebumps washed up and down his body and his organs all tensed inside him.

He could have laughed at himself. Yes, it was a creepy old road, isolated and silent and dark, and there *was* a vicious dog on the loose, but he was a grown man and an officer of the law.

The captain was equal distance from the warmth of the Bright house and the cold glow of the motel parking lot when the scarce clouds clawed in over the moon, blotting his light out slowly and turning everything soupy in the mist. He walked a little faster, fixing widening eyes on that distant parking lot. He believed he was a brave man, but he believed wrong. He started to sweat. His skin tightened. He heard the distant wind chimes on the motel, and then a squealing creak of rust and chains.

He turned his eyes slightly and saw the playground glinting. It was practically invisible so far down the road. But he could see one swing start drifting.

There was no wind against Captain Reilly.

He stopped walking.

He watched in slow-motion terror as the swing moved a little more, and a little more. The chains were squealing, dissonant against his racing heart. He wanted to believe it was the wind, but the arc was getting too big, picking up pace. He thought desperately of his own son when he was young, pumping his legs to get higher higher *higher*!

The swing stopped suddenly in a grating crush of pea gravel. Captain Reilly breathed out shakily, but had no time for anything else.

There was something in the road.

It raced past him with a rush of wind and a fluttering sound he didn't quite recognize. Laughter rang up around him, a child's soaring laughter that seemed to turn his blood into crystalline glass, to tear paper-cut slivers through every vessel. He whirled around, hearing it echo from the playground, down the road, and from the small sheath of trees. He stared into the shadows there. The air was suddenly too thick, bloody and syrupy all at once.

He saw a flash of red in the bushes, two eyes, and heard a growl start up.

Captain Reilly gave a guttural, low moan that he was hardly aware of, his face sheet-white and dripping cold sweat, his boots still stuck to the ground. He heard something shouting at him from that foggy haze, too far away to hear beyond his fixed panic.

Emily Novak had been a warm-up.

"We didn't run away, Captain," he heard two voices say from his left side. The voices screeched right down his spine, clenched his stomach. "Chuck wasn't an accident. The monster got him, and it got us, too."

He heard the playground gravel crunching, someone walking closer to block his right-side exit. Just as he thought to turn completely around and run into the high grass, he saw some spare moonlight glint off white teeth in the bushes ahead. His skin was waves of hot then cold, rolling threats of nausea, a prickly haze in his head. He caught a glint of red in the bushes (*Eyes*, he thought, *dear god, those are eyes*) and suddenly the voice in his head was audible: it was primal, prey-ish instinct, and it told him to *Run*.

Adrenaline shot through his too-tight veins, and Captain Reilly unstuck his feet. He turned—his ice-cold, fumbling hand on his pistol—toward the dark and lonely road stretching back to the Bright house where his son slept in the cruiser.

If he had wanted to scream, it caught in his dry throat. The air smelled like blood and rotten things, sickly sweet and metallic.

He didn't believe in ghosts, but something was materializing ahead of him, something small and almost familiar, almost childlike. Already ghostly when they lived, they were skeletal now, starved. Their clothes hung on twig-thin bodies, see-through-soaked with sweat to show blood-red bruises, and broken ribs moving in disjointed rhythm to the rest. One grinned with two missing front teeth and watery blood dripping down a fish-belly-white face, and the other's grey-brown arm hung dislocated out of the waterlogged sling around her neck. The two held hands. They had died that way, hand in hand down in the tunnels.

Captain Reilly turned to the high grass but stumbled back from a large boy, or something like one, covered in mud that flecked his hair and dusted his clothes and pasted him with forgotten cobwebs. His limbs moved in all the wrong places, snapped from the fall. His flashlight had bashed through his temple and orbital socket, and he looked like he had one glowing eye.

Captain Reilly heard the bushes shake and the growling rip into a bark. He was shoved from behind and fell to his stomach like a man being arrested. The things all laughed. They stood over him at the side of the road, the tall grass whispering behind them.

Captain Reilly's eyes swept over the grim council, one by one.

"Meyers?" he asked.

"Johnson," Ellie said.

"Levi," Ben croaked, and shook out one hand.

The third was silent, but Captain Reilly recognized him as the Warren boy, whose body he'd excavated from the basement of the abandoned mill. That boy had been buried, unlike the others, and now they were all here.

The growling started up again behind him, and he felt something tugging curiously at the leg of his pants. The street was blue with moonlight and shadows, and too empty. One, two, three. Where was the fourth?

"Captain," the final voice said, approaching from the direction of the motel . . . and the mill. The growling spiked into half-barks, bubbly with blood-tinted slobber. It landed hot on the back of his neck. "You should have looked for us."

A dog, Captain Reilly thought while he lay sprawled. *They're dogs, Espino girls. Bite and never let go.*

"I didn't go fast," the voice said, passing behind him to join the snarling thing. "You could have found my body, for my parents. You owed them that."

The voice was waiting for Captain Reilly to turn around, but he would give it no such satisfaction. He stared at the smug faces of the three others, who the town was better off without. It hadn't missed them.

The growling thing barked sharp, loud.

"There's a monster in this town," the voice said. "And we're going to kill it."

Something bit down hard on the back of Captain Reilly's knee, splintering the tendon like a snapped leash.

He writhed and screamed as the creature tore into him, clawing up and flipping him while he tried to scramble into the ditch and the high grass. The creature sank tooth and nail into the good captain's soft stomach until its face was wet and hot with blood. Captain Reilly screamed himself hoarse, hoping someone would hear it, someone would come, someone would save him.

What happened to the safe haven of a small town?

If anyone heard it, they were minding their own business.

PAZ

Paz died realizing that the monster wasn't the slimy, scaly thing she'd thought, that it wasn't a flesh-and-blood thing at all, but that it was *alive,* and sure as hell had made its home in lovely little Bridlington. All by herself when the end came for her, Paz had two choices:

She could lay down and die.

Or she could stay and fight.

Someone has to kill the monster, she thought as her soul tried to part from her body. *And if no one else will, I'll do it myself.*

The soil shook. The universe wrenched and spat and gnashed its teeth. Paz Espino smudged her memory onto the town. She would not choose death. She would not leave. She would kill the monster, one way or another.

And then she awoke on her back, staring up at the gap in the floor of the old mill. She knew she was dead and remembered everything. It was pitch black down there, but she could see all. As she stood, her body felt heavy; the stormwater of her death pulled her down, like bone-deep exhaustion.

The rope was gone, the gap was far away, and the darkness pressed in on her. She slowly turned in circles to look at every inch of the mill basement: the refuse of Chuck's accident, a few rats blinking warily at her. But no Chuck. No Ben. No Ellie.

She had been ice before, but now her anger was thawing everything into racing river water.

"Sammy?" she called, hands around her mouth. She couldn't see Sammy up there, but she had to try. "Sammy, someone took the rope. I'm trapped."

No response. She narrowed her eyes. *Come on, scaredy-cat.* Her heart beat heavier, pulsing cold water beneath her gray flesh. "Sammy, come help me."

Still nothing. She was beginning to shake. She was answered only by the scurry and squeak of rats. Darkness bore down on her.

"Sammy!" she called, louder, so loud the earth seemed to shift beneath her feet. "I know where to find the monster now."

They had promised they'd kill it. And now it was more than just avenging Chuck or proving the town wrong. The monster had killed Paz; if the mission was personal before, now its importance was tenfold. Now it was tit for tat. *Come on, monster, it's time to d-d-d-duel.* "We have to take the monster's teeth, Sammy!" How would they rip the crumbling teeth from the infected jaw? Well, there were no more playing-card-spoked bikes in Bridlington, right? And how had that been managed?

"We have to kill the bad people," Paz said, and knew it to be true.

Still no response. But Paz kept trying. She kept trying for days, a week—more. Everything was rushing together, blurring.

She didn't need to sleep or eat or drink, and so she just waited. And listened. And shouted.

And finally, one day, there was a sound. She sniffed and looked up to the gap where the rope should have been. She saw blank, black eyes and a furry face.

"Oh," Paz said. Her face was flat. "Hello again."

One of the Meyers' King Shepherds (Petey or Pauley . . . even Ben and Ellie could never tell them apart) stared down at her through the dark. She heard scratching behind him, and saw the shapes of Pauley/Petey and Blitz. All three had been off leash in the cornfield as always and heard the vibration of Paz's calls. She stared up at them.

Petey/Pauley whined and wiggled his haunches, prancing at the gap. Blitz stuck her white head and quivering pink nose in so far Paz thought she'd lose her grip.

Paz grinned. *Here we go, folks. The warm-up before the show.*

"Bad dog," Paz said, and saw a flicker of red play through Blitz's ice-blue eyes. "Jump, Blitz."

Blitz's head sparked up into a cherry-slushy wonderland. There was no hesitation. All four paws left the mill floor.

She crashed at Paz's feet and died almost instantly. No more chasing anyone through the corn. No more hurt. No more fear. No more. No more. *Crack* went the next one. And the next. Paz would starve the monster. She smiled, with a deluge of stormwater slipping between her teeth to dribble down her front.

//\\//\\//\\//\\//\\//\\//\\//\\

When the time finally came that the rope was dropped again and Paz was allowed to crawl from her grave, her friends came back. She stood in the mill basement, revenant with leaves plastered to her, and said, "Can Chuck and Ben and Ellie come play?" And they did. They popped back into Bridlington with their bikes, and their slushy cup, and their devotion. But just like Paz, none of them could gain a hold on the living in more than a tingling-if-you-stepped-on-their-heels way. This job needed hands, or teeth.

And after six years of waiting, Paz Espino had a plan.

Paz watched as the creature who had once been called Bird tore spongy stuff out of Captain Reilly's stomach, blood dripping from his feathery jaws. Her three friends had gone off to play on the jungle gym where they could almost push Ellie on the swing if Chuck and Ben both helped. Ben didn't like the blood so much: it made him think of *Goosebumps*, so Paz oversaw the wet work alone.

But Paz was not a monster. She was justice on two wheels with a playing card in the spokes. She listened to the screams fade off into gurgles and she called Bird back to her side, walking carefully over to peer down at Captain Reilly's glassy eyes.

She wore a kid's smile, two thick braids, and muddy scrapes. Unlike the others, who were enchanted by such cool powers, Paz found no glory in wearing the face of the end she was force-fed.

"You could have saved me," she told Captain Reilly. Bird had made quite the mess of him, and was now nudging his hot nose into Paz's hand. "You could have listened to me about the monster, but you didn't."

Captain Reilly had very little fight left in him, but he narrowed his eyes. "You're a . . . you're a *dog*," he growled. Blood dripped from the side of his mouth and was splattered on his face. Blood-red on bone-white.

"I'm not," Paz said. Her crew laughed and sipped their slushy that never emptied. Together, free. But they weren't done. This was just the start. "There's a monster in this town, Captain, and I can take its teeth so it starves."

With that, she left him there to bleed. Paz and her crew grabbed their bikes and raced to Quinn's house with Bird galloping alongside them. Captain Reilly watched them go, fading as his blood pooled onto the summer-warm pavement. He died unceremoniously, alone.

Caleb Reilly, Junior, slept drunk in the back of his father's cruiser. He didn't hear the bikes or the creature approaching.

THE HOANGS

Beetle, once called Sammy, had come out to his mom a few years into his six-year stint in Harville. He called home from a payphone by the museum he frequented, because he didn't want to tell her in person and risk seeing her disappointment. Over the crackly connection, he let it all spill out in a few uninterrupted paragraphs: he wasn't a girl, and he wasn't quite a boy either but somewhere close to it, and so he was her son and he could be called he or him and he could be called Beetle.

She was silent.

She said his deadname, and then she said, "I just want to know if I did something wrong."

Beetle, fourteen then with a very DIY-blue haircut, felt himself go numb. He hung up and started imagining exit plans and couch-crashes for after graduation, but was pleasantly surprised when she still showed up for the monthly visiting day. She bought him boba like always while he showed her which new bugs he'd found.

"I'm scared for you," she finally told him. She was looking at his hair, and he wasn't sure if she was talking about that or about being genderqueer when she said, "I'm scared this will make it even harder when you come home, *Beetle*."

His name sounded stiff in her mouth, so unpracticed and strange that he had to remind himself that it was in fact his, and he did want her to say it. He was scared of a lot of things, but not this decision.

"I feel like this is my fault," she told him, and he prepared to snap at her for insinuating that being trans was the fault of anyone, but she continued. "That you're here, in Harville. That home was so terrible."

Oh. He knew there was no reason for her to feel guilty about a shitty little town. He hugged her then, which he didn't do exceedingly often, and put his face in her shoulder. "It wasn't your fault about Paz, or me," he said, and believed it.

She didn't. There were a million things that went wrong, but Ms. Hoang hugged her son and took full blame for everything: that he was at an alternative school for high-risk teenagers, that he was so far from home, that he had suffered what she was sure was a psychotic break after his best friends all ran away. She hugged her son (*My son*, she thought, to get in the habit, *my* son) but could only remember how wrong she had let things become.

The night he'd come home from the mill, the night Paz Espino "went missing," his mother had carried him up to his room and tucked him into bed while the wind and rain thrashed. Beetle had fallen asleep with her fingers drifting through his hair, like that might protect him.

The storm raged well into the next day, and Beetle didn't speak. He felt like it was perpetually night, like there were perpetual monsters. He was slowly catching pneumonia, which his mother thought was just a bad cold at first and assumed that's why he wasn't speaking. He drank bún bò huế in bed, the non-spicy kind, and slept awfully. The rain swelled against their house and a very feverish Beetle thought it sounded like waves, like he was underwater and drowning. He could taste the water and the runoff sludge in his throat. He opened his eyes and saw lightning flash through the grid of his window, throwing drip-marks of rain over his Bakugan poster and small army of Webkinz. He was delirious with chills, fluid building in his lungs.

Paz Espino was dead by then, and had just found herself again under the mill. Beetle saw it with his eyes open. Childhood pacts, stronger than diamond, or distance, or death, especially in a town where things had gone ungrieved. Beetle should have been dead along with the others, and that tied him to them.

He could see the pit as if he were staring up at it, saw that there was no rope anymore. He could feel the water pulling at him.

"*Sammy?*" he heard Paz whisper. He felt his own lips murmur, shoving out the crackle that had built from not speaking for a while. "*Sammy, someone took the rope. I'm trapped.*" He sat up in bed, the room still warm with the smell of toned-down spices just for him, the wind and rain gusting and rushing and drowning him alive. "*Sammy, come help me,*" he said. His eyes were wide and tears dripped slowly down his round cheeks.

His mother was in the next room and heard the mumbling. She thought it was the wind, and then she thought it was his Nintendo DS. She put down her book.

Beetle felt his vocal cords contracting as Paz's did. It was her voice from his lips. "*Sammy!*" he said, a little fiercer. "*I know where to find the monster now.*"

Beetle's mother stood in his doorway and he didn't even notice her. She watched in horror, her child sitting bolt upright with his face drained pale. "*We have to kill the bad people.*"

"Sammy," his mother choked out, almost a sob. She was covering her mouth and staring at him with the air Blue River–cold around her.

Beetle turned slowly to her. "Má," he said. His voice crackled again. He felt like he was breaking slowly. He wanted to cry and scream. But all he managed to choke out with his crackling voice was, "Paz is talking to me."

Tattletale.

His mother knew this was worse than sticks and stones. Something was very, very wrong.

///∧∨/∧∨/∧∨/∧∨/∧∨/∧∨/∧∨\\\

A week later, Beetle was exactly twelve years old, and found himself in a brightly painted room with construction paper crafts on the walls and very inaccurately painted butterflies. He wasn't altogether sure how he had gotten there, only that Paz had been screaming at him all through his fever, and then it broke and she still screamed, and getting in the car felt like a dream. He couldn't hear her anymore. There were necessary introductions to the kind-looking psychiatrist. He was polite, and then they got into it.

"Are you looking forward to grade seven?" she asked while he rolled some playdough into a ball and then into an egg-ish shape.

He shrugged, small in his Inuyasha shirt that his aunt had sent him without knowing he was so far behind the growth curve. "I guess," he said. He broke a small piece off the big block and rolled out a little line, and then two more. He connected all three into an accurate insect leg.

She waited for him to say more and he didn't, so she said, "Your mom says your teachers like you."

Beetle made some more legs, not looking up. He fixed his glasses. "They think I'm weird. I heard them say it."

He heard her scribbling. "You're old enough to know what bullies are," she said, not a question.

He fixed flat wings onto the egg shape, and then the legs. "I know what bystanders are, too."

He looked up only enough to see her frown. "Do you think you're a bystander?"

He gave a dismissive shrug.

"Do you know any bullies, Sammy?"

He looked up from his playdough beetle. "If I tell you," he said, his face cold like stone, "no one will believe me. Just like with Paz." He felt something welling up inside him, but it wasn't tears or fear: it was magma, and it was heating up under his skin and cooking him alive. His eyes were hot and prickly, too dry. "No one ever believed Paz and now she's gone. She's gone because that's what happens to weird kids. It's what's gonna happen to *me*." He smashed his hand down into his beetle and it splayed out into a flat purple disk, legs creeping out from under his hand. "And I *wish* it would, because I don't want to be in Bridlington anymore. I want to be gone too, like Chuck."

There was an awful silence, and his therapist's eyes widened behind her glasses.

That's what did it.

Her reaction shocked him into realizing the gravity and *truth* of what he'd said, and he almost choked on the tears that came on suddenly, thick as sewer sludge and fast as Blue River. So there he was, sobbing and spluttering for air, wishing he were dead, knowing his friends were, knowing home was hell and not knowing how to change it. He cried for seven hours straight.

His mother cried for three of those, looking over pamphlets in the late-night light of the kitchen. He was just upset, scared, she thought. What he needed was his mother.

But she'd have to be up early to open the diner the next day for breakfast, and she'd leave him again, with a key waiting for him next to the door.

Ms. Hoang loved her son deeply. Holding on was easy. Instead, she picked up another pamphlet.

Beetle liked the tiny, tidy room he found himself in at his new boarding school, with his sketches of bugs and things Paz had never touched. He wanted to resent her—sometimes did—but decided to move on instead. And so things got better, slowly. By the time he was fourteen and could go to the park by himself, he hardly thought about Paz at all. Every summer, his mother asked him if he wanted to come home, but every summer he refused to step foot anywhere Paz or Ben or Ellie had, and so he talked her into enrolling him in his school's overnight summer camps. He frequented the library so much bigger than the one in Bridlington, looked at people like him at the museum he eventually worked for, kissed a girl in his grade ten biology class even though it wasn't very good, and kissed a boy at a summer dance, which was also a little subpar, mostly because he still wasn't sure what he wanted. When he finally did pile into his mother's car and chug back home with his Bug Book on his lap and the skies turning more familiar (as if the sky had been any different in Harville), he knew the world was vast.

He just had to survive summer in Bridlington. And then he'd be off to university, and gone forever.

Beetle had expected Paz's voice to come screaming back the second he came into town, but she was quiet. Maybe he really *had* hallucinated the whole thing, created a false reality to escape the idea that she was gone forever. He didn't believe it, and it wore at him all summer while he worked. Every time Mr. Espino looked at him pityingly, every time he saw the missing posters of Paz and Ben and Ellie on the corkboard in the motel office, every time he avoided Marcela, he felt Paz's ghost.

He needed closure. It was the grown-up, therapied thing to do.

When it was nearly August, he took his lunch break and marched himself over the bridge, down the path, into the gorge, along the river, under the bridge, and up to the boarded ruins. He pried off two of the re-hammered boards and wormed into the mill to stare into the pit.

He saw nothing down there.

"I'm sorry you're dead, Paz," he said. It was an apology six years in the making. He wondered what she'd have been like, if she'd have gone to Harville with him for university, if she'd look like Marcela, or if she'd have grown like him. "But I don't believe in ghosts anymore."

He turned to leave, and then he felt something tickling in his vocal cords like a bug. *"If you're so sure,"* Beetle felt himself say—he swore he heard it, too, from the pit where they'd once thought a monster lived, as if the monster were one thing in one place—*"then gimme the rope."*

Beetle gritted his teeth, looked to the stairs and the shadows under them, and saw a dusty mound shoved under there. The rope. Whoever had pulled it up didn't even have the decency to get rid of it. He stormed over and flung the rope into the pit in a whirl and rattle of mud, kicked the wall with his Vans, wrenched at the stairs, clawed at his hair, screamed. He was pissed at his mom for sending him away then bringing him back, at Mr. Espino for giving him a job but never talking about Paz, at Captain Reilly for turning his back, at Ellie and Ben for being willing to follow Paz anywhere, at Chuck for dying in the first place. And at Paz. Sometimes he hated Paz for being brave. That day, he hated her for getting a chance to leave Bridlington, even in death, and not taking it.

The rope was down. He stood above it with his jaw locked tight and his muscles on fire, breathing heavily.

"Thanks, Sammy," they both said. *"I'm gonna kill the monster."*

"You should have left," Beetle said, with his eyes on fire. "I'm gonna leave, forever."

"Scaredy-cat," Paz said, but not without a little humor.

KID WHISPERER

It was near sunrise when Asher opened his eyes behind his sunglasses and blinked away a dehydrated itch while a jackhammer went to town on his skull. He swung his legs off the side of the bed, sat up, and ground his hands up under his sunglasses. He took them off for just a moment, and the thin line of parking-lot glow leaking through the window seared against his eyelids. He stared at his reflection in the dark pools of the lenses.

Asher's eyes were dull hazel, set above soft cheeks and a faint dusting of acne. Nothing special, really, but he could smooth his chest, he could wear thick clothes, he could change his smile into whatever he needed and drop his voice low and find the best words, choose the right mask. He was an actor. But what he couldn't change was how soft his eyes were, how doe-like and lost. They shone a spotlight on him, and they told the world his biggest secret.

It wasn't that he was trans, or that he was a homeless runaway sprinting from everyone who ever knew him. It was that he had no idea what he was doing, and was terrified.

But he could survive. He wanted to believe he wouldn't have his throat ripped out and his blood smeared across lawns, his body dragged down the gorge, that he wouldn't die penniless and abandoned in Harville. He didn't know why he somehow felt that possibility drifting closer, but he did. It was a premonition that could only be had while blearily hungover in an unknown, night-hazy motel room, where even terrified teenagers become prophets. Mostly because they won't remember it in the morning.

He fixed his sunglasses back on, squinting hard behind them at Marcela in the other bed and Beetle on the floor with one arm under his head and his honey-comb glasses and chest binder folded next to him. Asher felt like he was forgetting something, but he was still too tired to piece the night together. He patted down his pockets—phone, keys. No wallet, but he didn't have one, just left all the evidence buried in his glove compartment.

He stumbled into the bathroom and rooted around for some Advil as quietly as he could. He figured Marcela could spare some. He took two dry.

Bird.

Shit.

Asher poked his head out of the bathroom and looked around the room, thinking maybe Marcela had taken pity and let Bird in after all, but Asher knew that stupid dog would have been all over him. And there was no slobbering, wiggling, fuzzy mess at his heels. Shit shit *shit.*

Asher stepped over Beetle and ducked out the motel door

into the cool night air, hoping Bird would be sleeping right outside (no), or maybe his drunk self had had enough presence of mind to put Bird in the car parked just ahead (no).

He could smell something metallic in the air, just enough to get his nerves up. "Goddammit," he muttered, and thunked his fists against the top of the driver-side door. He cupped his hands around his mouth, hoping his whisper would carry. "Bird!"

No scrabble of paws. Asher bounced his knees nervously. He knew Bird didn't know "Come" so he called the next best thing. "Wanna go for a drive?"

Still nothing. Instead, he felt watched. It prickled at his neck, trickling down into his hands. Asher bundled a little farther into his hoodie. He walked quickly toward the jungle gym side of the motel to see if Bird was on the back lawn. He vaguely remembered him being there, at least in the high grass between Quinn's and the motel. How had he gotten so careless?

Asher zipped around the side and waded out to the middle of the lawn. "*Bird*," he whispered. "A drive! Treat! Walk!" Anything Bird knew. Asher felt as if the lawn were writhing and shifting beneath him, like water that he might sink into at any moment. Even the air felt like rapids. Asher was starting to grow delirious in the forever-expanse of the grass. Bird never ran far, so where was he?

Asher spun in a slow circle, looking from the thin forest separating him from the Mac's to Quinn's, to the motel, and then to the road that became Main or the Blue River bridge. There was no sign of Bird. A sense of serene acceptance dripped from his tongue into his throat. He swallowed Bird's name.

A thought passed through Asher's mind, something that had been building since he'd arrived in Bridlington: Bird was better off without him. Someone would take him in, give him a real home. He was a cute dog, and he knew "Stay." Someone would make him their business and feed him properly and brush his fur and take him on drives, while Asher found Caleb and grovelled.

And maybe, *probably*, Asher would be better off too. Bird was the reason he wasn't staying in the motel in the first place and had to sleep in his car. It was Bird that barked that first night at the cemetery, why the minister had come out to check and taken Asher's money, leaving him to steal Clif Bars and dumpster dive and let Bird eat soggy cheeseburger bits covered in coffee grounds and swamp-water soda. Why he was out of options.

Asher blinked hard and swallowed a nearly-crying lump in his throat. What the hell was this? Crying over a dog? Crying over himself? People like that didn't belong in Bridlington, he knew.

Come on, he told himself. *Don't be such a sissy.*

Just as he prepared himself to turn back for the motel and go to sleep and hope to wake up more masculine, he heard the fluttering of a playing card in spokes behind him, and then the crunch of gravel. More than recognizing the sound, he recognized that there was only one person he knew who seemed bold enough to be out so late, and so alone.

Paz.

Things really were coming full circle.

Asher turned. He was hungover and Bird was gone and that last part might have been a good thing, he wasn't sure. Paz had ridden her bike up to the edge of the playground, putting one sneaker down onto the wooden barrier that held the pea gravel. In the faint light of the motel, she was barely a silhouette.

"I'm looking for my dog," he said, which seemed like a good excuse not to talk to her. "I don't have time for games."

A cloud shifted, and Asher could have sworn Paz's eyes were dead-thing silver, but then they were dark again. Seeing her now and having something to compare to, he realized she looked almost identical to Marcela, just younger. It was disturbingly uncanny.

"You left your dog. I found him," Paz said. "He's mine now."

Asher nodded, slowly. He didn't know what to say.

A few birds were starting to wake up. The sky had begun to lighten.

"You don't look so cool anymore, Asher," Paz said, tilting her head a bit. She gave him that old look-down. "You look like you're getting monster-y."

Asher didn't know what *that* meant, and he narrowed his eyes. *You know what, screw this.* He managed to peel one foot up and then the next, starting to rush at her. "What the hell do you wa—"

She grinned. The first light of dawn reared, and in it Paz's face was sick-gray, her eyes dead-pale, her lips drowned-blue. She dripped storm drain floodwater onto the pea gravel.

Who said ghosts only come out at night?

"Boo," she said, just a flicker of her dead-face.

Asher's eyes widened, and he fainted.

BEETLE

While sleeping on the floor of Marcela's suite, Beetle watched as his childhood friends circled Captain Reilly's cruiser. He could see it like he was there: Ben, Ellie, and Chuck, looking for a way in, along with a bloody beast he barely recognized as Bird. Caleb was dead-asleep in the back, and he didn't wake up even when Bird charged the car, snapped at the door handle, raked his bloody claws along the sides. Ellie flailed her too-gray hand with chipped nail polish at the door handle, but she couldn't quite get a grip to pull it open. Ben tried to pick up a rock to break the windshield, but neither he nor Chuck could lift it, so Ben just shook out his hands nervously and Chuck huffed and swayed.

Paz wasn't with them; she'd gone off to see if she might find someone to open the door for her, someone with hands who had never died.

Someone who still owed them some involvement.

Each individual viewpoint was stacked up before Beetle, like microscope slides, and in one of them he could see Paz staring at the back of the motel, at the high window of the suite he slept in. No, he couldn't quite call it sleeping anymore. He was dreaming awake, as he had in his terrified youth.

"*Are you going to be brave?*" Paz said, and Beetle felt the words croak from his throat too. He could see Asher passed out in the grass, his sunglasses slipped from his soft cheeks, yellow-pink light rising over him. He could see Ben and Ellie and Chuck riding their bikes from Quinn's house, Bird galloping beside them with blood caking his fur flat to his thin sides.

"*It's time to kill the monster. It's time to kill Caleb. He pulled up the rope. He's next.*"

The other three bikes bumped off the road and cut across the motel lawn. Bird sniffed at Asher a few times, snuffled his nose right into Asher's chest for a second, and then tore after his crew with a booming howl that Beetle was sure the entire town must have heard. But Paz let them go—she would meet them later.

She had called on Beetle alone before, and would again. He saw through her eyes as she walked up the side of the motel, beside the jungle gym, and turned to look down the row of motel doors in the gray morning light.

"*We got the other two without you,*" she said, and he knew who she meant. He knew Paz too well *not* to know who she would target first. "*You can still come with us if you stop being a scaredy-cat. We can finish it together.*"

Like we should have before, Beetle thought. He shivered, wondering if it was Paz thinking it, or if it was him, or if it mattered. He didn't want this. From his hazy own-vision, Beetle found himself staring at Marcela. And she was staring right back.

Beetle saw Paz walk down the line of doors, saw her stop in front of theirs. He was drenched in sweat by then, shaking like he'd shatter. Marcela was eyeing him warily. He waited for her to call him a freak or call the police and have him led to Harville's hospital.

"*Caleb next,*" Paz and Beetle both said. "*Because he pulled up the rope.*"

Beetle's stomach dropped, and that alone seemed to bring him back into reality. He could feel the hard carpet under him, knew he was sitting up, and he was suddenly only himself. He wasn't surprised Caleb had done that—he might have guessed so himself. What horrified him was that Marcela had to hear it too. Her face suddenly tightened. She got to her feet and rushed him. He thought for sure she was going to kick him, but she stopped short.

"Liar," she spat, pointing her finger. "Paz wasn't even at the mill. Caleb said—" Marcela closed her mouth. She waved her hands like she was trying to sweep the pieces back together, but she never got the chance.

There was a light sound from the door, a muffled *thud.* Marcela jumped up and whirled around, her lips shaking, one tear dripping down her face. Beetle snapped his head to look at the door, expecting it to open on Paz. He shot to his feet, stumbling back beside Marcela, his shivering shoulder to hers. He heard nothing but his racing heart and the buzzing bedside lamp.

And then a voice, muffled but so very there. "Come out and play," Paz said, and there was another *thud* as she kicked the door. It seemed louder, like she'd gotten more power behind it, as much as a ghost could. Beetle's frantic eyes never left the doorknob, waiting for it to turn. Beetle wasn't sure what he would do if it did. What he might say, if anything.

But it all ended unceremoniously, because Bird was too risky in the daylight and Paz had no plans without him.

Beetle didn't see her go, she wouldn't let him, but he heard the clinking sound of her picking up her bike, and then the playing-card rattle fading off. He wasn't sure if she was going back to the mill with the others or if she had errands to run before the next night.

Once he couldn't hear her anymore, he managed to exhale, but just barely.

"What the hell, Hoang?" Marcela breathed, without ever taking her eyes off the door or her shoulder from his. He couldn't turn to look at her either, to see if she was still crying. He heard her swallow, hard, but couldn't give her an answer.

He knew one thing for sure: Bird had killed Emily and Captain Reilly, which made Asher the last person who should be out in the open. He might be just as hunted as Beetle.

Beetle stepped carefully for the door, sure Paz was gone but still feeling his throat scraping every time he swallowed, still blinking sweat from his eyes. "We get Asher, then we talk," he muttered.

"About Caleb," he heard her say, but didn't turn back. "About the rope."

About the rope, he thought, because there were so many pieces coming together now, and they needed to weigh options. He needed to know how hard it would be to escape it all.

Asher Gordon woke up in the field with Beetle's hands on the front of his hoodie.

"Wuz happening . . ." Asher muttered. "Bird. P-Paz."

"We know," Beetle said. He was cold and sweat-soaked. Marcela was close beside him, her shoe almost touching his.

"She looked like a horror movie," Asher said.

But then there was the wailing of police sirens, and red and blue lit up the field along with the sunrise, and before Beetle could decide what that meant for them, Marcela was already grabbing Asher by the shoulder and hauling him toward the toolshed.

"His dog bit Caleb," was all she said, and then the three of them hid like criminals, or maybe just like outcast kids.

INTERLOPER

The police had finally realized Captain Reilly wasn't responding to his radio, and they found his body. Only the dead captain knew about Bird, so they figured it was the same animal that had killed his niece—some sort of wolf or very gung ho coyote. The cops all stood around the remains, eyes wide, skin cold, hands on their guns. No one was safe now, not even people like Captain Reilly who could walk the streets at midnight.

Paz Espino was teaching the people of Bridlington about fear.

While they speedily took pictures and cleared the remains, desperate to have this done with before any innocent civilians saw the carnage, Asher Gordon was sitting in a wheelbarrow, cross-legged. The air in the toolshed was scratchy and thick, already heating up as the sun inched higher to throw pinkish light through the dust-caked window behind the shelf. Marcela and Beetle were shadowed in the dark behind his sunglasses.

Beetle had explained everything, clambered and rushed and doubled back, because he had to tell the story of the Shepherds, and how Paz had been there because she was supposed to "apologize" for telling Captain Reilly about Ben—and also how there was Chuck and also the monster hunt and also the present-day situation including Emily and Captain Reilly, and explain how he knew about that, which was a complicated thing to do. Marcela had her arms locked tight across her body the entire time, her eyes a mile away from her skull and her teeth so tight Asher thought she would open a black hole between them.

"And she's going to kill Caleb," Beetle finished. His trembling calmed. "But I'm leaving, and you can too."

The end. Okay.

Asher held his hands together like a man praying, pressed them to his lips, and then pointed them to Marcela. "Marcela had a twin sister," he restated.

Marcela nodded stiffly. She was still wearing Quinn's flannel, and her makeup was smeared into dark shadows at her eyes, pulled red over her lips. She was shifting from heel to heel, like she was terrified to stop moving.

Asher pointed his hands to Beetle. "And Beetle was friends with her when he was a kid, and Ben and Ellie. And they all died the summer after grade six, but people thought they just ran away."

"Yes," Beetle said.

Asher closed his eyes tight behind his sunglasses. "And these are the same kids I met at the Mac's, including another kid who died."

"Chuck," Beetle said. He breathed in slowly and looked to Marcela. "The day you met her, she would have just gotten out of the mill."

Marcela's voice was like a car's backfire. "Because you *let* her out."

"I thought it wasn't real!" Beetle snapped. He'd spent six damn years learning the difference between breakdown and reality. "How the hell was I supposed to know Paz was gonna 'go ghost' and start up a murder spree?"

"You couldn't have guessed it?" Marcela said, and that seemed to shock both of them into silence. Asher didn't know what Paz was like before she died, so he couldn't have known how it was a long time coming.

"Okay, can we also acknowledge this is, like, *really* messed up?" Asher squeaked, before managing to rein his voice back to an even level. "You all seem a little chill about ghosts."

They both blinked at him.

"I'm leaving soon, so it won't matter," Beetle said numbly.

Marcela was looking out the small window, swaying faster and faster. "Good for you," she spat, tapping her toes now too. "Some of us have to stay here and tough it out."

"Your twin sister is a ghost and you're gonna choose now to call me a coward?" Beetle said. "I didn't get to *choose* having her voice in my head. And frankly, coward talk is rich coming from someone still dating a murderer."

"He didn't kill anyone," she snapped, so quick to defend. Asher watched her eye twitch once, like something in her was revolting. "He was only twelve."

"That was older than Paz."

"Stop," Marcela said, hands near her face in jagged claws like someone fighting off a migraine. "Shut up about the rope."

"How'd he even know about—" Beetle stopped himself, eyes growing wider. His voice dropped low. "Oh my god. How did Caleb even know to check the mill, Marcela? How did he even know she was going after the monster?"

"I thought he would help!" She was shaking so violently that Asher thought she was going to shatter and fall between the wooden floorboards. She was turning gray and clammy. "I was eleven too. So were you." She pressed her hands to her face. "Oh god, oh god . . ." She kept repeating it. Over and over.

Asher thought Marcela and Beetle were both losing it and he wanted no part. If he hadn't seen Paz go all *Paranormal Activity*, he might have thrown the whole thing out. But he knew they were telling the unfortunate truth.

"Okay," Asher said, trying to settle the tension. He told himself to keep it together, and turned his face into a cold, hard mask. "And now she's out—and Ben and Ellie and Chuck," he said, getting ahead of Beetle's open mouth. "She's running around town with a ghost-bike killing bad people with my . . ." That last bit caught in his throat and burned with regret. If he had just kept an eye on Bird, then maybe none of this would be happening. "With my possessed dog."

There was silence, and he suspected they were counting on him to do something. But what the hell could he do? Just because he was new to the mix didn't mean he was bringing any expertise or fresh perspective. If anything, he'd made things worse by bringing Bird.

He almost choked up, and swallowed it. "So, where we're at now," he said, just to be a hundred percent clear, "is that she wants to kill Caleb, and she wants Beetle in on it."

They both nodded, Marcela through her shaking, and Beetle gray-faced.

"I'm not doing it," Beetle said. "If I have to waste every paycheck I've made this summer on a taxi to Harville, I will." Marcela cut Beetle a dark look, but he kept talking. "I mean, it's your dog, Asher . . . what are *you* gonna do about it?"

Asher pressed his fingers to his lips again. Yeah, all right, he was complicit. But he was just a boy far from home who no one would miss if he died. He thought that if someone flicked him off this cosmic plane like a crumb, no one would ever know where he went and, frankly, no one would care. He was much more like Paz than he could ever have known. And he was so far out of options it wasn't even funny. He could crawl back to Caleb, maybe win some favor by figuring out how to warn him in a way that didn't sound totally crazy.

Or?

Asher Gordon breathed in slowly, looking from Beetle with the morning light reflecting through his gold glasses and off his black eyes, to Marcela whose hair was falling out of last night's ponytail. The sun was rising and Paz was baring down on the town, poised to spill more blood. Asher felt something building hot and solid in his chest. He was unhoused, and alone, and neither of those things scared him as much as his fear, which was a revolving door that he just had to step out of. He thought he had only ever been himself since the day he ran away from home, and so Asher Gordon knew his stance on this whole ghost business. It was three very simple words:

No.

Thank.

You.

Asher bolted for the door so fast that the wheelbarrow clattered over behind him, barring Marcela and Beetle, for just a moment's head start. He went scrambling out over the grass, fumbling his keys from his pocket. He hit the alarm instead of the unlock button a total of seventeen times before he got to his wailing car and couldn't figure out why the door wouldn't open. He wrenched the handle so hard the car rocked and he screamed and shook.

He wanted nothing to do with this. He wanted to shut up and ignore it. He wanted to mind his own business. He wanted to be Caleb Reilly regardless of anything. He went to the gym, he drank beer, and he would go hunting and be game for anything and maybe he *would* go into the reserves just to get some money in his pockets. He was just one of the guys.

He was not a ghost hunter, and he had no plans to die noble.

Asher reared his knee up and kicked his car door so hard it dented.

CALEB REILLY

Caleb Reilly woke up fatherless, hunted, and with a hell of a hangover. One out of three would have been awful—two would have been catastrophic. Three meant he nearly punched the cops who stopped him from stumbling down the road and into the scene, and he screamed until his throat was raw. His father couldn't be dead. He couldn't. He had to see for himself, but when he'd finally fought past them, there was hardly anything left from the ribs down, and from the ribs up, his father could have been something hanging in the butcher's shop.

One was awful, two was catastrophic, three made him feel so powerless his brain shut down. His father was killed, they said, by a wild animal. It felt impossible, and yet what other answer was there? Caleb Reilly stood frozen in the middle of the road, feeling like he could do anything (scream as loud as his lungs would bear, punch the officers, pull the flesh off his bones like an animal, like a *dog*) but it wouldn't be enough. Nothing would change.

"Come on, son," the acting chief said, a cop who still gave him generic birthday presents every year. He put his hand on

Caleb's arm and turned him toward his waiting cruiser. "I'll take you home."

The second Caleb sat passenger, it all seemed to sink in deeper. On the way, the cop told Caleb that his cousin had also "passed away." Caleb stared out the windshield at Bridlington. The town seemed unreal, too bright and sunny as the painted signs were flipped to *OPEN* because no one knew yet. It felt disgusting that the town should appear so normal when things weren't normal *at all*. How had the town his family built, the walls and roads they'd made to keep the bad things away, so suddenly collapsed on them?

"You can cry, sport," the cop said. "I won't tell anyone."

"I'm not a crying person," Caleb said. "I don't think he wants that." He felt a wave of tears build in him and heave up through his chest. He sank them back down.

The cop nodded. "That's brave, Caleb."

Caleb thought about punching his fist so hard through the windshield it shattered, and the car crashed, and they both died.

When the cruiser turned east onto Main, Caleb looked far ahead and saw the sun rising up over the trees way back beyond the barely visible speck of the bridge. A shudder crept through him, even though he wasn't quite sure why yet.

His mom was waiting at the door with her face put on. She did her best to act exactly as you'd expect of the chief of police's widow, or the mother of a boy like Caleb Reilly. She let Caleb into the house, accepted the condolences of the cop, and closed the door.

She looked up at Caleb and put her hand very gently on his

shoulder. He looked at her but through her at the same time. Caleb Reilly was past the point of crying or wanting to put his head in her lap like when he was very small. He knew she would let him, treat him gently, like she did when he was twelve with muddy hands from the mill that she didn't ask about. Like she did when he concussed himself playing hockey at thirteen but tried to play through it, racing over the ice and smiling at his dad with wonky pupils. When she took his water bottle to wash at fourteen, and it smelled too sharp for water, and her husband told him that "Reilly men don't act like that" and thought the problem solved. Like when he wrapped his car around a tree the day of his seventeenth birthday because he thought about Paz Espino, about pulling up the rope, and he had one brief flash of regret that was too much for him to bear.

The morning after his father died, Caleb Reilly's mother kissed her son's cheek.

"You can talk to me about anything, Caleb," she said.

"Okay," he said. But he let the monster straighten the lines of his face, dumped Coke into a glass, wished for two fingers of whiskey ordered with the severe attention of a little girl pouring a green slushy, and went up to sit in his room to mentally assess damages.

He didn't get the time for it. The problem came to him, just as he closed his door behind him.

"*Caaaay-lebbb*," he heard someone sing. He froze. The voice had drifted in through his slightly open window. "Caleb. Hey."

That voice. Almost like Marcela's, but decidedly *not*. And wasn't it so fitting, he thought. Something was wrong in town, and wasn't there only one person who stirred up trouble quite like this? Hadn't they always said that it would escalate? And they'd never found her body to confirm her death; he never knew if the rope was her only exit. Six years of planning for a grand return, was that it?

Caleb set his Coke on his desk corner and rushed to the window, staring out into the barely lit morning air of Bridlington's most affluent neighborhood and to the figure on his lawn. He expected to see a bastardized version of his girlfriend, dressed wrong like Beetle Hoang and covered in blood. Someone he'd feel no regret smashing in the teeth of. Someone who could take his wrath.

No.

He had forgotten how ordinary she was, with her hair in braids and her Super Mario shirt and cargo shorts. Round copper cheeks, some Band-Aids, and a smile so wide he could see a missing tooth in the back. She was smaller than he remembered.

Not just small for someone his age, but small because she was still eleven.

She's just a little girl, Caleb thought, with his anger dripping down into knee-shaking terror. She was no older than he had been when he had his first drink. An ordinary little girl who suddenly seemed far younger than he remembered her. And so he knew she wasn't ordinary at all.

Caleb's eyes widened and his breath, building from stunned puffs to frantic gasps, began to cloud the glass. Every organ felt like it was shriveling up inside him. Everything was spinning. It wasn't enough for Paz Espino to cause trouble for his father when she lived.

Apparently, she had to prolong it.

"You can't stay inside forever, Caleb," she called with a quaint smile. He could hear the faintest bubbling gurgle in her throat, like speaking through sick spit. She took a long sip of her Mac's slushy. "You either come out, or I come in."

Nothing was beyond Paz Espino, not even coming back from the dead. He should have spent those six years planning for this day. He should have kept the same watchful eye Marcela had—did she know? All those years when she'd turned gray and huddled into him, and he'd played hero to make her better?

The only person he'd ever trusted was dead, and that *thing* out there had surely killed him.

"Come play, Caleb," she said, and smiled. "It'll be fun."

Liar.

He shut the window, and started making a plan.

BEETLE

Beetle was frankly appalled that some pissbaby was going to throw a tantrum instead of deciding what to do about his own damn dog. Beetle also had a stronger center of gravity.

"Hey!" he snapped, and when Asher turned, Beetle reeled his fist back and socked Asher right across the cheek. Asher went down like a gangly scarecrow. Beetle had never punched anyone before; a shock of pain exploded up his arm. The human skull is dense.

Asher crumpled onto the pavement and slid back so violently that his hoodie raked halfway up his torso. Beetle saw the hem of what was clearly a binder. Suddenly, he got a lot more context for why Asher was such an insecure dickhead. But he had zero time for it. Asher had ended up here; he was part of this now. They all were.

"Now is not the time to feel sorry for yourself!" Beetle half shouted, which he knew was hilarious coming from him.

Asher scrambled to yank his hoodie down, fix his sunglasses, and was suddenly back on his feet. "I'm not even from here,"

Asher said, trying to lift his chin high. He looked like a grand-standing goose. "Why the hell is this my problem?"

"It's your dog," Marcela added, drifting over to them and warily watching her parents' door.

Both Beetle and Asher snapped their heads to her. "It's your sister," they both said, and simultaneously wanted to throttle the other for taking the words out of their mouth. Asher made a yowling sound like a cat, reared his arm back, and then, instead, spun on his heel, scraped his hood up, and grabbed fistfuls of it and his hair.

Marcela narrowed her eyes and stomped closer to the two of them. Beetle thought she looked ready to rake both their eyes out from behind their glasses.

"What the hell are we doing?" she asked. "Besides you two being macho pieces of shit."

"I'm not the one beating up a car," Beetle said to Asher's back. "That making you euphoric, egg?"

Asher made stiff claws of his hands and gesticulated wildly, raising them up like he was going to tear down the sky. "This is all ridiculous," he said without turning around. "What are we even supposed to do with this?"

"Run," Beetle said, because it was the same old chestnut he'd been cracking at all summer. "Get the hell out of here."

Marcela tilted her head carefully. "You think that's the only choice?"

There were quite a few, actually. Between Marcela having some good favor in town and Beetle having six years of dis-tance, they were in better shape than they thought they were.

There were timelines where they went to find Paz and tried to reason with her; they wound up dead in those. They could try to find Paz to try and take back Bird, or put him down, and they'd die that way, too. There was one option where Beetle did as he had done before and followed Paz into the bleak without question, but this time, he followed through: he killed Caleb Reilly with a knife through his gut, stabbed him again and again for every hurt, and was caught by police the same day. There was another iteration where Beetle committed to his summer plan, took that student housing offer, scraped his paychecks together, and got the hell out of Dodge. In that one, Bridlington was an inferno on the evening news, Beetle lived a very long, very unhappy life, Asher died in a back alley from trying to DIY his hormones, and Marcela went down with her perfect little town.

A part of Beetle knew this, or at least felt that death was coming for them in so many ways down all the usual avenues. They needed to be smarter. He wrenched his brain around, fought it, heard the scared, young part of it scream at him to *just run, please just run, just do the easy thing and get far away.*

"You're not running now," Beetle said. He said it to Asher, too proud to say it to himself.

"So we're helping Paz kill Caleb?" Marcela asked. Her voice was so quiet it might have been the breeze. Her eyes were all fire. She opened her mouth, maybe to condemn, maybe to defend, but she said nothing.

Beetle tightened his jaw. "No," he said, to a groan from Asher. Beetle was six years past the mill, but he hadn't ever really left Paz's crew. He was supposed to ride with them, and he knew it. Her voice was in his head.

He'd stopped believing Paz should let it go. "They're bad people, the ones she's going after," Beetle said, even though he knew "bad" was sort of a flat word, more a noun than an adjective. But maybe that was idealistic, to think that people could *do* bad without *being* bad. "Bridlington turns away from people. It's messed up and needs to change. Maybe Paz has the right idea—I won't help her with it, but I won't stop her." And the second she was done with this, Beetle was getting the hell out.

"Would she . . ." Asher started to say. He looked off up the road, where the police had already cleared out. Beetle wondered if he was thinking about Bird. "Would she kill us, too?"

They paused again.

"I don't know," Marcela said, looking at Beetle. She seemed to think he had an answer, or else didn't want to give hers. "Do we have the monster in us?"

Scaredy-cats, and Asher looking a hell of a lot like Caleb.

"Her grudge is with Caleb," Beetle said. Caleb, who'd let his cousin push Beetle into an open grave; Caleb, who'd pulled up the rope; Caleb, who had dripped his father's smile onto all of Bridlington, and had probably done god knows what else when no one saw. "He has a grip on this town—everyone jumps when he jumps. Maybe she'll stop when he's done."

Marcela's voice got tighter. "How do you—"

"I don't!" Beetle said, exasperated. He may have been Paz's friend, but a murder spree was nothing like a laser tag birthday party or any of the things he'd done with her. Even putting cards on their bikes after the Meyer incident, to become othered and inevitable, was more symbolic than violent. He understood why she was doing it, that she really had no choice, but how did he know how the rest would play out?

Even the birds in the trees were silent.

Marcela closed her eyes as if to gather her thoughts. "She killed a girl who made everyone's life hell," she said, slowly. "She killed a racist cop. She'll kill . . ." She couldn't seem to say Caleb's name there, but tilted her head as if it would let the piece fall into place. "And you think we should just let her."

Beetle could do nothing but nod. Yes. Yes, he did. He was Paz's friend, and he was going to trust her to do what needed to be done. He was raised on a playing-card-spoked bike, where people looked away. Away from names on the playground, away from kids walking into graves, or else shoved into them.

"This is Bridlington," Beetle said. He had a stake in this place, and he believed in beaten things showing their teeth. He would never be sure if the next words were his own or Paz's through him: "*We mind our own business.*"

MARCELA

Marcela shoved everything down until her stomach burned to charcoal—and the rest of her, too.

She was going to let Caleb die, because that was easy. However, it would be harder if she had to look him in the eye and know she was going to let him be mauled to death. If that meant spending the day holed up with Beetle and Asher, then so be it. At least Beetle's house was empty. The three of them drifted there for the day, keeping a moody, jumpy distance, waiting for the night to come and for Paz to take Bird for another bloody walk. Beetle would leave town on his anticipated schedule. Asher would . . . she didn't really know what Asher's plans were, and she got the feeling he didn't either. And really, neither did she. Caleb would die, and then what?

They waited, and it felt like someone had hit slow-mo on a snuff film.

She texted her parents, sure they'd want her away from that crime scene once the police regrouped enough to start door-knocking. She texted Quinn to make sure she was okay. Quinn messaged her back a total of seventeen times, all to the effect of "oh my god Marcela are you okay I'm coming over," but Marcela knew she couldn't look Quinn in the eye.

She thought to tell Quinn how much she'd rather bunk down with her, but that seemed to be giving too much away, so she shut off her phone and shut herself in the bathroom to stare at her smudged face. When she dragged a makeup wipe over it, cakey beige peeled away to show her freckles. When her eyes cleared, all she saw was Paz.

She remembered how thin Paz had been in those final days, how she'd seemed cold and silent. There had been a month or so between Chuck's death and Paz's, where Paz ate very little and talked even less. The town had driven her to her end, and Marcela had let it happen. She'd trusted the wrong people. Made the wrong choices.

She choked back a sob, but even with her eyes squinting and tears building, she couldn't look away from the blurry image of Paz in the mirror. She thought about running, like Beetle, her and Caleb leaving town together and never looking back. She'd love him still, or try to think she did. But she knew Caleb would refuse to go with her and call her a traitor for suggesting it. She'd grovel and still end up alone.

But staying would mean always waiting for Paz to show up behind her, and that seemed even worse than being alone. She imagined how her face would look rotting in the river, and cried.

The day passed. Marcela was sitting in Beetle's desk chair, fiddling with a Tamagotchi that had only enough battery power to show the sluggish ghost of an image, when Beetle's mother came home. She seemed surprised about the two new additions to her son's room, but she didn't seem to have the energy to question. She did pull Beetle into the hall for a moment, and Marcela strained to hear the words "motel" and "captain"; what horrified her more was how low and level Beetle managed to keep his voice when he said he knew nothing about it and was sure it would all clear up soon. It would, wouldn't it?

She hated this. Every moment closer to Caleb's death felt like a step closer to some huge fire, one that was already blistering her skin up. And that made her angry, because why cry over Caleb goddamn Reilly? Why be upset for *him*?

She wasn't, not really, but she couldn't quite grab the idea in her raw hands.

Ms. Hoang regarded Asher warily, but not Marcela, who was given a familiar smile before she was offered a home-cooked dinner. The three of them drank their chicken soup ("Nothing too challenging," Ms. Hoang had called it, which seemed to be a dig at Asher) and ate mostly in silence, though Asher was tricked into admitting his only experience with Vietnamese food was "*bonn me*" at Whole Foods. That made Beetle snort. Marcela couldn't find any humor.

In both Beetle's and Asher's glasses, she just saw Paz staring back at her.

It was nearly evening when Marcela stepped out of Beetle's room, silently moved to the front door, and went to stand on the porch. Part of her wondered if she was going to sprint to Caleb's house and ruin it all. Instead she froze there, looking out over the lawn and listening to the chuffing of the sprinklers and the scrape of a group of young boys playing road hockey beneath a candy-colored sky of red and orange and purple. It seemed too quaint, like every other simple life on the block was mocking her with its normalcy.

Ms. Hoang came out after her, closing the door quietly.

"You and Beetle are friends now?" she asked, raising one eyebrow. Her voice was staccato, and yet still soft. "He said you two weren't talking."

Marcela crossed her arms tight across her chest and her shoulders drooped a bit. "Necessity thing," she said, amid the quiet clamor.

Ms. Hoang rolled her eyes a bit. "You Espino girls," she said with half a laugh, which made Marcela tense. She waited for the punch. "Always so businesslike."

It was the closest anyone had gotten to talking about Paz. Marcela didn't know what to do with it, like when a cat brings you a still-twitching mouse. She thought about Paz's face in the mirror and felt the weight of the entire mill on her shoulders.

She pried her lips apart, fought the urge to clamp them shut again on what she was about to say, and forced herself to speak, breaking six years of silence.

"What did you think of Paz?" she asked. She needed it said before she let all of this happen. She *would* let all of this happen, because that's what she was good at.

Ms. Hoang sighed but stared off down the street along with

her—two solitary pillars. "She was so good for Beetle," Ms. Hoang said. Marcela turned her head slightly to look at her out of the corner of her eye. She seemed far too genuine, smiling, small. "They all were, those three. There was just something different about them."

Marcela shifted her eyes to her shoes. "They *were* different," she said, which was a nice way of saying they would have sat alone at recess if not for each other. She swallowed. "I liked them, Paz's friends," she managed to say. "Ellie had so many of those stupid Silly Bandz, so I always thought she looked so cool. And Ben gave me his Gushers once when I was crying from something Emily said—he said he thought I was Paz, but I know that wasn't true."

"Chuck helped me with the gardening sometimes," Ms. Hoang said, just as quiet. "I always wonder . . ." She looked over to Beetle's window, and Marcela saw her eyes shine a bit. Marcela hated seeing adults cry—it felt wrong. It was why she couldn't stand to be around her own parents for too long. "I know it does no good, but I always wonder what would have happened if Ben and Ellie and your sister hadn't run away, and if Chuck had survived. I wonder if anything could be different here, or how much."

Marcela's throat constricted. She wondered too, but it did no good. She was seventeen, her boyfriend was going to die, and he had been the only thing keeping her from being just like Paz, right? Unloved. Unmissed.

"You know what they say about Espino girls?" Marcela choked out. She felt cold in the summer breeze. "They" was just the captain, but boy, had that caught on. Things could spiral out so quickly. "They say we're like dogs, 'cause we bite and don't let go." It really was dog-eat-dog out there: Marcela had taken her fill when she'd left her sister to stamp and scream, and she knew what that made her. She'd been tricked into a self-fulfilling prophecy.

Ms. Hoang grabbed her arms, firm but kind. "None of that, Marcela," she said, but Marcela couldn't look her in the eye. "This town, it's . . . small, not quick to change. You can't listen to what it says about you."

Marcela felt as if she were disintegrating. "I don't know who I am," she said, shaking her head in the hopes it would stop the tears, but it didn't. Swimming or drowning—both meant you were in the river, while people like Caleb watched from the banks. "I've just been trying not to be Paz and now—and *now*—"

Marcela fought for air, racked by wave after wave of sobs. Ms. Hoang hugged her, and Marcela collapsed to put her face in the woman's shoulder. Marcela had never cried in front of her own mother, and now she felt protected in a way she'd never been before, not even with Caleb.

The truth was, she'd always been waiting for Caleb to hurt her, and apparently he already had, without her knowing.

"I let Paz go." Marcela couldn't breathe. "I heard her get up the night Chuck died and I didn't stop—I didn't stop her because I thought she was just going to get me in trouble. And she told me—told me she was going out when she . . ."—*died*—"ran away, and I let her go, again."

Ms. Hoang breathed in. "I saw Chuck that night too," she said. She was nearly crying too. "So if you think it was all your fault, then at least know . . . that's two of us. There were so many things wrong, Marcela. So many things."

Marcela cried and cried. And Ms. Hoang cried too. They stood there together, each feeling hollow and horrible, like the worst people in the world. There was comfort in being two of the worst people, but it wasn't much. And it was only Marcela who knew that those mistakes had gotten bigger and bigger and would end in carnage and punishment that had gone on far too long to stop.

Or so she thought. The sun set behind the mountain range of cul-de-sac roofs, and the street lamps came on.

ASHER

A sher was brooding in the corner. He was feeling less like punching something now that he was well fed, but dinner had only given him the energy required to sulk and huff, not to plan. He still had very little idea where he would go from here. Run, like Beetle? Staying seemed nearly impossible, especially if it ever came out that Bird was the one who killed Caleb, as he was sure it would. Two mauling deaths in a family was coincidence, three would be a pattern, and then what?

The longer he looked at it, the more ludicrous it seemed to let this just happen. At the same time, the longer they sat waiting, the harder it seemed to stop. Asher figured that was how most problems were, and his stomach made a dull, self-sorry flip.

A bundle of fabric hit him in the face. He scraped it away angrily and looked up to see Beetle standing next to his closet, having presumably just pulled out whatever item had been thrown at him.

"It's big on me, so it'll be huge on you," Beetle said with

flat-toned diplomacy. "You slept in your binder, and it's definitely been more than eight hours. That's two strikes."

Only then did Asher realize Beetle had thrown a button-up shirt at him, XXL. He'd be swimming in it.

"It's pink," Asher stated.

"Vertical stripes hide your chest. You're gonna collapse your ribs if you keep going like you are," Beetle told him pointedly. Asher had noticed Beetle leave and take his binder off earlier in the day—he had an alarm on his phone for it, which was so strange. Beetle had resorted to wearing a baggy shirt that did nothing to hide anything. He didn't seem to care, which made Asher even more unfairly frustrated. "And you could wash your binder, too, before you get some sort of infection."

"I can wash my own clothes," Asher said, teeth tight together.

Beetle didn't even look at him. "You don't seem like the kind of person who would fare well if someone saw his binder at the laundromat, egg."

Asher had no idea what "egg" meant, but suspected it was a little patronizing.

It was. Beetle knew that while Asher was certainly aware he was a man, he clearly had no idea what kind of man he wanted to be. Beetle might have had a lot of issues, but he'd never had much of a problem being himself.

"Why are you being nice?" Asher asked. "I don't want to be your friend or anything."

Beetle hid the lurch in his shoulders. "All right, dude," he said, and drew the last word out so he sounded like the kind of person who would also say things like "bruh" and "YOLO," which Asher had been known to do.

Asher knew he was being mocked. "Turn around," he said, preparing to change, and Beetle sat down on his bed and faced the headboard. There was a poster there (fifty generic bugs—it would have wigged Asher out if he had to sleep under so many twitchy little limbs) and Beetle stared at it.

For just a moment, Asher looked at the profile of Beetle's suddenly younger-looking face, carved by a thin shine of gold street lamp light coming in through the window. Asher stared at Beetle's flashy glasses, at a forelock of pink that fell down between his eyes and how it tangled up into baby blue, and pastel pink, and seafoam green. But more than that, he looked at how Beetle didn't hunch in over his chest like Asher always did.

He felt something light on fire within his crunched-in ribs. Envy, he realized, and hated the feeling.

He clawed off his hoodie and struggled out of his binder, feeling it bunch against his sweaty skin and peel away like a scab. The open air stabbed at his back like needles. He didn't look up into the full-length mirror of the closet door. He pulled the new shirt on and let it swallow him whole before he adopted the position: shoulders forward and hands in his jeans pockets so that the shirt bypassed his chest entirely. He nudged his sunglasses with his shoulder, adjusting them to sit straighter.

"You good?" Beetle asked.

No. Yes. Asher didn't know. It had gone on too long to think about.

"Sure," Asher conceded. He spun around, and Beetle turned.

They looked at each other for a moment, and Asher thought the silence was too much. He threw his arms out. "Do I look like you'd beat me up or what?" he said. He tottered his weight back and forth from one stiff leg to the other, looking like some sort of deranged carnival target. "Wanna punch me again?" It was trying to be a joke, but without any of Asher's usual faked confidence.

"I'm not sorry for that," Beetle said. He looked at Asher longer, and Asher scrambled back to his bell-ringer hunch. "You were being a man-baby."

Asher thought that was almost fair. He did regret kicking his door, a bit. His knee ached at the joint, and he had the cheek bruise throbbing like penance.

"Does it feel okay?" Beetle asked.

Asher shrugged.

"You really can't wear it too long. I know this one trans guy who—"

The word sent something sparking through Asher's brain like a cattle prod. "I'm not—" he started to say, but knew that wasn't right. "I don't really like . . ." He tried to pull on his Caleb Reilly face, but he felt too small and decidedly too pink to do it. Which he knew was ignorant. Before Bridlington, he would have adamantly reminded people that gendered colors were a social construct or whatever, but it was hard to stick to your morals when you'd taken a swan dive off the poverty line. "I'm not out or anything. Like, I'm *out*, like I'm—" he gestured haphazardly to his entire body, "but . . ."

"Stealth," Beetle said, and Asher blinked at him. Another word he didn't know. He'd never met another trans person

243

outside glimpses on Tumblr, and even then he'd always been too terrified to go closer to the people who knew more. Beetle shook his head. "Like . . . you're trans, but you don't let people know you're trans."

Yeah. Because what a great pillar of his community he was, homeless in his car and angry and envious and hurting. Asher sighed and flung himself on the floor to sit against Beetle's bed, pulling his black hoodie into his lap. He stared down at it through his sunglasses. "I'm a guy," he said, like he had to state it. "No one has to know the rest."

Beetle sniffed. "Sometimes I don't want people to know about me either," he admitted.

"But you don't care," Asher said, thinking of Beetle with his shirt always open over his binder and the hair that practically screamed *something gender-y is happening here*, which was commendable. "If people see . . . you know."

"Everyone here already knows," Beetle said. He slid off the bed to sit beside Asher on the floor. He did it carefully, warily. Knowing Bridlington as he did, Asher figured Beetle hadn't gotten to talk about this in a while. "So I might as well look how I want. I don't think anyone knows you're trans."

Asher rolled his eyes, smiling with his tongue stabbing angrily into his cheek. "Good," he said. He leaned his head backwards. "When are you leaving?"

"A week, I guess," Beetle said at a crackling whisper. His room was unchanged since he was twelve, and it really felt like some eleven-year-old friends could walk in at any moment. "I can get into student housing."

Asher hummed. "That bodes well for me," he said, twitching out a bit of a smile. "You can take my dirty little secret out of here."

Beetle's shoulders tightened. "It's not dirty for you to be—"

"Not that," Asher said, quickly, like he almost regretted insinuating it. And maybe he did. Maybe it was nice to get to talk so openly. Maybe Beetle wasn't a total asshole. "I mean Bird. I shouldn't have left him and I . . ." He looked at his sweaty hands. "God, we all screwed this up so bad."

"Yeah," Beetle breathed.

Asher shouldn't have asked it. He knew it was going to bring more questions than answers, more hurt than comfort, but he wrenched it up anyway. "Do you think there's anything we can do to stop it?"

Beetle opened his mouth, closed it, and closed his eyes when he tried again. "I don't want to," he said, quiet. "I used to think Paz's 'monster hunt' was useless, but something's gotta give. Maybe this is the wake-up call we all need."

Asher didn't know what to say to that. Beetle might be right. And he was, technically. They just hadn't quite gotten there yet.

Asher sat in Beetle's shirt thinking about the staccato clarity of his voice and how he looked a bit like a freak but in the best sort of way, and Beetle sat staring at the sliver of Asher's eye he was allowed, underlined by his thrown punch. The two of them said nothing and did nothing either. Because the fact remained that they were both lonely kids who had suddenly found someone else on the island, and neither wanted to mess it up. Asher wanted to keep not-hating himself, and Beetle wanted to believe good things could happen in shitty old Bridlington.

If they followed the easiest path to the end, let Paz go about her business that night while they minded their own, Beetle would see Bridlington burning on the evening news, and Asher would be slaughtered across someone's lawn. There would be no happy ending for anyone. Because no one would know why they were hunted, no one would have a chance to fix their mistakes, and nothing would get better.

But, in the best ending, Asher would grow up into a right and proper freak of the highest caliber, and he'd be proud of it. And Beetle would think Asher was not-so-annoying with his plastic pink gauge earrings and sauntering walk and (thank god) clothes that weren't hoodies. But that was the best ending, one that forced them to be wholly brave and grow larger than they were. To split from their skin like cicadas seeking the sun.

Beetle looked at Asher and wished for no more scared kids.

He kissed Asher's cheek, very quickly, and then choked out that he was going to go brush his teeth. He raced out the door. It was so fast it almost hadn't happened at all.

Asher sat alone in the room, staring after the door as it swung shut. His face was red-hot behind his sunglasses, his cheek hummed with the bruise and the brush of lips against it, and he only now realized that he was okay with that kiss. He was really okay with it, and almost began to sit forward as if to follow.

But then, instead of feeling happy or even embarrassed, he could only think about just how much he didn't feel like Caleb Reilly. The knowledge hit him with the force of another punch, landing him seated again, knowing that this wasn't some dream world where everyone got to be who they wanted to be. Asher

Gordon wasn't just unhoused, but unhoused and trans. Not just unhoused and trans, but unhoused, trans, and *that g-word I don't wanna think about.* And what good ever happened to kids like that?

He felt his chest itching irritably, felt the skin at his jaw prickling. He had been sitting with his legs open, but he pulled his knees up fast, scared it was obvious that the only thing in his pants were two socks safety-pinned into his boxers. He felt like a kid playing dress-up, like a fraud.

The monster was clawing at Asher, nails raking down his chest, telling him how he needed to be if he was going to survive this town. How it didn't matter if Beetle made him feel all right—no one else would, and Beetle was leaving anyway. How Bird was going to kill Caleb. It all felt too big to move or change or worry about. And yet he wanted to. And yet he did.

Asher closed his eyes tight, and the monster told him there was a way to stop hurting, and it was as easy as falling asleep.

THE MEYERS

When darkness fell and every house became its own fortress, Paz and her crew scoped out the Reilly home. Though they saw Caleb looking at them from his lit-up bedroom (Ben and Chuck made faces at him, and Ellie dramatically presented Bird so Caleb would know just what he was in for), the only way in would be to smash through the kitchen's picture window. Mrs. Reilly was making herself a tea in there, staring, numb, into her mug—they'd have to deal with her first if they wanted to get to Caleb.

Paz debated this. Sure, Mrs. Reilly had never pulled up the rope or been mean on the playground like her son or niece, and sure, she hadn't locked Paz in a cell and called her a dog and said she was very badly parented and also carried a gun and ran the town. Sure, she was a very sweet lady who brought pies to the church bake sale, but Paz knew two other people who did that, and they would be visited that night. Mrs. Reilly was, after all, a Reilly, and she had minded her business while Paz and her friends died.

As the entire town had done.

It was decided that if she got in the way when they came back, she'd go down with her son. Bridlington would have to start making choices. It was time for fearless people to be scared too.

And on that note, they put a pin in Caleb, and all kicked off again to pedal south.

The crew rode out of the cute little neighborhood and past Main, weaving through the houses and finally out to the southern roads, where the rushing of cornstalks whispered like ghosts. Ben and Ellie took the lead, bumping off the main road and onto a dark lane lined with little lawn ornaments: tin windmills like bike wheels and stone angels smiling sweetly. Paz and Chuck rode behind them, one straight line of four children and a dog bounding after them. Ben's star necklace gleamed on his bike handles, and it would have been visible for a second to anyone who was paying any attention at all. No one was, as per usual.

Paz had no reservations about this one. They approached the Meyers' porch, where the pie had been thrown like a declaration of war, and none of them were frightened.

They went to the back of the house and dropped their bikes near the derelict doghouses. Ben shook out his blue-tinged hands and turned to Ellie. She smiled from under her too-dry hair. He smiled back with missing front teeth. They bumped fists, and then tangled their fingers together. Bird nudged the broken screen door open enough for the four children to weave into the linoleum kitchen, where Bird's claws made jaunty clicking sounds. The lot of them slipped past the old rotary phone, the kitchen table with fresh-cut flowers in the center, and turned down the narrow hall. There was a cross up there, and it stared down.

The door to the master bedroom was open, almost like an invitation.

///\\\//\\\//\\\//\\\//\\\//\\\//\\\

Mrs. Meyer was sleeping soundly until some dusty smell sheared through her sinuses. Her sniffling cough might not have been enough to wake her entirely, but there also came a harsh, gold-orange light. She only had time to blink at the black silhouette standing beside her bed like a reaper.

"Mummy?"

She sat up and turned sharply, hawk-like. A curly-haired boy was sitting on the end of the bed, with an arm-slung girl next to him, hand in hand. She didn't feel them there; the bed hadn't sunk. She blinked, and her Ben and Ellie were smooth-cheeked and bright-eyed. Mrs. Meyer was still half asleep and thought to wake her husband, tell him those two who ran away were finally home. They had both been clumsy and never listened, but she was a fine Christian woman who loved them enough to correct it, and now they could catch up on six years of misbehaving.

Then it suddenly hit her: it had been six years since Ben and Ellie ran away. And yet Ellie's hair was still as straight as if she'd just left the salon, and she'd always paid good money for that. Both were still scrawny and obviously eleven, silver and bronze in the moonlight.

"We came back, Mummy," Ellie said. She started to smile.

She looked at her dear sainted parents; she let her alive-face melt away slowly. "Isn't it good to see us?"

Mrs. Meyer watched Ben and Ellie's clothes turn wet and see-through, revealing splotchy bruises. She watched their skin suck in, turn gray, carve shadows into their once youthful faces. She smelled dust and blood, and a patch of water was dripping onto the floor where someone else was standing, cloaked in shadow so Mrs. Meyer could see only a grim frown. She heard something starting to growl, louder, and snap like it was laughing, but she couldn't see it over the foot of the bed.

Mrs. Meyer numbly flapped her hand into her husband's shoulder.

Mr. Meyer woke, blinked toward his wife's shaking figure, and then followed her gaping mouth and trembling hand. He sat up to see Ben's grinning mouth and those two missing teeth. The boy had nicked the good knife—that was Paz teaching him to disobey his parents. Mr. Meyer heard a dull *pop* and watched Ellie's arm shift under her too-tight skin, hanging dislocated. He had only grabbed her to stop her from leaving; it was the consequence of still chumming with a girl like Paz Espino, who shouldn't be trusted around normal little girls like dear, impressionable Ellie.

Had they survived that night, the Meyers would have maintained that they didn't kill those children. Obviously, the children had starved to death, from the way their ribs showed under their sweat-soaked clothes. They had not starved them. They had not murdered them.

You can believe that too.

"Get 'em, Bird." Ellie smiled, and the last thing either Meyer saw was a great mass of teeth and cherry-red eyes as the creature leapt between the ghosts of their old foster children and feasted.

MARCELA

Marcela had fallen asleep in a sleeping bag on the floor, Asher next to her, Beetle in his bed. She had been sleeping drearily but deeply; that is, until a pounding from somewhere in the house lurched her awake. The room was completely dark, but in that stillness she realized that the pounding was someone knocking on the front door. She clicked her phone screen (12:56 a.m., and many notifications) and shone the light around.

It took Marcela all of two seconds to realize that: a) Asher's sleeping bag next to hers was empty, aside from a mess of pink fabric; b) Beetle was sitting bolt upright with his eyes wide, stuck in one of his freaky trances with his hair sleep-mussed and his glasses off; and c) someone was knocking on the door loudly enough to wake the whole street. Marcela looked at her phone screen again.

Reece: *Yo, weird message from Asher—*

Quinn: *Caleb left me a scary text—*

Quinn, on Facebook Messenger now: *Cela, I'm really worried—*

The knocking echoed through the house. She looked up and saw Beetle snapped out of his trance. He and Marcela stared at each other in the dark, and both looked down to Asher's empty sleeping bag, while the front doorknob rattled like someone was trying to get in.

"*Asher*," Marcela said, like a curse, and tore into the hall with Beetle just behind her.

Ms. Hoang was bustling from her room with quite a lot of angry muttering, presumably about how late at night it was to be knocking like that. Marcela dove ahead while Beetle shoved on his glasses and stammered a very rushed, "It's okay—Má, go đi ngủ. It's no one—Không có ai—It's just my bạn—Asher locked himself out."

While Beetle successfully coaxed his mother back to bed, Marcela flipped the lock and wrenched open the door to a rush of slightly chilled night air. What was Asher doing outside, especially when Paz would be prowling? "Asher, what the hell—"

She stopped dead.

Someone was on Beetle's front porch, trembling, with sweat dripping down his face and a stripe of blood swished across one cheek. His eyes were wide, his mouth slack, his knees shaking. Marcela's mouth hung open.

Beetle flicked on the porch lights, but Marcela had already known that the hulking shadow wasn't scrawny Asher. Now the humming bulb showed the grim face of Bridlington's own Caleb Reilly.

Marcela felt anger rip through her. Her hair fell past her shoulders in loose waves, she had bare feet, Quinn's flannel, no makeup, and a hard-pressed, copper-faced sneer. She was not the girl he'd known since they were ten. She was ready to shove him back, lock the door, and let Paz have at him.

"Mar," he muttered. His lips shook; his face was stone-white except for that horrifying bit of blood. Instinctually, with terror, she knew it wasn't his. "I'm so sorry." His knees gave out and he half collapsed on the welcome mat. She watched the Reilly man cry himself hoarse, managing half-formed apologies for ropes and dogs and perfect towns.

Paz had turned the tide on Caleb, and it was time to swim.

BEETLE

Though it was a convincing lie to send his mother back to bed, Beetle had known it wasn't Asher frantically banging at their front door in the middle of the night. He knew what had happened, how this mess of a Reilly man had ended up on his doorstep, scared into apologies.

And he knew that Asher was already half dead.

Through Paz's eyes, Beetle had watched the past half hour go like this:

After the Meyers, Paz and her crew rode back into town. Every house was a silent, grinning skull of dark windows and closed garages. The air smelled like watered lawns and cherries and blood and dead kids. Yes, it smelled like dead kids. Beetle smelled it in his room, staring wide-eyed at his door with his mouth hanging open. He tasted the cherry slushy while Chuck sipped, and couldn't stop or close his eyes.

Look away if you dare, Bridlington. If Paz and her crew remind you of anyone close, remind you of things you forgot or didn't listen to, or responsibilities you shoved onto too-young shoulders, then you can stop reading here . . . but it won't stop anything. What's done is already happening, in towns like this and towns like yours.

Who are you tied to by childhood pacts?

Paz pedaled with all her fury, cold in the whip of the breeze, water spraying off behind her and being replaced by more. She coughed out a mouthful of it along with a leaf and two dead bugs, and rode with storm-drain runoff dripping down her graying face. She tried to blink it away for her alive-face but couldn't. She felt too cold and wrong for an alive-thing. Bird galloped alongside her, wearing a coat of blood and spongy tissue.

Paz turned onto the Reillys' street and she and her crew tore forward in a rattling of cards in their spokes. Paz was so, so brave, always and constantly and without falter, forever and ever, amen. She hadn't been scared to face the monster in the tunnels or to go on alone without Ellie and Ben, and she hadn't been scared a day in her life on the playground or in that holding cell with Captain Reilly.

Paz Espino was never scared, according to all the town. That's what the people who ignored her chose to believe. But Beetle's own face was wet with tears that were hidden on her already-wet face, and he knew otherwise.

They stopped their bikes in front of the Reilly house, at the end of the street near the gorge. Bird was already bristling, staring at the dark picture window with a quivering nose and glinting red eyes. He growled slowly, like a question, huffing and threatening to bark. Paz started forward: Caleb was only a pane of glass and maybe a flimsy door away, and she might not get a better chance. It was the closest moment to perfection, and if Mrs. Reilly woke up and got in the way, then *fine*.

Paz wouldn't have to make that call.

Before Paz could go through with her plan, the Reillys' front door flew open, followed by a *ka-chunk* sound she didn't recognize until she turned and her soaked heart tripped.

Paz saw Caleb Reilly, huge, with his partridge-hunting shotgun pointed right at Bird and a shell punched into the chamber. Paz's throat constricted—Bird was flesh and blood and could be killed, and then how would they finish their mission?

"Call it off," Caleb said. One tear slipped down his hard cheek, but that was all. His words were steady and rumbling, his stance set. "I'm not afraid to end this here, Paz. For the town."

For the town. Of course, for the town. She put her hands in her pockets and forced herself to feign confidence and composure and everything else she'd had when she lived. "What are Espino girls, Caleb?" she asked him. Bird snapped and stalked forward. His shoulders moved under his skin like shark fins, flaking half-dried blood off onto the neat stone walkway.

"Call it off!" Caleb almost shouted, but then he hushed his voice. Paz knew he didn't want to bring the neighbors out to see him talking to no one but a rabid-looking dog.

"I can get another dog," Paz said. Bird took another step. "I'm going to kill the monster, Caleb. And that means you."

"I'm not!" Caleb squeaked. "I was just a kid."

"So were we," Paz said, sharp. Her bones slid all waterlogged and wrong when she stepped forward from the group, who watched with avid attention. "But you're not anymore."

Bird was a few paws from the steps up to Caleb's door. His nose quivered and his teeth gleamed. Chuck sipped the slushy with the maddening sound of a drink on the dregs. Bird snarled louder. Ellie and Ben giggled. Crickets thrummed.

Paz whistled sharply between her teeth, and Bird leapt.

Caleb tried to pull the trigger—but a gangly figure in hyper-masculine black jumped between him and the creature and was tackled to the ground in a spray of blood. One drop swished across Caleb's face. His aim stuttered down.

Through Paz, Beetle watched in horror as Bird ripped his claws across Asher Gordon's chest, snapped at his face. They could both hear Asher screaming, trying to speak, the words "It's okay" bleeding from him, his red-slick hands fumbling over his dog as it lunged for his neck. He looked like he was pushing him off, but trying to hug him, too. "I'm sorry, Bird—I'm sorry, boy—a drive—let's go for a—"

But Bird didn't seem to hear him. And one apology was not going to fix this.

ASHER AND
BRIDLINGTON

A sher screamed and everything flashed red and bright behind his eyes. This was not the end he'd had in mind when he'd crept past Beetle and Marcela, fallen into anxious sleep.

He'd gone into the cold washroom and pulled his binder back on over his chafed-red skin, even though it pressed splint-sharp pain through his ribs and bruised against his organs. His eyes were wet with tears, but his jaw was tight. He let the smooth fabric of the Under Armour hoodie fall back over him and pushed a hand over his chest. Flat. He stared into the mirror and a very loud part of him still wished—wished against his real face in there and a home-cooked dinner and Beetle, oh yes, even against Beetle, who was sweet with an edge and didn't hate himself for being trans or liking boys and who almost made Asher feel that way too—wished against everything to be Caleb Reilly. To be the kind of person who fit into

Bridlington, or anywhere, really. He was an actor not for the applause but for survival.

The monster was swimming in his chest and in his small hands, the shape of his eyebrows and thin wrists, in every inch of his five-foot-two frame. But especially behind his eyes. He put on his sunglasses and left the bathroom, tiptoeing past Ms. Hoang's closed bedroom door and to the front door, grabbing the lanyard with the house key and silently locking the door behind him before dropping it into the mailbox.

He was going to fix this, somehow.

Asher sat on the porch and opened Snapchat, hoping the one name he mostly recognized would still be awake. Lo and behold, a shirtless Reece appeared on the screen. No time to think on that.

Where duz Caleb live? Asher asked, with the camera blocked so it was nothing but black. *Said he'd let me stay over.*

Reece was more than happy to comply. And the address for the Reilly house wasn't far, according to Google Maps. Asher could walk that, or rather sprint it. Paz and her crew could be on their way already.

Despite his tight chest and his aching ribs and exhaustion, and with thanks to some proper food in his body, he took off as fast as he could, like Beetle on his nightly run to avoid the dark.

He arrived barely in time. He didn't even see Paz and the others—only Caleb pointing a gun at his dog. Bird. The entire world was Bird: covered in blood, snarling, and ready to leap. His stupid, damn dog.

The monster screamed at Asher to let it go, let it all happen, shut up, turn around, walk away, be selfish and ignore it all.

Asher made a thin whining sound and fought it. Not for Caleb Reilly holding that large gun with his stance tight and strong. Not even for Asher himself as some sort of feat of macho bravery. Maybe he didn't want to be macho-brave; maybe that was tiring.

It was too late for apologies to his only friend, but he could try and act, even if he tried alone.

"Bird," he said, and he saw one of Bird's ears twitch, but only that. Asher's chest felt like it was made of lead, and his mouth was so dry and coarse he could have lit matches on his tongue. "Stay."

But it was too late for that, and maybe he had known it while he was running. That rules went out the window in desperate times.

So when his dog leapt for Caleb, Asher did too, and inserted himself between them. The collision sent his sunglasses flying from his face. It was all he could do to try and hold Bird. His claws raked through Asher's tried-and-true hoodie, his teeth grabbed it and shook his Boy like a rag doll, but Asher's thoughts were all about how he would try to make it right. How it was his fault, and they'd go for a drive when it was over. They'd go find some good food or a dog park. He'd make it up to Bird. He'd be better. He'd try to fix this. He'd try.

He tried to say it all to Bird, but the blood loss was too much.

He'd never make good on the drive or the dog park. But that was okay.

He understood it wasn't Bird's fault, and he made peace with this.

//∧∨∧∨∧∨∧∨∧∨∧\\

As Asher collapsed and was torn to bits, Beetle felt Paz's mind turn to a livid flurry.

Asher sobbed when Bird jerked him onto the sidewalk by his ankle, snapping the bones there and letting his foot hang crooked and mangled. No no *no!* This wasn't who was supposed to die! But he *did* have the monster in him—Paz had felt it the night before, when he'd left Bird to fend for himself, starving and alone. Did it matter that he was trying to fix things now? Apologies don't fix anything, right? But she had felt a kind of kinship with Asher, weirdo to weirdo.

A light flicked on down the road, washing the street in yellow. Both Paz and Caleb turned to see another light turn on, and another, alerted by the screaming.

Paz looked to Caleb. "You're not off the hook," she said, but she wasn't getting at him with that gun out, and now there was Asher to account for. She'd work with it. She *had* to.

She and her crew grabbed their bikes and rattled past the Reillys' lawn and across the small road beside the gorge. Paz looked back to see Bird following, dragging Asher behind them by the ankle until the tendons snapped and he passed out. Bird readjusted, chomping into his shoulder with Asher's head lolling into his neck, and kept on pulling. Bird was more fluff than muscle, but Asher was thin.

Paz faced forward again and led the charge through the blurry storm-drain water in her eyes. Her face was sliding more and more, less bright-cheeked and alive and more drowned and dead. Finish the plan. Kill the monster. Justice was very simple. Very simple indeed.

Put down the dogs, she thought, and shivered.

Caleb Reilly stood in stunned silence, watching the lights of neighbors flick on up and down the street. He held his breath, closed his stunned mouth, and swallowed hard. This was Bridlington, and maybe it wasn't always perfect, but it was a town that would protect you if you protected it. If you kept it happy, you'd get everything you wanted. People would come check on him, or call the cops, or *something*.

But he realized with mounting horror that he did know Bridlington, deep down, and people here minded their own business: surely the screaming was some joke, or else someone else would have called the cops—no need to inundate the department. Caleb Reilly had never been the one screaming for help. Now that he was, now that *he* was the one needing people to get off their asses and believe him, he saw the town the way Paz did.

It really was full of monsters.

One by one, the lights flicked off, and Bridlington went back to sleep.

The town was broken, and he didn't know how to fix it. His world was shattering apart.

Caleb Reilly looked at the long, smooth barrel of his shotgun. He thought about how clean and simple it seemed against the mess of blood where that Asher kid had been gored by his own dog. He thought about how easy life was when he was drunk, and the fantastic moment when his car wrapped around that tree. He thought about pulling up the rope, and every playground taunt he had thrown as a kid before he'd learned to hold the monster in a quiet, Bridlington way.

He realized the town was silent, and his father had let it be so, and his father's father, and his father's father's father. And trying to break that (if that was even what he wanted, which he wasn't sure) would mean severing himself from every other Reilly man. Caleb knew it would have been simpler to die right there.

But simple wasn't okay. Not anymore.

PAZ

Paz swore there were good guys and there were bad guys and there were people who had the monster and people who died from the monster, and no one changed. Not ever. They'd gone under the guardrail and down the gorge and through the treacherous current, and now she watched Bird drag Asher up onto the muddy bank. The four children stared down at him while he spluttered up mouthfuls of bloody water.

"P-Paz," Asher breathed, semiconscious now. "Paz, stop. T-talk to me. L-l-let's t-t-*talk*."

She saw the monster rippling through him, but in the form of self-hatred and self-preservation. Could she fault him for that? And if she let Asher off the hook, then did she have to forgive Marcela turning on her and choosing Caleb for the same reasons? Where did the line get drawn?

"No one looked out for you," Paz told him, numb. She gritted her teeth, *hard*, like her jaw might stay that way forever. "They won't come for you."

"They didn't come for us," Ben said, shaking his hands. Chuck nodded over and over.

"They made us hunt the monster ourselves," Ellie said.

But when Paz looked at her three friends, she saw the moonlight through them, like they were fading. No. No no no. Ben and Ellie had taken out the Meyers, and Chuck was part of the gang . . . were those the only reasons they were allowed to stay here? Were their tethers snapping now? It was all ending.

"We can f-find . . ." Asher tried to say. He was drifting off again. "All—all of us . . . try to . . ."

"Shut up," Paz said, not unkindly, though her blood crackled and told her to kill him then and there. A dog that bites once will bite again. A town never changes. "The town left you."

She couldn't know, but Asher didn't quite believe her then. *Beetle, Marcela*, he thought, out into the ether. He didn't feel alone, just unlucky. *Help me out, dudes. Lend me a hand—I'm drowning here.* His vision faded, then darkened, and Paz watched him slip away with a little more finality this time, looking almost peaceful.

Bird dragged him into the mill after Paz, and one by one they all leapt down the drop chute. For the ghosts, it was nothing, even though Paz had to pat Chuck's shoulder a few times before he had the guts to jump. Ellie and Ben cannonballed in and went rolling over the floor, laughing and scattering the rats below, who were sniffing at the grizzled bones pulled all about the basement. As for Asher, he landed with a horrible thud like a body bag being tossed, and Bird was only spared the same fate because he landed *on* Asher.

Paz listened to them, the echoing sound of the slurped slushy and Ellie singing about "Go Go Power *Rangers*" while Chuck whooped and clapped. She stared up at the pit, the rope still dangling.

"Asher's coming with us," she said to Beetle way, way out there. This was it: no more forgiving. If there'd have to be a line drawn, then Paz would rather smudge it out. "He'll die down here like we did, and then you'd better start running, because we're gonna get you next."

BEETLE AND MARCELA

Beetle had really convinced himself that he wanted no part in any of this, but that night's blood oiled the gears in his head: Asher, fumbling apologies to his dog; Caleb, sobbing on his doormat. Whatever it all meant, something felt different. Not in the town, but in Beetle. He didn't feel chitin-shelled or like a too-small boy in a too-big mason jar.

And now they were all outside on the porch, and he had to decide what to do with this difference.

"Asher's not even from here and he tried to stop this," he told Marcela and Caleb. Caleb was curled up against Beetle's closed front door, Marcela leaned into the railing of the porch as far away from her technically-still-boyfriend as she could get, but Beetle was pacing across the path up through his lawn. His usual simmering anger was trying to spin itself down, thread into logic. "We all messed up, and now Asher's paying for it."

They were silent. Marcela chewed a little at her lip, squinting out past Beetle. "What changed your mind? You said she just killed the Meyers—don't tell me *that's* what's making you regret this?" She was stone-faced in the small bit of porch light. The next part was an accusation, because she knew, like so many others probably knew. "Ellie had a sling when she died. I heard Ben was missing teeth."

Beetle's eyes were hard. "They'd have been split up if anyone found out," he said. It was why Ben couldn't tell Captain Reilly, and why Paz was branded a liar. He hated that he saw some of the blood as justified. He figured he shouldn't, but he was too human not to. "That's not what's changing my mind, it really isn't." He swallowed, and looked to the wreck that was Caleb choking back sobs.

Marcela seemed to know what he was thinking. "It won't end with Caleb," she said. She seemed to be trying to make the pieces go together, squinting, with her lip wobbling, her voice turning shrill and afraid. "The town's crooked anyway, and it might not get better just because Captain Reilly is gone. We could let her keep going."

"You want that for her?" Beetle asked slowly.

Marcela wanted to fume, but she only stared hard at him. She wanted to say "Is it still her?" Because, was it truly? And could you feel bad for putting this weight on an eleven-year-old if the eleven-year-old was already dead? What more was there to steal from her? It's not like she'd be depriving her sister of soccer games and Disney World or whatever.

Did Paz ever really get to enjoy those when she lived?

Marcela took a pinched breath. She loved her sister. It was that horrible mix of envy for Paz's muddy knees and close friends, and resentment that Paz had attention when Marcela had resigned herself to none. And yet it was love. Maybe Marcela didn't love her own face in that mirror, still felt like a kicked dog, but Paz . . . what would you have looked like at seventeen? What could this town have been if you were here? Marcela wondered what futures had been lost with Paz gone.

She wondered what futures might be lost if they let Caleb die, considering this asshole had the love and trust of the entire town and was seemingly ready to jump when they told him to. She didn't know how long it would last—maybe it was only the shock of realizing he might die too—but even temporary solidarity could be used for something.

"I don't want everything to be like this forever," Marcela said, low and quiet. She surprised herself with it, almost stopped, but kept going. "I want room for us."

There was a pause where no one spoke, and all they heard was the thrumming of crickets and street lamps.

Caleb had quieted in his sobbing, so that they had forgotten he was there. "I hope it can," he said suddenly. Both Beetle and Marcela looked at him peering up from the shelter of his arms, eyes red-rimmed. "I thought it was the right thing to do, keeping everything quiet. I thought she was bad . . . but she was just a kid—" He stopped himself on the edge of hysterics, grinding his knuckles into his eyes. "If I make it out of this tonight, I . . ." He stopped there, as if he had suddenly come up on the end of his plan.

How the hell did you make this right?

"I don't know how to fix this yet," Marcela said. If she said what she was thinking to say, she could never go back to being a Reilly girl. She didn't know what she'd be instead, but that felt like cliff-diving. Dangerous, sure, but exhilarating. "But I don't think I want to talk to you any more after this. The rope, Caleb. I need space to figure that out. But for tonight . . ." It was a horribly big step, but she'd try. "We need to get down there. To talk to her."

"Talk to her," Beetle repeated, like he was thinking it over. His face was draining of color, as though his resolve was fading. "You think we can get her to stop?"

Marcela looked away down the road, chewing on her cheek. She said nothing.

Caleb swallowed like it physically pained him. "Okay," he relented, shaking his head and raising both hands. "Fuck it, *fine*. Fine. If a bunch of grade sixes had the guts to go down there, then what's one possessed mutt?"

Marcela looked to Beetle, who was standing stiff and awkward and looking at Caleb like he might run over and kick him. Might get even after all these years. Marcela thought he'd be justified if he did, but they were older and knew it wouldn't end when the bruise healed. This was unfortunately larger than the three of them.

So, on with it.

Beetle left a note inside for his mom, and the three of them ran out of the neighborhood. No bikes with bone-white-blood-red playing cards in the spokes. No slushies. No kiddie weapons, no proper flashlights; instead, Marcela's and Beetle's phones stuck in their front pockets with the lights on, Caleb holding his. They were too old to be ninjas or believe in monsters in a slimy, real way. But they believed in scared people doing what scared people do, and believed they could maybe stop it. They followed the exact path Chuck Warren took on his bike six years ago. They went down the trail toward the gorge, under the fence, and down the side of Blue River.

All too soon, they approached the dark specter of the old mill. Beetle saw a gleaming trail of scarlet slathered on the rocks and cement, leading from the river and up to the loose board over the window where the bloody body of Asher had been dragged in. Paz wasn't counting on anyone coming after him. Maybe this would prove they had changed.

Marcela swallowed and walked forward first. She was wearing a pair of Ms. Hoang's running shoes. With Blue River rushing in their ears and the moon covered in clouds, Paz's twin locked her fingers around the final board over the window. She was a silver outline with the light from her phone diffused and pink-orange through Quinn's flannel. She gave the board a solid yank and it fell away to clatter onto the rocks, with a puff of dust swarming around her face and into her hair.

Marcela climbed in first, seemingly fearless, with Caleb following. By the time Beetle went into the mill for the second time that summer, Marcela was already descending the rope to find her sister like she should have done before. Caleb followed.

Beetle did not.

Their phone lights disappeared into the black. Beetle Hoang crouched with his fingers jagged on the edge of the pit, staring into the smell of blood and the sound of breathing. He heard the crickets, a maddening fury, and his head was a riptide of memories and mud and pain and fear. He was still going to run. Marcela and Caleb could fix the town—they'd always wanted to stay—but he was made to leave, and never promised he wouldn't.

He could leave earlier than intended. Drop the rope right here and leave everyone *including* Paz to pace and suffer down there. Marcela and Caleb would be trapped, surely without cell service. The town wouldn't really know what happened, but it would no longer be stalked. And he could leave without ever having to face the terrible dark and everything he'd done wrong.

Can you run fast in those checkerboard Vans? Can you be a superhero in those?

Beetle took a deep breath of the bubbly, blood-smelling air.

He didn't want to be angry and scared forever. He didn't want to be driven from this town. If he was going to go to Harville, it was going to be his choice.

And as he decided to climb down to finish this properly, he swore he felt the ghost of a pebble-shaped, owl-eyed little kid watching him. He hauled over, grabbed the rope, and saw the figure staring back at him. Beetle swallowed, and the mask called Sammy—ghost or memory—evaporated before he was sure it was real. He forgave that kid, and loved them.

I'll do it right this time, he promised. He left his childhood weight in that mill, and climbed down to help his friends.

MARCELA

Marcela watched Beetle descend next to Caleb, where the old splinters of the drop chute's wooden cap chuckled under his feet, and the sound of Blue River rumbled like steady breathing. When they all turned their careful lights around, they realized they were in the middle of the huge, refuse-filled space, with very little idea where to go and very little light to pierce the black.

Marcela crouched, goosebumps racing up her arms. The light of her phone showed a splatter and smear of blood heading off into the darkness. Before she could panic and hate herself for it, she strode onward, leaving the others to follow.

Marcela hadn't thought it could get darker than the mill, yet here she was parting the bleakness like it was ferns in the forest, her light ripping through and shining strange on all of the forgotten equipment. The hair on her arms was starting to tingle.

Something raced by her, she swore, and she scanned quickly with the light.

Nothing.

"Did you feel that?" she asked, without turning around.

"Yeah," she heard Caleb breathe. He audibly shuddered and then jogged up closer to her, which made her bristle even worse. "Let's just go."

She turned her light back to the ground and kept following the blood. It reached almost the end of the room (that was a lot of blood for a not-very-large person to lose . . .) before it sluiced down into a wide drainage tunnel. Marcela crouched, trying not to shake. The tunnel was just a black eye curving into an L-bend, and she kept expecting some sort of face to pop out at her. She wasn't sure what she would have done then, but when she was so low she could hold the metal edge where floor stopped and tunnel began, she heard nothing but the quiet trickling of water below.

"It goes into the sewer," she said, and looked up. Caleb was crouched ahead of her. "You first, Reilly."

Either it was just her light, or he'd paled a few shades. "Why?"

"You're the biggest," she said. As far as she could see, they'd have no problem slipping down, but she wasn't sure if it narrowed past the bend. Plus, she wanted him going first so he wouldn't run off the second she stopped watching him. "If you can get down, then we all can."

"I'm sorry, Mar," he said, and she was about to snap at him to prove how sorry he really was, but he was already putting both legs in, sitting on the edge, and catching his breath. Without a word, he slipped off and was cramming himself through. Good. Now she and Beetle should—

Wait. Beetle. Caleb's face had already disappeared past the

bend when she shone her light around and didn't see him anywhere.

"Beetle," she whispered, too scared to shout. She stood, and that's when she heard the growling. She swept her light across the room and caught Beetle standing frozen a dozen paces back. His phone light cast a faint glow back onto him, lighting up his solitary figure and shining on the gentle, smoke-like wisps forming around him.

The growling grew louder.

Marcela thought about running through the corn with Quinn and her twin sister, who she treated like a dumb kid. The day Captain Reilly set his ironic end into motion, and Marcela decided she'd do anything if it meant not having the pointing finger turn on her. The day she found out how to survive Bridlington . . . how to grovel like a dog.

Beetle was being closed in on by the feathery shapes of huge, ghostly King Shepherds. The Shepherds were not so corporeal as Paz and her crew, were more memory than physical form brutally anchored, but their eyes glowed red in the dark.

Beetle's face was a slack square of paused terror, and he stood so still he seemed wooden. He turned his head slowly, watching one of the black shapes stalk him with its head lowered. The dog's teeth glittered and dripped heavy white fog. It puddled and pooled at his paws, falling like sea foam. Beetle didn't dare try to run: she could just see pale movement behind him, and knew his exit was blocked, too.

Marcela felt just as cemented, just as panicked. She covered the light from her phone and dropped her eyes low. She felt the corn whipping at her face. She felt Quinn's hand in hers. *Leave the dumb kid, Marcela. Aren't you smarter? Aren't you practical?*

Dog eat dog.

The growling stopped as the Shepherds did, each of them compressing slowly, like grasshoppers. The white fog was puddled up to Beetle's bare shins under his shorts, and he closed his eyes.

Marcela thought to run like a practical Reilly girl. But she and Quinn had hung back that day while Paz went to apologize. Marcela remembered staring at her best friend from over their locked hands and thinking they'd be friends forever, that the world was endless.

It will be, she thought.

"Hey!" Marcela shouted. She waved her hand in front of her phone light so it strobed. The two visible dogs turned to look at her with gleaming red eyes. Marcela stepped closer and stared them down with her eyes just as fierce, and her jaw tight and true. "Miss me?"

They turned from Beetle far too fast. All three Shepherds scampered forward, tumbling against each other, racing with a rattle of claws like the rattle of corn husks. Marcela remembered Paz wanting to stand against the Meyers' dogs like she was invincible. Ten years old, a mirror image of Marcela, with the sunlight on her face and her determined frown. Her twin sister who she would do anything for—drink a slushy in October, speak up, and stand bold-faced against the Meyers' beasts.

Marcela wore her sister's lockjawed stance. No, not Paz's. Marcela's. All hers.

The largest dog tore ahead of the other two, bone-white fur and blood-red eyes, and leapt in a whirl of claws and a snap of teeth. Marcela felt the dog's foamy breath splatter her face and smelled the rot of a dead thing. The dog's teeth snapped sharp across Marcela's forehead and nose. Its claws raked hot on her shoulders.

This one's for us, Paz, Marcela thought, sure of it, ready for her sister. *A girl is not a dog.*

The Shepherd flew right through Marcela, landing in a scrabble of paws behind. It was just a memory, could sting but couldn't kill.

Marcela grinned a wild, half-arrogant smile. The other two dogs, looking much smaller in comparison to the third, whined when she snapped her head over to look at them. There were thin scratches down her face, just enough to draw blood, but she was alive.

"Sit," Marcela said, and the two dogs did, watching her with guilty eyes and downturned noses. She looked up to Beetle, who was already racing back to her. He tore right through the dogs, who whirled like smoke and reformed behind him.

Marcela grabbed Beetle's shaking shoulders. Both of them opened their mouths to say something, and neither did. They weren't running, and they weren't cowering, and they weren't even going to fight like Paz had. They were bigger than desperation.

Beetle went down the drainage pipe next, and Marcela followed. She got one last look at the three King Shepherds sniffing after her. She wouldn't have known, but the image of those three dogs staring down at her was quite like what Paz had seen, staring up from the basement.

"You're not so scary," Marcela whispered.

And then she slid down the pipe and into the sewers under Bridlington.

BEETLE

Beetle watched Marcela wriggle out of the drainage pipe and splash down beside him. He let her grab his shoulder to steady herself. They had washed down into a wide sewer, dripping and dark with the tunnel reaching out in either direction and the water soaking up to their ankles. Their phone lights didn't go far, just rippled into the water and reflected on the slimy walls, making them look like they were moving. Any blood trail had been washed away or else smeared down Caleb's clothes. He was being a surprisingly good sport about that.

Beetle blinked in the sudden blinding light of Marcela's phone. She had to raise her voice above the echoing of Blue River rushing loud above them. "Which way?"

"I can't do it on command," he said, tightening his face and fixing his glasses. But she looked at him a little longer, more softly, and he huffed.

Beetle tried to sink into his head. It was less that he was trying to see through Paz's eyes and more that he was remembering Paz sitting with him under the jungle gym when they were very small, friends since pre-K when she talked too loudly and he didn't talk enough. He could have told you almost anything about Paz when they were eleven: she liked green slushies best (she called them "Ben 10 slushies") but loved Ellie enough to cave to red requests, and Digimon more than Pokémon, and was awful at Uno. Marcela and Paz were twins, but Paz and her crew were locked together like soulmates.

He didn't follow the path she took toward her grave but rather some tugging in his chest that told him the quickest way to the same end. Beetle Hoang turned left, downriver, and started walking.

It was not an easy trek. Blue River was so loud that crossing under it made even Caleb cover his ears. There were patches where they were so cold their breath showed in the air, and yet places where they were so warm that he undid a few more buttons, and Marcela shoved up her sleeves. The idea that his friends had done this six years ago made Beetle cringe. He couldn't tell how far below the town they were, or if they were actually above the mill within the gorge walls. Could Asher have survived being dragged this far? And if he had, would Paz let him go? Could she really be talked down?

He hoped that if she was going to kill them all, she'd be done then. And he hoped the messages they'd left behind would do something about the town. He wasn't sure at all.

They walked up to another circular maw to crawl through. It felt almost right, seemed to ring with a Paz-feeling. There was no blood, but Beetle figured Asher had been washed clean. Or his heart had stopped beating.

"I guess I'll . . ." Caleb started, and he gestured to the tunnel. He paused as if waiting for anything contrary, and then bucked up and crawled in. Marcela and Beetle watched his soaked running shoes disappear, one and then the other. Blue River rushed loud and close.

They had in fact been going the right way, but it was little consolation.

Beetle smelled cherry slushies. He heard growling. He only had time to turn wide-eyed to Marcela before Caleb screamed. They both dove forward to grab his ankles, but something yanked him through. They heard him land on the other side, and the distinct sound of something snarling and snapping and getting its teeth bloody. They both froze at a crouch, staring off down the pitch-black tunnel with their lights not reaching the end.

"So you both got the guts to come down here," they heard from past the tunnel.

Caleb screamed, shrill and tear-soaked and swearing he wasn't his father, he was going to do better. Bird snarled from deep in there. Beetle grabbed Marcela's hand, fast. She let him.

"Come on," Paz said, echoing above Caleb's screaming. "You're next, scaredy-cats."

In the living world above, it had started to rain.

ESPINO GIRLS

P az had let her crew go. The three of them had finished what they'd stuck around for: Ellie and Ben had stopped any chance of the Meyers fostering again, and now Chuck wouldn't have to go alone. They would have stayed longer if Paz had asked them.

Whether this would be better or worse for one Paz Espino, she swore she could carry this.

Before they left, Paz's friends all hugged her tight. Paz felt them breathing against her, but at the same time it was like they were on the other side of the room. She stood in the middle, silent and cold with her alive-face long gone. Fine. Work to be done. Someone had to do it. Paz had to do it. Yes, yes.

"You can come too," Ben said, too thin against Paz.

Chuck hummed, agreeing.

Paz swallowed, slow and cold with stormwater dripping off her. She tried to take off her dead-face, to flip through other masks like Asher or like Marcela, but the toothy parts of Paz had been creeping out long before she died. The scared things were coming up through the cracks. Ready to snap.

"Someone has to kill the monster," Paz said.

Ellie hugged her tighter. "You've got this, Paz," she said. Paz felt six arms around her, three bone-thin, one limp and dislocated, and two heavy and bent at snapped angles. And then she stood alone in the cistern, her back to the huge gate of the city's stormbreaker staring down from over her shoulder.

Bird had started growling at one of the intake pipes.

She watched with dull triumph as Caleb poked his head out. He had only enough time to get one arm through, and then his phone light fell on Paz where she stood. Before he could even scream, Bird sank his teeth into Caleb's thick arm and hauled him in, to drag him off to the corner. His screaming echoed.

And then came Marcela, and then came Beetle. One by one, they dropped down the short distance into the pitch-black storm cistern, the one that had filled up and killed Paz Espino. They landed in only an inch of water, Caleb's blood swirling around them while they scanned with their phones. Paz had the benefit of dark-accustomed eyes. She watched.

Just because they showed up didn't mean they were good.

Put them down, Paz thought.

In the dark, Marcela wanted to catch sight of Paz or Asher or even Caleb, though she had little hope for the last two. Caleb's phone was drowned; his screaming had stopped echoing. What she saw instead was a shadow of Bird trotting through the thin sheet of water, his fur slick-red. She smacked Beetle's arm so he'd look. They both watched Bird jauntily tip-tap up onto the small lip of a drain and past the crumpled form of Asher, semi-sitting,

285

with blood swirling around him. But then the spotlight from Marcela's and Beetle's phones touched another figure.

"Paz," Marcela breathed, and put both hands over her mouth with a squeak.

She watched Paz's lips pull back into a grin, wrinkling soggy dimples into her face and showing too-white teeth and too-pale gums. Paz wore her dead-face, and it made the air reek of rotting fish and wet clothing. Her hair dripped in two heavy braids pulling her scalp crooked, loose strands plastered to her skin along with leaves and thin twigs. One arm was a sloughed-off mess, just white bone visible from under a waterlogged Super Mario T-shirt, and she was missing a shoe. Bird crouched ahead of her, just as he had once protected Asher from Paz calling him to the back of the cemetery to avoid the minister, and as he had once protected him from Caleb. He turned his snarling mouth to Beetle and Marcela, and his red eyes reflected the light.

The water at Beetle's and Marcela's ankles glistened and the dripping sounds sped up. The rain was coming in.

"The monster's in you, too," Paz said. It was hardly words. It sounded like a broken faucet. Water gushed down her face and rounded her stomach. Her eyes were silver-pupiled. Marcela wasn't sure if she was smiling or if her skin was just hanging like that. "And I'm gonna kill it."

Bird took a step forward, crouched and ready to stalk. Marcela could barely see Asher, knew he was half dead, and she was sure that Caleb would be screaming if he had the life to do it. Time was running out . . . and yet her eyes dropped to her soaked shoes. It was one thing to say she'd come down here, another to stand against the ghost Shepherds . . . but it was a whole new beast entirely to look at her drowned sister. Being brave was easy in theory, harder in practice.

"Paz," Beetle managed to say. His voice wavered but was still clear. "You've gotta stop. You've gotta let us get Asher out of here."

"Why?" Paz asked. "The whole town either kills or dies. If you really think he's good, then he's better off down here."

The water swirled into the drain at Paz's feet. So far, it was going down easy, but Marcela suspected it wouldn't take long for the water to build up. Bird's paws sluiced quietly through the water, creeping farther.

"Caleb came here to prove he would make it up to us, and you," Beetle said. "We all did. The three of us are going to fix this."

Paz stepped forward, jangly and wrong with her legs water-logged and rotten. "He's not changed," Paz snapped. Her words went loose as her jaw slid; she had to press pruney fingers up to fix it. It cracked into place like a crunched water bottle. Marcela flinched. "Coming down here doesn't change what he did to me."

"You don't have to forgive him," Beetle said. Marcela kept cracking open her lips, trying to manage something. They only had so much time. "I don't. But if you kill him, then—"

"I'll be just as bad?" Paz asked. There was no humor in her voice.

Bird took another slow step. Marcela wrenched her neck up just enough to see that, and the water was up past his paws now, pulling away the blood. He walked with a cloud of it swimming around his ankles.

"No," Beetle said, hard. "But if you kill him, no one will know what—"

Marcela felt Paz's stare land on her, like icicles piercing her skin. "You can go with him, *Reilly girl.*"

"I won't," Marcela said. It lacked bass, but she knew it was true. She clenched her fists to pull some assurance through her too-thin veins. She wouldn't. The water was up to her shins. Everything was green-and-black shadows, with light barely touching the edges. "I came after you this time."

"You left me!" she shouted, and it echoed. Paz's head was all water. Her brain was melted. She was *tired*, and what did these half-apologies mean anyway? Her lungs floated strangely between her ribs.

"And so what then, Paz?" Marcela said, low. Bird crept forward with more resistance, the water lapping at his chest. Paz watched Marcela's face struggle up, her skin pale and terrified, but her eyes clear. "Everyone liked the people who died. No one knew they were wrong. So you keep that up, killing 'good' people, and then what?"

Caleb groaned from behind Paz, and Bird whipped his head to bark at him. The sound smacked around the walls and hit Paz from every side. The drain was gurgling, a vortex spinning slowly around her. She fought back old panic and let the flood rise.

"The town minds its business," Marcela said, her voice growing louder. "You can't kill things no one talks about. They'll say Caleb died in some tragic accident." She swallowed. "Paz, no one will notice the pattern unless we show them."

Paz was an eleven-year-old girl, pinned down with no exit.

The ice was crackling in her skull, pulling at her skin, sticking her organs together. "Fine, then!" she shouted. It echoed all around: *then then THEN!* Her skin slipped farther from her bony face. "We're all bad anyway, so we'll all die!"

Die die DIE!

"Paz," Beetle squeaked. "No one's good or bad."

She wasn't hearing him. "I don't care!" Paz screeched. Her voice cracked and a rip sliced down her cheek from under her eye, almost like a tear. Her knees were shaking.

The water rose: Bird couldn't move at a crouching stalk, only a stiff-legged shuffle. Caleb was spluttering behind Paz, and she heard his weak legs slipping from under him. Asher was silent.

"Just make it all stop then, all right?" Paz said. "Either we have the monster or the monster hurts us, so just make it *stop!*" Her jaw slipped loose again and she had to put both hands under it to hold it, half collapsing on swinging-loose knees, nearly lost under the water *again*. Her voice was nothing but bubbles. "If everyone's dead, then the monster can't get anyone and I can LEAVE!"

Marcela, Espino girl, in running shoes with her hair down, finally saw her sister. *Really* saw her. But Paz wasn't Paz at all then, swimming in shadows and light refracting off the glistening water. Her hair was a swirling mess and her skin was starting to fall away completely. The air smelled like a cherry slushy left out too long, rotten-sweet.

It was Marcela's turn to hold the weight.

"What if we helped you starve out the monster? Us, not you," she asked hurriedly. Tears were spilling out of her eyes then; she let them come. "I don't want it all to end with you dying twice,

Paz." Marcela forced herself forward through the nearly thigh-high water, and thought about Ms. Hoang hugging her, about being haunted by the past, wondering if it would ever get any better. "The world's really messed up. But if you think people want to be bad forever, then it's never gonna change. People need to know how to put this all right. We'll try to teach them."

Bird was starting to whine through his growling. The water was lapping higher, and he was too stiff-necked to turn nervous eyes back to Paz. The blood was swirling off him.

"We're not gonna look away," Beetle said, shuddering forward another step too. The water felt thick as tar and threatened to take them all off their feet. "The town would have been better with you in it. We're going to prove it. We love you, Paz."

Paz swallowed and managed to hinge her jaw back on. Marcela let the current tug her closer, past Bird. He made one snap at her thigh. She held her breath, but he didn't lunge farther.

"I hate Bridlington," Paz wheezed. The water was spinning at Paz's belly in the center of the vortex, but gravity couldn't seem to touch her. "I want it gone."

Marcela stepped onto the drain, where water sucked and bubbled at her shoes, and her phone light glinted on every ignored part of Paz. Everything the town had made her: waterlogged and dead without a choice.

Whoever looks long enough to realize *why* people show their teeth?

This would end, and not with little girls forced to be brave. "It won't ever be like this again," Marcela said, and hugged her sister. Paz practically collapsed into her, arms wrapping tight and far too small. But still, in that moment, they felt warmer than drowning. Paz felt alive, if only for that peaceful second.

No more, Marcela swore, while understanding that convincing Paz was only half the battle. How were they getting out of here? *No more.*

Bird whined in the cold water. The blood was washing from him; his eyes had flickered from red back to black. He whined high, and there was the sloshing sound of Beetle picking him up above the water without any complaint or cherry-slushy aggression. The tunnels were chuffing out water with aggressive coughs; Marcela knew they'd have no chance of fighting back through it. She looked up just long enough to see Beetle rush past her and Paz to where Asher was slumped, with only his face floating just above the water.

Just as Beetle got one arm under Asher's shoulders to hoist him up easily, just as Marcela realized the only thing that had saved Asher from having his chest torn open by Bird's claws was his binder, just as Caleb managed to put his torn-up legs under him and stumble closer, Paz opened her brown eyes against her sister's shoulders. They all heard the water rushing louder, all felt the ground vibrating, but only Paz knew what it meant.

Whatever they'd decided, it might not matter.

"The stormbreaker just opened," Paz breathed, and a wall of water came flooding through the gate behind them.

PAZ

Paz had felt the basin fill before, knew what was happening, and knew she couldn't stop it. The water rushed in, tossing all of the living into the back wall where their bones smacked into the cement. The current swept them right to the top, and then the whirlpool for the drain threatened to pull them down against it. Paz hadn't been moved and stood staring up into the black, metallic-tasting water. She heard Bird's whining reverberate down to her and could see the others up high above her, fighting for the surface. The intake tunnels were sealed; there was only one way out.

Paz looked down at the drain grate under her feet. Six years ago, the storm had washed her in and sucked her down against it, pinning her there like a leaf while the basin took an eon to drain. There were worse ways to go, she'd thought optimistically. It was almost pretty, and there was a sort of dandelion-soft flippancy that came with knowing you could just sit there and let it all happen around you. But there was no good way to go when you had so much left to do.

Paz stood where she had died, staring up at what her life had led to. What everyone's lives had led to, she figured, because it wasn't just she who had made this so. Was it all a mistake? She didn't know, and didn't think anyone could say. Things just *were*, and you had to figure out where to go from there.

She could let them die. And then the monster would be gone from them, and they'd probably rest. She could keep going.

Paz Espino thought about running through the corn with her sister, when they had been so similar. And scared, in different ways. And thought about sitting under the jungle gym with Beetle. Or reading with Chuck in the lowest reading group where neither of them belonged, or when she'd braid Ellie's hair, or every water gun fight with Ben. When the four of them would ride through town as the sun was setting, and the air smelled like hot pavement and wet lawns. And even if the town didn't like them, they had each other.

She looked down at the drain. She had long studied it in her years trapped and shouting. She watched it shift with the water flow, every bolt rusted loose except one.

Paz was the one with choices now, and she had to decide what to do with them.

CALEB

A t the top of the basin, they were all losing strength. The current yanked at their ankles. The darkness was so thick they weren't sure they were still above the water. Caleb could hear Bird's paws frantically slapping at the surface but couldn't tell where Beetle and Asher and Marcela were. Caleb thought to call to them, but his torn body was in so much freezing pain that he thought he might already be dead or drowned.

And then:

"*You gotta trust me*," someone said in the nothingness. Beetle, he thought, but somehow wasn't sure. "*Caleb—they said you were gonna do good things now?*"

"Yes," Caleb spluttered. A wave of grainy water washed into his mouth and he spat it out frantically.

"*Get in the current*," Beetle said. His voice was interrupted by wave after wave of water down his throat. "*Come down— come down here.*"

"What?!"

"*Do it*," Beetle said, but now Caleb realized why he hadn't been sure of the speaker: it sounded almost like Paz, like some sort of poorly timed comedic impression. "*It's time to—*" Another mouthful of water. Another wincing groan and a spluttering cough that sounded like it might have come from Asher. "*—apologize.*"

Caleb blinked. He didn't trust this. He hadn't been raised to trust this. But he hadn't been raised for a lot of what had already happened. So where did that leave him?

Espino girls are dogs, Caleb. You're not some kid with a playing card in the spokes. You're my son.

Not like this, he thought. *You were wrong, Dad.*

He let himself go under.

The current sank him like an anchor, and his feet hit the drain so heavily that his bleeding legs almost collapsed. The grate squeaked. He stared into the blackness around him with his lungs already starting to burn and his ears ringing from the pressure and every puncture and tear in his body bringing searing pain. He knew that he'd never make it back to the top of the basin.

"Now that we're alone," Paz said from somewhere far too close. He almost choked out a scream but kept his lips sealed shut. He couldn't see a damn thing and the voice was circling him. "Time to see if I can really trust you."

He couldn't have responded if he'd wanted to.

Eventually, the current was too strong, and they were all sucked down into the black water.

BRIDLINGTON

The night Asher Gordon was taken, Bridlington witnessed a storm unlike anything it had seen, at least in the last six years. Ms. Hoang hadn't quite fallen asleep again after the banging on the door and had checked after to find that both Beetle and Marcela were gone. She figured they'd be back shortly, wouldn't run far with those animal attacks. But they weren't, and Beetle's phone went to voicemail. And then it started to rain. The thunder rolled and the rain was thrown into the house like waves. She waited at the kitchen table, tapping her feet in her slippers.

The time ticked very, very slowly. She knew it was ridiculous to try to cook past midnight, but she was possessed with the need to make soup: two batches, not too spicy. He'd be sick when he came home, she thought in the back of her mind. Like before.

Like before.

The memory bowled her over. Her eyes went wide and she covered her mouth with her hand. Yes, like last time. Here she was again, waiting on her son and his friends to come back from some grand adventure. It could have been Beetle six years ago. It could be him that night.

She felt hopeless.

The power flickered and lightning cracked. It sent a streak of white light through the kitchen, and only then did she see Beetle's incredibly green Bug Book on the counter. She looked at it as if in a trance. She thought of Beetle when he had been so small and bright-eyed, when he'd run into fields with his book, nose to the grass. She'd let the town hurt him, she'd made him into a glum shadow after Paz died, the sobbing wreck she sent to Harville. She'd cut him down. And now it would happen again, she thought, and she hadn't caught it in time.

There was a note next to the book, on the same floral-patterned paper she wrote her grocery lists on. She stepped toward it like someone in a trance, picked it up and read it under the flickering power.

Má ơi

I'm doing what needs to be done. I'm not going alone.
I never blamed you for anything that happened to Paz or
to me. There's like nine thousand people in this shitty
little town. It's not just you, Má.
    Con yêu má nhé.

Beetle

She had no idea what this meant other than that Beetle had put himself in danger again and she had missed it.

Be brave. The world was bigger than her mistakes. The entire town was outside her door; it didn't have to be a fearful thing.

Ms. Hoang swallowed, plucked up bitter nerve, and pulled the phone off the wall to jam it in her shoulder, trying not to cry more. She pulled her contact book out of the kitchen drawer and flipped to find Beetle's Grade Five Parent Sheet. She felt stiff and distant, but had to try.

They picked up almost immediately.

"Marcela?" Mrs. Espino asked.

"No, it's Tam Hoang," she said. She tried to keep her voice from turning frantic. She wasn't a bad mother. She wasn't a bad mother. "Is my son with you?"

"No," Mrs. Espino said.

Ms. Hoang breathed in slowly and looked out at the sheets of rain tugging the tree in the backyard around like a dog with a toy. The air cracked and rumbled.

"Marcela's not home either. She's usually so good about texting us."

"Beetle too."

Mrs. Espino sniffed and her voice was tight. "Quinn Bright just called us," she said. "Something about a text—she said Caleb Reilly was looking for Marcela and she sent him to you. Did he get there?"

Ms. Hoang tapped her feet, thinking of the pounding on the door. "I think Caleb was here," she admitted. So where was that new boy? Asher, yes? She pressed one hand into her lips, hard. "I'm so sorry. I went back to bed when he came."

"We didn't even realize she was missing until after dark," Mrs. Espino said. Her voice was tear-soaked.

Ms. Hoang reached for her cellphone across the kitchen table and tried to type in another number one-handed. It made her mind ring so much louder than the thought of calling the Espinos: she typed in the Reillys' home phone.

"The weather . . ." Mrs. Espino started to say. It was nearly the same as when Paz had "gone missing." They were all aware.

Ms. Hoang's eyes watered. Not her son. Please not her son and please none of his friends. She was sure she'd be ruined forever. She felt, and rightly so, that this second storm was bringing something huge on its back.

"I'm calling Renée Reilly," Ms. Hoang said. "I'll put her on speaker."

She tried not to think about it, just forged ahead and waited while the line rang, and rang, and rang.

"Hello?" Mrs. Reilly's voice was very awake.

"Hello, Renée," Ms. Hoang choked out. She suddenly wished she knew Asher's parents. A parent ought to be worried their child is out in a storm like this. "It's Tam Hoang, and I have Marianna and Tomás Espino on the call as well. Marcela and my son aren't home and we think Caleb was with them. We were wondering if you knew anything? They seem to have been at my house last, but . . ."

But she let them go.

All three lines were silent. Ms. Hoang wondered if the

Espinos were waiting to be called bad parents like she was, if they were waiting to hear that their child was just some basket case who was better off away from all of them.

There was something strong about being scared for the same reasons. Something that forced them all together like kids with playing cards in their spokes. And that included Renée Reilly.

Ms. Hoang heard the jingle of keys. "I can look around the school," Mrs. Reilly said, because she'd never been her husband and might finally get to prove it. "If you can search the neighborhood, Tam?"

Ms. Hoang and the Espinos paused for a second, but then Ms. Hoang agreed. The Espinos said they'd take the south side of town. None of them knew each other more than from various town events, but they had all decided their children were "friends."

Ms. Hoang was a catalyst that night, because of Beetle, because of Asher, because of Paz, because of because of because.

//\\//\\//\\//\\//\\//\\//\\//\\

Two other places in Bridlington were sparking up to set off the fuses.

Quinn was pacing wildly around her room, rereading Marcela's text to her. It was simple, very simple, in a way only Quinn could ever understand.

I want blue slushies again. Have my back, please.

"Caleb was saying weird shit in the hockey group chat," Reece said through speaker phone. "Something about getting his shit together and not sitting on his ass."

Out her window, far in the distance, Quinn saw faint head-light beams leave the motel parking lot. She knew something was horribly wrong if there were cars out past dark, especially in a storm like this. "Have you heard from Caleb since those texts?" she asked.

"No," Reece said, swallowing. "Asher was texting me about him—both of their phones are going straight to voicemail."

So was Marcela's.

"Something feels really wrong about this," Reece said.

Quinn agreed. She, like everyone else, thought Paz had run away. She always wanted to think she would act if something went wrong. She'd pull kittens from a burning building, wouldn't she? But real life was hardly so dramatic, and the small problems never felt like her business.

Marcela had grabbed her hand to run from the Shepherds because they were in it together.

"Come pick me up," she told Reece, and gave him no option when she hung up the phone. If he came, he came. In the mean-time, she slammed her father's door open and argued herself hoarse until he called Renée Reilly and asked what the hell was going on.

"Marcela, Caleb, and . . ."—he didn't seem to know the other names—"Beetle and Asher are missing," he said, and caught the panicky alarm on Quinn's face. He sighed and motioned back to the stairs. "There's people looking, honey. I'll bet they just—"

Thunder rumbled and the power fritzed a bit. Quinn nar-rowed her eyes. "They could be in a ditch somewhere," she told him, her voice threatening to tremble. "And there were those animal attacks. Literally *anything* could have happened."

Her father squinted at her a bit and looked out the window while the wind gusted against the house. "True," he muttered. "But it's not—"

"It *is* our business," Quinn snapped, and she was already storming to the closet to get her shoes. She chucked his coat at him. "They live here too."

Mr. Bright was bullied into his car to search the local parks, around the same time Reece showed up. Reece took less convincing ("Do it for the boys," she said, mostly sarcastic, but he had already decided he would), but he was a mediocre driver at best and wasn't thrilled about Quinn's suggestion to go drive along the long road that bordered the incredibly steep town side of the Blue River gorge.

Still, Reece hauled his F150 onto the dark road, white-knuckling the wheel. Quinn leaned out the window and pointed a camping flashlight into the gorge, scanning the rocks while the rain pelted the top of the car. It sounded like they were being shot at. She squinted through the rain, already soaked.

They were nearing the border of Bridlington, the quaint neighborhood on their left fading out into dangerously swaying trees and Blue River rushing far below on the right.

"Quinn," Reece said warningly, slowing down. She knew the cement road was ending and would give way to rough gravel and then soft mud. The truck would certainly be fine off-road, but the street lamps ended out here and the clouds were twisting up.

"Reece," Quinn said back from out the window, soaked and shaking now. "Drive the stupid car."

The truck rumbled over the gravel with just the high beams to show the way, dipping and waning in a way that wasn't all too safe with Quinn hanging out the window only a few feet from a very steep drop with only a very small guardrail. They were near the edge of Bridlington when the sky split with lightning and Quinn almost screamed.

No one would believe her. *She* wouldn't even believe her. But Quinn Bright would testify until the day she died that she saw a very young Marcela Espino standing in the middle of Blue River, stone-still despite how fast the water was rushing, like it wasn't even touching her. She locked eyes with Quinn and smiled.

But then the lightning ended, and Quinn swung the flashlight to that spot.

She was gone.

"Stop the truck," Quinn said. She was out the door before Reece could even slam it into park. She raced through the small lookout where Asher had slept for five days, ducked the rail, and slid down the side of the gorge with the rain pelting her and turning everything muddy. Reece followed after. They didn't even have their feet under them—they just let themselves skid right down the near-vertical drop with mud coating their backs and shoes.

They both hit the slippery concrete lip of a drainage pipe, landing heavily and clambering for each other so neither would tip forward. They stared down and over at the water tumbling out into Blue River.

Quinn shone the flashlight over at exactly the right time to see that the water flooding from the pipe was stained red, and to hear someone spluttering against the metal mesh at the opening. They watched a hand reach out, copper-brown.

"Marcela," Quinn muttered, and Reece was already fumbling for his phone.

"Dylan's always awake late," he said, while Quinn was already getting down to her knees to peer over. "He can—Yo, asshole, wake your dad up and ask if he has a crowbar or something . . . I don't care, just start waking him up and I'll fill you in."

"We're getting help," Quinn whispered. She couldn't see over, but she grabbed Marcela's hand. It was ice cold. "Just hold on."

A crowbar didn't cut it. By the time they managed to get Bridlington's only tow truck over to yank the grating free, there were a dozen people awake and invested in those four bodies pulled from the tunnel.

It was six years too late, but they were rescued. And was that ever a wake-up call to see that Bridlington had some problems.

BIRD

Bird woke up. He lay on his side for some time, breathing in shakily and breathing out in soft whines. He was alone in the dark, smelling old stone and dust. He heard Blue River breathing around him.

Slowly, he wagged his wet tail against the cement with the dull smack of waterlogged fur and panted like he was smiling.

Bird found his paws and stood up. His fur weighed him down and made his skin feel slimy on his bones. He tried to shake it out but the feeling didn't go away, and he almost whined before he forgot what he was so distraught about. His tongue lolled serenely out of his mouth. He looked around at the basement of the mill. There was a smear of blood that smelled like his Boy, so he put his nose to it and snuffled his way over to the drainage pipe.

Bird heard someone coming up through it.

He stuck his face into the pipe and watched a face emerge.

"Hey, Bird," a familiar voice said. Bird wagged his tail, spraying water that wouldn't land where any living person could see it. "Just you and me."

Bird barked happily, and it took the person down there some time to move him so they could climb out and he could lick their face with a too-cold tongue. He spent a long time sitting between their legs with his head on their shoulder and their arms wrapped around him. The drain was open, and they could leave whenever they wanted, but they took some time to just sit. And to think of monsters under the town.

Bird sighed that deep, incredibly pained sigh only dogs seem capable of, and thought that even if he was cold and wet, at least he wasn't alone.

Paz agreed. She felt a little warmer, and figured she could find a way to leave for the next place if she wanted that. For now, there was Bird for company and comfort.

As for the others, Paz couldn't do much for them anymore. They had to make their own choices.

BRIDLINGTON

The Man came into town on a string of good luck that he felt very, very aware of. Traffic had been light on the 400, his horrible little car wasn't putting up too much of a fuss, the present had been bought without much hassle, and the sun had been warm enough for him to put down his windows. With evening rolling slowly over, he was grateful for the calm chill to the summer heat.

The little shitbox car rolled over the bridge and the Man looked for the mill: an impulse. He felt a strange sense of serenity when he saw nothing but rocks, newer and cleaner than the rest. There were three bike frames sticking up, decorated with ribbons and playing cards and something small that flashed a glint of starry light in the sun and lengthening shadows. Cricket (the aforementioned present) put her too-big front paws on the car's windowsill and sniff sniff sniffed toward the memorial. Her tail swung warily.

"What are you seeing?" the Man asked, petting her back. She was a Labrador-something-something and her blond fur was short between his fingers. "You seeing ghosts?" She attacked his hand with her tiny pink tongue, and he grimaced and wiped it on the front of his button-up. They had been getting along cordially, but frankly he would be glad to hand the lead role to a more experienced pro.

They drove past the newish Circle K and the gas station, the pavement hazy in the heat, turning the out-of-season saltbox to a yellow blur. The sun was bright in its slow descent when he passed the motel. Kids on bikes were streaming down the road beside him, riding toward the forest. One of them was wearing huge owl-eyed glasses and smiled at him through the window. He wondered if kids still put playing cards in their spokes.

The Man crawled up on the central section of Main Street, where Mrs. Espino was putting up the letterboard for Digital Heritage Day at the library and talking avidly with a few of the junior helpers; they weren't helping so much as they were chasing each other. Cricket snuffled moodily and he petted her quickly before he snapped his hand back onto the wheel to white-knuckle himself to an achingly smooth stop at the single light in town.

"How was that?" he asked Cricket. She stared back at him.

The Man drove off a little farther down the road. He gritted his teeth and parallel parked in front of the available meter. It took him quite a few tries, and he was well aware that the baristas in the coffee shop across the road were staring at him. One of them, whom he recognized as a newcomer to the town but still knew the name of, caught his eye and waved their hand a bit, as if to signal he had a liiiiittle more room. He took it, straightened out, and they touched their pointer to their thumb to signal he was A-OK. He gave them a sheepish smile (and pointed from his hair to theirs and gave a thumbs-up to say he thought their green-dyed locs were rad) and turned off the engine. Cricket whined irritably.

They had parked in front of where the old diner used to be.

"No telling anyone about the parking," he told Cricket. She was a very opinionated little dog who looked more like she was pouting than smiling.

The Man stepped out of the car while Cricket whined from the passenger seat, only her tiny pink nose visible. The Man heard people passing behind him, walking out of the diner with a clattering of the chimes above the door and a rush of warm, lemongrass-scented air that went past him and through the open windows of his car. Cricket wiggled her nose harder.

"Smell good?" he asked her.

She gave a very decided huff.

He grabbed her and tied the leash to the dog stand. He took a deep breath and looked up and down Main Street.

Bridlington.

Good to be back. It really was. The Man, also known as Beetle Hoang, saw a general store worker across the street organizing the community fridge and making friendly conversation with an elderly couple Beetle would otherwise have given a wide berth. The guy's mouth was hidden behind a surgical mask, but his eyes were easy and smiling.

Caleb Reilly caught Beetle's stare between the heads of those old folks and gave a shy little wave. Beetle waved back. They weren't close, really, had their own circles now to smooth old hurts, but it was nice to know that old jackass was still using his Reilly smile properly.

Beetle too. He smiled, wrestled into his slightly crumpled N95 mask, and turned quickly. He felt eleven years old when he rushed through the door of the remodeled diner, wearing his Inuyasha shirt, with the air thick and spiced. He saw his mother through the window to the kitchen and she signaled she'd be a minute, as always. He let her work.

The restaurant's head waiter (turned delivery guy in their current "unprecedented times") strutted out from the break room, weaving between the tables. He was good at his job, and Beetle had to wait while he conversed with people picking up their orders, doing the whole "Oh that looks *so* good" and "Next time, you have to get the chè, it's like the greatest thing ever" and "Trust me, I should know. Look over at the guy by the door and tell me I don't have superb taste," which made Beetle's face burn red. Ms. Hoang heard it through the window to the kitchen and he gave her his best pained look. She winked and went back to handing off a bag to a delivery boy that Beetle swore was the grandkid of one of his old teachers. Oh, small towns.

Asher finished his usual banter, waving to Ms. Hoang, all the while juggling a tray with three cups of chè. When he walked, his pant leg hiked up just enough to show the metal socket of his prosthetic foot. There was local speculation among the library's youth group that he was a Transformer.

Beetle caught the tray before Asher dropped it. Yes. It was so good to be home. A degree in his car, a dog outside, and very good people.

"You're late—your mom and I thought you went fender-first into Blue River," Asher said, hazel eyes and a soft face and small pink gauges in his ears. When Beetle put his hand on Asher's shoulder, there was only one layer between them, and Asher finally had the hard-won posture of someone who breathed easy.

"Your car is a piece of shit," Beetle said, keeping his voice low. His hair was all fluffy and pastel in the light from the big window out to Main Street. "If I went into the river, that'd be on you."

Asher waved it off. "See anything *spoooooky*?" He grinned, wiggling his fingers.

Beetle smiled. "Not a bit."

Asher threw his arm around Beetle's shoulders and the two headed out into the street so Asher could pull his mask down to kiss Beetle's cheek, then croon over his new dog.

//⋀⋁/⋀⋁/⋀⋁/⋀⋁/⋀⋁/⋀⋁/⋀

Marcela was sitting in the playground outside the motel, swinging slowly and typing on her phone while the call played on speaker. Beetle and Asher were en route, Asher sending her nearly constant Snapchats of Cricket, or Beetle driving with very intense focus, captioned *He can't 3-point turn so we're driving the whole street* and peppered with a million slightly sarcastic heart-eye stickers. She smirked and swung a bit on the swing.

"Drive faster, Beetle," she said into her phone. "I miss your dumb ass."

"I'm focusing," she heard him say. She kicked her feet through the pea gravel, watching the shadows pull out longer and hearing the crickets start to thrum. The wind was soft on her short curls.

"A bunch of the kids at the library want to make their own Bug Books," she told him, because that old thing had become something of a trophy there. On thinking about the library, she clicked out of Snapchat and opened her texts to Caleb: *What was the library budget again? How might one make it bigger?* "They're all obsessed with you," she added. "That might be because Asher doesn't shut the hell up about how you pulled him out of a sewer."

"I did pull him out of a sewer," Beetle said.

"I also pulled him out of a sewer," she added.

"Yes, that's right, Cricket," she heard Asher crooning. "I was pulled out of a sewer by your lovely second dad, my favorite mean lesbian, and her comp het ex."

"Screw off," she told him, but she was smiling. "Drive faster, Beetle."

"For that, I'll drive slower."

She tapped the call off and swung some more. The motel had been slow lately, but the library was a good gig. She'd been helping get them onto what her mom called "the socials," which was helpful when everything was still mostly digital, but she'd been really enjoying it. She was debating going into communications or marketing or something, maybe just an online degree? She still had another few months to think it over and she wasn't in a rush to decide. Caleb said there was a budget meeting in a week. She asked if she had to be there or if he had it handled.

She closed her phone with a click, pocketed it, and held the swing chains as she stared out at the lawn and trees back there. "Had a bit of trouble today," she said, mostly to herself while she scuffed at the gravel. "There was a kid tearing down posters for the Pride readings. Some little teenage prick. He called me a bitch, but whatever." Can't win 'em all, but it was good to try. "Tobi told me not to worry."

Tobi was . . . well, technically speaking, they'd come to rent in Bridlington with a few other U of H students before things got pandemic-y, and now Tobi was Zoom University-ing and working at the coffee shop near the library. More formally speaking, Marcela had what Asher called "a big fat crush" and what she called "assessing the situation." She and Tobi were supposed to watch some A24 movie that weekend and she figured she'd decide if it was a date *after* it happened. The embarrassingly bubbly feeling in her stomach said she was hoping it would be. It was a bit mortifying, but she smiled anyway.

Marcela was still on the swing when Asher and Beetle rolled into the parking lot. Asher was holding Cricket at eye level and they were playfully growling at each other until she nipped his nose.

Marcela stood up to go hug her friends.

She was aware that the swing beside her was drifting in a few smooth arcs and that the pea gravel crunched a bit. She didn't ignore it so much as she let it go about its business.

She didn't know anything about that. Nuh-uh, no way.

She felt like a kid with their fingers crossed behind their back, and she locked her jaw in a grin.

//∧∨/∧∨/∧∨/∧∨/∧∨/∧∨/∧∨//∧∧

The fourteen-year-old boy Marcela had spoken with was still out when the sun was going down, riding his skateboard around the parking lot behind the high school with the sky growing dark and the first few stars straining through. He'd already forgotten about that bitch from the library and her dumb little readings. Boo-hoo. Cry me a river.

He carved around and kicked up his skateboard, the sky orange and the pavement black. He was starting to sweat and thought it was just from the summer heat. Cold dripped down his spine, but he tried to ride it off.

Something raced behind him, a shadow and a feeling. He ground the tail of his board into the pavement and stopped suddenly.

He pulled his AirPods out and heard crickets starting up in the field beside him. But that was all. Crickets, and the smooth breeze, and the muffled thump of his music.

And then, slowly, a *plomf, plomf, plomf* sound coming up behind him, and one wet shoe slapping the ground. The boy stared straight ahead, frozen, with sweat creeping down his cold face. He looked out across the parking lot at the sky leaching into indigo-dark, smelled cherry slushies and heavy blood. The sun crept lower and lower. The street lamps flicked on gold.

Plomf, plomf—

Silence.

Something breathed on the back of his right ankle and his dry eyes looked down to see white fog foaming around his shoe and the tail of his board. It moved slowly up toward his other foot and then folded back on itself and dripped down to swirl on the pavement like dry ice.

"Hey, kid," a voice said from behind him. It sounded young, but bubbly. A little wrong. "I think you should really think about changing your act." The slow slurp of a drink on the dregs. Something sharp closed at his ankle, not breaking the skin, just nibbling, considering. He moaned quietly, his knee buckling.

The thing took its teeth off and seemed to hold its breath. The boy waited five seconds, ten seconds, feeling watched still, but maybe like whatever was behind him had backed off.

He blinked a few times, smirked to himself to try to remember how tough he was, and prepared to swing his other foot down and ride off for home.

Something snorted heavily on his ankle.

"Consider this a wake-up call," the voice said, and the boy's vision was suddenly a cherry-red sheet of pain. He screamed and rode for home in a whip of white fog, the back of his calf scarcely bleeding but still burning up sharp.

Maybe she did have her jaw locked on what she wanted. But sometimes people needed a little reminder, and it sure was fun to hear them squeal.

AUTHOR'S NOTE

I didn't actually set out to write a horror—believe it or not, I thought I was writing a fluffy little romance novel. I'm not sure why I tried that, considering I hardly read the genre on my own time, but I think I wanted something to distract me. Like Beetle, I've always felt more at home in the big city of Toronto than in the suburbs where I grew up; unfortunately, this book was written only a few weeks into the COVID-19 lockdown, when protections had me grounded at my parents' place with no way to see my found family in person. I get why I wanted to write something light: I needed to get away from it all.

Six chapters in, I knew I'd made a mistake. I wasn't really having fun, and I can promise you that I'll never make you read something that I didn't enjoy writing. The story felt boring, typical, and frankly inauthentic. Who was I to write anything about connection when I was so very alone? I stared at this story about a runaway teen and his dog and this cute town he ends up in, and asked myself what I wanted to happen. What would be the most exciting thing?

A monster, I decided. An ignorant town that doesn't care about its most marginalized. A spooky mill inspired by the first place I ever explored. Kids on bikes, kids like I was, with Mac's slushies and playing cards in the spokes.

I set out to write something to distract me from the world, but instead I chose to sit in my terror and my loneliness. I had multiple readers suggest that the characters were too angry, too abrasive, that it made them unlikeable, but I was too when I wrote this. We're not really our best selves when we're desperate. I needed a story to speak to everything I was scared of, and that's where *Lockjaw* comes from. In fiction, we can build the tragedy, and we can also build the solution. That's why we need horror: we need to know we can get through hard things.

When the world is bearing down on us, when transphobic laws are coming to pass, when racial reckonings seem to bring little change, when workers are being underpaid, when children are still ignored every time they cry injustice, and youth are forced to the frontlines of activist movements, we have to steer into the skid. We have to look at what scares us. We have to sit in it, and think on it, and ask ourselves how we get through.

The answer, as it has been all throughout history, is "together."

This book was my search for community. I can say I've certainly found it, and I hope you do too. I know we'll never stop being scared or feeling lonely, but I know it can lead us to wonderful things.

In solidarity,

Matteo L. Cerilli

ACKNOWLEDGMENTS

First, as promised, thank you to Victor, with a shoutout to Ru. I love you both for just being my friends and sticking by me even when I shut myself into "writing jail" and you lose communication with me for like six weeks. But perhaps most importantly, thank you Victor for giving Beetle his Vietnamese, and Ru for assisting. Thank you for the in-depth conversations about dialect and connotations and the nuances of "Viet-glish." It brings so much to the page. I have this snapshot in my memory, of you two around the table of that place on Prince Arthur Avenue (you know . . . where the pipes were so janky that the laundry water backed up into the kitchen sink?), huddling at my laptop and parsing over four sentences like they were an entire thesis. I believe love is shown through actions; I felt so horrifically loved in that moment.

And now, for the rest. My journey from "three-year-old with a homemade picture book" to "published author" is a series of handoffs from one person to the next, so I'll thank them in that order. Thank you to my little sister, Megan. You're first for a reason: growing up on bikes with you, with those Mac's slushies, and with Zoseph (our fifteen-pound mini Labradoodle who inspired Cricket, not Bird) has made me who I am. I love you more than I'll say out loud. And then thank you to my parents, Giuseppe and Wendy, some serious STEM-major folks who somehow got on board with this whole writing thing. Thank you to my first "professional contact," Brian Henry, who noticed me in the workshop room, and to Hannah Mary McKinnon who he asked to beta read my very first (very rough) novel, and who warmly encouraged me along my journey.

Thank you then to Cassandra Rodgers who heard my query and passed my contact along to the one and only Ali McDonald, my fabulous literary agent. Ali, I'm sure you'll fire back with "I know talent when I see it" or something, but thank you for taking a chance on a nervous seventeen-year-old and letting me grow alongside you. You're as much a friend as a business partner. While I'm praising the Five Otter Literary ladies, thank you also to Olga Filina who let me brush up on my editing skills at the office. Thank you, similarly, to the wonderful Jess de Bruyn who has edited so many of my projects, including *Lockjaw*. This book wouldn't exist without your tireless eye, passion for your work, and your willingness to get on board with my more eccentric choices. All four of you remind me that I can actually do this. I cherish that more than I can say.

Thank you also to my beta readers, Luke and Roxy. Luke, I forgive you for thinking that Bird is a corgi, and for guessing the twist far too early and making me panic. You make up for it by being a phenomenal friend and a loyal reader. Thank you also to Roxy who thought she was just going to edit a book for a stranger . . . you're stuck with me, dude. Thank you also to all my professors at York University, especially those who took the time to not only understand my weird speculative stuff, but to encourage it. It means the world.

Thank you now to the Tundra team! Thank you, Peter Phillips, for picking up this gory little story, and for all your enthusiasm, and also for not laughing at me when I got so nervous at lunch that I spilled my drink (twice). I promise I'm usually smoother than that. Thank you to Catherine Marjoribanks, to Erin Kern, to Stephanie Ehmann, and to Sophie Paas-Lang for directing the *brilliant* cover. Thank you, thank you, thank you to the one and only Corey Brickley, the cover artist, who blew the assignment out of the water. I've admired your work for so long—I'm still reeling that I get the honor of creating alongside you. Thank you to everyone else who helped get this book from manuscript to print, including the booksellers and librarians working tirelessly on those front lines, and to readers. You're all as integral as any editor.

As we finish this off, thank you to the found families who have held and supported me. Thank you to the Starbucks crew who kept me sane during lockdown and beyond. Thank you, also, to the rest of the Smackhouse family: Bloom, Chance, Kai, Miriam, and Niña. Every action you've made and word you've said has been systematically documented and injected into this story. I also love you all.

And, finally and with utmost sincerity, thank you to my partner. Thank you for reading the prologue and encouraging me to go out on this limb. Thank you for being there at every one-hundred-page breakdown. Thank you for the little things, like not caring if I accidentally break the sauce for lemon pasta, for braving the fluorescent hell of the grocery store, and for the deep conversations that make me stronger every time. Thank you, perhaps, for the hard things too . . . like being forced to watch the first two *Godfather* movies with you even though they're too long. If you have bad taste, I'm glad I'm part of it. Thank you for accepting me, and letting me return the favor.